GIA'S ADDICTIONS

JUST GIA, BOOK 2

LUCY H. DELANEY

United States, 2019

To my girl, Matea.
You've suffered and survived so much and still strive to move forward
for your girl and boy.

PREFACE

"SO YOU MOVED?"

Gia looked away and sighed. A scornful smirk curled at the corners of her lips just before she shook her head in disappointment. She looked back at the questioner, "Yes," she nodded slowly, "Stupidest thing I ever did."

"But would you be here if you hadn't?"

There was a challenge in the inquisition and Gia knew her answer to this one question may be the deciding factor. "I don't know. I'd like to think so, but I can't say for sure. All I know is I did move and my life took a nose-dive from there."

"Well, by all means, carry on with your story... I am quite intrigued."

CHAPTER 1

IF EVE'S EYES were opened when she ate the fruit of the tree of the knowledge of good and evil, my eyes were opened with a bong hit in a hot, stuffy bedroom. I left the loft house in my cozy little alpine mountain town of Leavenworth in hopes of finding a better life, but a darker future than I ever could have imagined is all that awaited me. I knew evil existed. I saw it on TV and read it in the Bible and even had my own brief and horrible encounters; but I never really knew human depravity until I left. I thought I was moving from one parent's house to another one simple summer break, but before school started again in my new city, I would be a different person. I would know a different way of life. I would be well on my way to a drug and alcohol addiction I couldn't escape. I saw what I was in for in that bedroom, but it didn't start there. It started slowly and snuck up on me the way darkness and depravity usually does, a little at a time. And then, my eyes were opened.

I didn't realize how much I truly missed Gio until I was back with him every day. It was like having an arm reattached after a horrible maiming. I forgot how we could finish each other's sentences and the silent conversations we could have a room away from each other. I forgot how endearing his annoying habit of pushing me every time he walked by was or how homey it felt being in the same room, breathing the same air as he was once again. I went where he went, no questions asked because we were us again. I was accepted into his circle of friends because I was his sister. I was safe with them too for the same reason. No one else in the world could push my buttons the way he could but no one else mattered as much either. I was back with Gio, so I was home.

Summertime with the family was predictable and slow, like all the summertimes before, and always lived to the sound of the piano playing background noise. Lester worked long hours in the orchards so I didn't have to see him much and was able to effectively dodge most interaction with him when he was home. He was up and gone before the birds started singing their summer songs and usually wasn't home until after Gio and I were already in town with our friends. The days when Lester and I were both home together in the evening and Mom was working were most stressful for me. I knew the most dangerous times would be when he got his movies out of the drawer, and in the dark, in my room, where no one else would see him do what he wanted to do. As long as it was light and the other kids or Mom were around I could handle him though. When I wasn't with Gio, I spent a lot of time in the room I shared with my baby sister Hannah who, at six years old, wasn't a baby anymore.

In stark contrast to the polka music and tourist conversation that leisurely yawned and stretched the streets of Leavenworth awake below my loft windows, the hot, school-less mornings at my new house in the orchard were still, boring, and eerily quiet. Trent was always awake before Mom, Gio or I, but knew to keep quiet. Like always, Mom slept until early afternoon because she worked nights at two different lounges playing pop piano songs and still, only rarely, got to play what she loved most. It had been Trent and Hannah's summertime routine for their whole lives. Lester took Hannah to daycare on Monday, Thursday and Friday mornings, like he used to take Trent before he was old enough to stay home alone while Mom slept. In my opinion, Trent could sometimes make enough noise to wake an army even when he was trying his best to be quiet, but Mom could sleep through most of it.

Before I moved there, we spent a lot of summer days down at the pool. Mom would sleep on a lounge chair, we kids would play, and I would feel like a normal kid with a normal family. I still liked the pool time with her, the little kids and her friend, Rachel, but after moving in, the "specialness" of the pool-side faded into the same kind of monotony that defined the mornings. Gio and I went with them less and less because we had more and more trouble to get into with the friends Gio had made while we were apart.

When Lester got home, things were worst for me. I really didn't like him; he made me afraid, fretful and angry. I can't say that I hated him, but it was pretty close to that. I wanted to stay as far away from his sniveling conspiracy theories and nasty video drawer as possible. As soon as he was home, as he'd always done, he "cleaned up" from a hard day's work in his and Mom's bedroom. He spent lots of time in there or the bathroom, then came out to watch family sitcoms if Mom was home or his secret stash of movies if she wasn't. Certain sitcoms still raise my dander and remind me of those anxious summer nights and the angst that squirmed inside me as my mother prepared for work. I don't know why I was troubled around him. I only remembered that one time that he touched me, but I lived in fear of it happening again or happening to Hannah. I suspected that it had happened more, but I tried to tell myself that my mind was playing tricks on me. I kept our door locked or booby trapped at night to wake me up if he came in. There were a few times he got on my case about barricading my door "in case of fire" but I questioned why he was even checking my door in the first place. It couldn't possibly be that a watchful father checked to see if his girls were sleeping soundly. I jumped to the conclusion that his intentions had to be evil.

Without a paper route or errands to run for shopkeepers, or money of my own, I fell into a depression of sorts and slept tons of the anxiety away. I fell asleep on the couch or in my bed in seconds flat. As long as I was sleeping I didn't have to worry, so I liked to sleep, a lot. Sometimes I woke up to the drone of popular sitcom theme songs and dinner being served before Mom left for the night. Sometimes I slept right through her leaving and Lester putting in his movies and the kids playing and would wake up in darkness and silence in the middle of the night and wander to bed down the hall at who knows what time. Many times I wouldn't wake up until dawn's early light pierced through the windows the next morning.

For all the anxiety and distrust I had for Lester, I know somewhere in him he had to be a sort of OK guy, maybe. I mean he let my mom's kids from her first marriage live in his house, even after I'd made the accusation against him. It has to count for something. There were plenty of occasions where I fell asleep on the couch in the living room and didn't wake up until morning, and I heard normal, loving conversations between him and my mom. It tormented me to try to reconcile the decent things he did with the dirty things he could also do behind her back, like watch his nasty movies in the room with us there or sneak into my room or check me out on the couch when he thought I was sleeping. He only checked me out once on the couch, that I know of, but it was enough to fuel the anxiety I was trying to imagine was not necessary.

I tried to convince myself that I made a mistake all those years before or that I confused him with Brad, but my mind wouldn't believe the lie. I knew what I woke up to that night so long ago, I remembered the fear and dread of his hands and fingers moving further down and inside me. I was awake and I didn't make it up. The morning I woke up on the couch to his fingers, I know I was not sleeping or dreaming either. It was that first summer after I moved in with Mom, the sleeping summer. I know it happened, and it proved to me he was absolutely capable of doing nasty things no matter how much he denied it when he was faced with the accusation. It was hot and I was in a loose fitting tank top with long fringes and frayed out jean shorts. I was covered with a light green, fleece throw blanket that we kept on the overstuffed coffee-colored micro-fiber couch for such occasions. It seems strange to me why I ever fell asleep where he could get to me. Why would a girl who was supposedly petrified of being touched by her step-father fall asleep in provocative clothes in a room she knew he would be in? Why would I put myself in that position? Was I asking for it? Was I the whore I was beginning to feel like? Did I purposely put myself in the position to have it happen to me? But then again, what was wrong with me falling asleep on my couch in my living room? Shouldn't a child of any age feel safe enough in their own home to crash on the couch if they want to? But I didn't feel safe there and yet I kept putting myself out there for him to get me.

That morning was the only other time I absolutely know he touched me. Through my sleepiness, I woke to my mom in the kitchen making him lunch, brewing the coffee and doing the kitcheny-wifey things she did for him on her days off. I heard Lester tromping through the house, going here and there from their bedroom to the entry way table and into the kitchen as he prepared for his day in the orchard. At least it seemed like regular getting-ready-in-the-morning stuff to me. I almost fell back to sleep when he came into the living room. I guessed he was looking for something, but that wasn't it, he was looking *at* something instead... me. Mom had gone into the bathroom and when the door shut behind her, he approached, stealthy, like a cat. I almost couldn't hear him, but I knew he was coming for me. But it was daylight, I thought he was only a night time creeper. I was wrong. He was opportunistic and would seize any available moment and Mom was in the bathroom and it was the opportunity he needed to be a voyeur. He hovered over me and lifted the blanket up.

My heart thumped wildly in my chest, frighteningly fast. Danger was near and I was trapped. I had no way out; like when he touched me before, or when Brad told me what to do, or Vickie-Jean beat Gio on the stairs. And, like every time before, my brain and body froze. I couldn't think of what to do or what was going to happen. I was paralyzed, like a deer in headlights, or an opossum playing dead or a stupid idiot of a girl letting herself be violated yet again. What was my problem? I laid there, again and let him do it. I knew what was coming next and I didn't do anything to stop what I was dreading would happen. I didn't move or open my eyes and stand up to him and look him in the eyes and call him what he was, a sick pervert. I didn't slap him; I didn't get up and walk away to my room, or shout with all my might that I always knew he was a sorry, sick man. I didn't threaten to tell anyone, not that they would have believed me. I didn't do anything. Not one thing. I froze. All I could come up with was to pretend I was asleep! That's it, I laid still while his fingers pulled on the fringe strings and lifted my tank up, way up, until the cold air assaulted my hip, my belly, and as much of my chest as he could expose with my arms positioned the way they were. I stayed there, on my side, letting him look, afraid to move. He had to have seen my heart pounding violently in my bra-less chest. I was glad that my arms were covering most of my breasts but I hated myself for doing nothing. What was wrong with me?

I knew Gio was definitely old enough to fend for himself if I didn't allow the touch, and Lester had never made a threat anyway. I knew it would start problems if I accused him again. I was in his house, eating his food, using his electricity. I didn't know where I'd go though if the accusation got me in trouble. I couldn't go back to Dad's, Vickie-Jean made me feel this bad every day, but for other reasons and I had no other options. This was my new home; to disrupt the balance would cause problems. So I froze, controlled my breathing, and let him touch me. His calloused hand brushed across my thigh, grazing the flesh as he moved up toward my behind, which I knew was barely covered in my frayed Daisy Dukes. Why had I worn such short shorts? I never would have been allowed to wear them at Dad's but my mom was the one who bought them for me. I thought they made me look pretty, apparently they made me look molestable. He touched the curve of my backside softly, like I was something for him to ogle and use however he wanted. Then the toilet flushed. He replaced the blanket and walked away from me as quickly and quietly as he could before Mom came out. At least I knew then that she didn't know what he did, or why would he have run off at her reemergence?

I wished he could be purely evil to me like Brad was, but there was some kind-of-good to him too. Lester wasn't a devil-man and it messed with my head. He was annoying with his conspiracy tirades and he was scary when he got mad at Mom and pulled out his movies. But he was also the guy that took me to the store when I moved there and bought me all new furniture. He was the guy that sat at the dinner table with us when Mom had nights off to cook a good family dinner. He was the guy that randomly made us kids cocoa with whipped cream and sprinkles some nights before bed. He was the guy who hugged his mom and petted baby pigs on her farm. He was kind-of-good. I tried to imagine that it was only that one other time and wanted to stop being afraid of him. Something inside always told me there were more than those two times. It didn't occur to me until later that maybe he spiked my cocoa with Benadryl or something to make me sleep so he could do whatever he wanted and I'd be none the wiser. That would explain why I fell asleep on the couch all the time. That would explain some of the mornings I would wake up extra fuzzy, unable to shake the groggy feeling for hours or remember what had happened the night before. That's only me speculating, I have no actual proof, although there was one time with Gio that we know for sure Lester laced our weed with PCP. That was seriously a slime-ball move, but that was kind of how Lester was. So, maybe he drugged me, maybe he touched me, looked at me, molested me more than I'll ever know. If that is the case, I thank God that I do not know about it, do not remember it and have no proof of it. I can pretend it was only those two times. I like it that way. There are some people who go to counseling and hypnotists to find out about the darkness. Not me, nope, I would rather live in ignorance than know if his hands were ever on me more than what I remember.

I wish I would have known then that there would be no more touches, it would have saved me years of anxiety, but I didn't get that luxury. I lived in fear that he would get me again. Thankfully, with the exception of a few nasty, disgusting things that any pervert would say or do, that was the end of Lester's trauma. I wish I understood the reason I froze both times, or why I fell asleep where he could get me. It doesn't matter now, but it doesn't make sense that I feared him the way I did but laid myself out for him day after day. Why did I do that? I didn't want to be responsible for it at all, and yet I felt like I was. I thought I knew it wasn't my fault in anyway, but I still wondered if I was kind of asking for it, at least that time... I was on the couch in loose, short, suggestive clothes. I knew what kind of a guy he was. I should have dressed like a nun. I should have been in my room, or in my safe little Bavarian town, in my own little corner, but instead, I was far away from that pseudo-safety, splayed out on the couch for his sick, pedophilic eyes. Maybe, in his perverted, wacked-out mind, he thought I was somehow encouraging him. I swear I was in no way, shape, or form trying to make him look at me I just fell asleep on the stupid couch in something I thought made me look pretty.

I raged that day real good on myself. How could I be so stupid? I yelled at myself, screaming all the horrible expletives I could come up with to condemn what I'd allowed to happen. I chased the scratchy, blood curdling words screamed into my pillow, with a tremendous hit to my head with a fist or both of them. The pain was magnificent! Scratching, screeching, searing my throat, jarring my brain into the reality of how stupid I was to have fallen asleep on the couch.

It didn't take away his touch, but it was a good penance for allowing it to happen. That day I cut for the first time too. Sharp objects made good pain and if I was careful to keep the cuts hidden, I could relieve a lot of anxiety and no one had to know. It seems to me like twenty-first century cutters show off their scars. I mean no disrespect to them, I believe their pain is as real as mine ever was, but I don't understand it. My pain was inside and the rages brought it to the surface, to the outside, but except for that one time when I lived with Dad and Vickie-Jean and wanted them to see my bruised hand, I tried to keep my pain hidden... well, OK, not every other time, but most times. I didn't want people to know, but maybe I did want someone to notice my pain.

CHAPTER 2

PAIN AND ANXIETY didn't stop me from having fun with Gio and my Wenatchee siblings. That first summer I was overjoyed to be reunited with Gio, my other half, the finisher-of-my-sentences and knower-of-my-feelings. We still ran around and goofed off together in the storage sheds and in the old run down house at the back of the orchard property that we weren't supposed to mess with. We still climbed trees and picked cherries but we were growing up and were less and less interested in the "kid" stuff. We preferred to hang out in town with Gio's new group of friends.

Within weeks of hanging up my newspaper bags to move in with Mom permanently I was a drug user and seriously questioned the existence of God. He most assuredly did not exist in our orchard house. Without work and purpose, I was bored; and my idle hands found plenty of devil's toys to play with. Gio had already established his place in Wenatchee with a group of liquor stealing, chew spitting, heavy-metal listening, work-dodging friends. Some of them had cars. Sometimes we walked the two miles down the canyon road into town, sometimes someone came and got us. We rode down dusty, dirty trails in the sage covered mountains in the canyons or found our way to the evergreen treeline heading west toward the Cascades. We chilled in smokey bedrooms, RV "rooms" and basements. Gio knew who lived where, what drama awaited us when school resumed, and where all the Wenatchee kids hung in the summertime. Summertime at the pool faded to a memory, though occasionally Mom could sucker me in to tag along with bribery money. All I had to do for twenty bucks was play with the kids for a few hours while she lounged. Since I had no job, it was sometimes a necessary evil, not that my siblings were evil, they were just no longer novel.

Gio introduced me to his friends but in short order, he and Mom decided I was too churchy to fit in with them. Mom took me out to find some Dr. Martens and oversized band tees, holey frayed jeans, and plaid flannels to play off the grunge scene taking over Seattle. Gio came along to be sure they were outfits he could be "proud" of me in. I cut my long, dull, dry, stick straight hair shoulder length with layered bangs and red highlights. I was a skater chick that could not ride a skateboard. It was shocking to me how something as simple as a new hair style could make me feel like a different person. And, oh my, did the boys ever notice me! I liked the attention Mom and Gio, and Gio's friends, lavished on me. I had my ripped Nirvana, Green Day and Pearl Jam tour shirts, I had my mismatched flannels to wrap around my waist and frayed jean shorts and Docs. I quickly learned how to hold a boy's gaze with coy, playful eyes then turn away innocently with enough of a "come-get-me" smile, that they always did. Mom clothed me, Gio introduced me and all of a sudden... I was one of them. I wore the group's signature style for the next two years. The funny thing was, we listened to Metallica, ACDC and Black Sabbath way more than grunge but we wore the shirts with crazy-fan pride.

I started smoking almost the moment I moved to Mom's. I'd found a cigarette on one of my morning paper deliveries before I moved and smoked it, to see what it was like. It felt good to be bad, but it was a fluke find and besides, I knew how sensitive Nonna was to the smoke smell, and how many eyes were on me in the little tourist town. I couldn't get into smoking in Leavenworth, I would have been caught too quickly. The first time one of Gio's friends asked me if I smoked, since they all did, it was easy enough to shrug and say, "yes," because I had smoked that one time. To fit in, I started smoking, bumming one here or there until it was obvious that asking anymore was going to get me labeled a "moocher." I didn't want to be a moocher, a free-loader, a parasite within the group. Those people got talked about an awful lot behind their backs and I wanted acceptance. Theft became a necessary evil. I started swiping smokes from Mom and stores if they were easy enough to access.

It seems like it took a long time to go from the goody-goody Mom and Gio made fun of me for being to the street rat I became, but really the whole process happened within a month. Most of Gio's friends were boys, there were really only a few girls that were fixtures in the group like I was. Another boy named Matt had an older sister, Kaylee, who often tagged along when she had nothing better to do with her upper-classmen friends. Because we sort of "belonged" to our brothers, we weren't propositioned too much by the boys in the immediate group, the way they propositioned other girls. But I had my favorite within the group, even if I kept it secret.

A boy in the group, Jackson, had spent several months living with Mom, Gio and the rest of the family so he and Gio were closer than most of the others in the group. He was very attractive. He wasn't big but impressively strong, exquisitely chiseled and not afraid to hold my eyes in his. Most boys, I was learning, weren't comfortable making eye contact for a long time. Some took it as a proposition to be physical (like most men did) and acted on their impulses, I had fun leading them on and dropping them when I knew they wanted me. It felt powerful and I usually felt so little; it was nice to possess that control over boys much bigger than me. Most boys looked away quickly, either out of disinterest, discomfort or because I was Gio's sister and therefore off limits. I thought I was in love with Jackson because of how we stared at each other when we thought no one was looking. The look felt as intimate as any kiss I'd shared with Tyler. I wanted to be with him because of his boldness but also because I already felt like I knew him. He lived in the house that had become my home. He had been there several times when I visited but still lived in Leavenworth. We knew more about each other than most of the others did. To me it felt like a relationship, even though it wasn't. To him, there was never anything, except maybe that one time.

I relished being work free for once in my life, but the piano paid for my lack of business enterprise. For the first time in my life I had a piano, a real piano, in my house! Even better than that was the fact that no one cared how much or how often I played it, because if I wasn't sitting at the bench, someone else usually was. Lester, the hippy-man, was the only one who didn't play but he plucked his guitar most evenings, and sometimes played along with whomever was at the bench. As much as I despised him, I liked the music he made, and paid attention to how he played. Paul, my middle school friend, had strummed a guitar, but he was novice. Lester, I hate to admit, was very good and his music, as much as Mom's could lure me into the living room, to listen and learn.

My sonata, though, never came out when anyone was home. It was raw and real and changing like I was from the abused and misunderstood mean girl I had been into a dark monstrous thing of chaos. I loved it more than ever but it exposed too much of me. I dared not play when anyone else was around for fear of being found out. Surely anyone who heard it would realize the movements were parts of my life, the closet, the hellfire from church and trying my best to be good when I knew I was bad, the crescendo rages and rhythmic routine of my paper route. A new movement emerged with my same signature flare, but it was different. Deep, dark, chaotic tones mixed with high notes that were the boys I fooled around with. I kept the pages and pages of notes hidden in my room, taped to the underside of the keyboard I'd bought and still played, with headphones, quite often. Some of the worked and re-worked pages were so well-worn I should have replaced them; but like the music, the pages were precious and part of me. Paul, the only one who had ever listened to my sonata, touched those pages. They traveled from the school music room to the church piano at the AG of LV stashed in my backpack or back pocket and they moved when I did. I couldn't replace them because they were me too. Every time I added a new page was like learning something new about myself, like how a hard-working WOP like me could turn into a lazy street rat in the course of one hot summer and feel not one ounce of guilt over the metamorphosis.

The house we called home was situated in an orchard that Lester managed, it still stands there, up the dusty canyon road, but I hardly recognize it anymore, with its new siding and white picket fence. It was excessively boring most days, so Gio and I often left home to find adventure. From the house to town was a half an hour walk. Gio and I trudged it plenty of times when we had no ride in. At first, I was a tag along and it was fine with me. Honestly, I think it was fine for Gio too. He would never admit it, but he missed me as much as I missed him. He had grown in height and mass over the year of our separation. His frame had broadened and made him look larger and older, even though he was still kind of a thin kid. My gangling awkwardness hadn't matured at all. At five feet six inches tall I was thin and bony; my holey fishnet tights were practically loose when I wore them. Gio and I, for the first time ever, no longer saw green eye-to-eye, he was two inches taller and still growing. His stature and bold attitude had earned him quite a bit of respect within his social group, and it made my transition into the group a breeze.

Even if it was because I was Gio's sister, it was a relief to be accepted. My whole life, save a few photography vacations my step-mom planned, revolved around the local happenings in a tiny tourist town, where I felt wrong, strange and awkward among my peers. Wenatchee was a metropolis to me, the high school was easily quadruple the size of my old one. Living with Lester kept me from moving to Mom's when Gio did, but I think unconsciously, I also feared moving because I didn't think I'd fit in and wouldn't have the "local card" to at least sort of help me belong. Because of Gio, I didn't have to worry if I'd know people that first day. I didn't have to try to make friends. I inherited everyone he knew, simply because I belonged with him.

Though we went down into town, almost any trip away from the house in the summer inevitably ended up in the mountains where we were sure to find friends hanging out. It was sort of like the church youth group activities… only with drugs and alcohol and without adult supervision. We talked about things that mattered to teenagers; complained about our lives, parents and siblings and dared each other to do stupid things for no good reason.

I lived for the weekends, which were slightly more rowdy and fun than the weeknights. Really, there was a party to find any day of the week if Gio looked hard enough. And he looked. Pretty much every night was a Friday night in the summer in Wenatchee for Gio and I. We stayed up late into the night partying in the mountains or canyons. We woke up late the next morning after Lester was gone. We chilled around the house, maybe played with Trent, maybe emptied the fridge of its contents as any hungry teenagers are apt to do, or cleaned the house to ensure permission for another night out. We usually left in the early evening before Lester was in for the night and stayed out until midnight, our curfew, or later... if we were willing to risk a rant from Lester, were he to find out.

There were a few usual mountain hang outs; the one we called "The Hole" was by far the most frequented and most likely to be checked out by the cops so we kept it to weed and alcohol at most of those parties. Since The Hole was far off the dirt road, if any cop ever trekked up to check us out, the headlights would give all of us enough notice to toss our cans or pipes and appear to be innocent, clothed kids, peacefully hanging out by the time they got to us. Further up, into the piney Entiat hills, there were places for more devious and dastardly parties, the kind that went for days. They were more like extended-stay camp outs than parties. It was hot enough that we slept in truck beds or tents. It was dry enough even us punks knew to avoid fire at all costs. They drank, got high, played in any near-by rivers, creeks, or bodies of water, we blasted music, and a lot of kids had a lot of sex! I didn't realize how lucky it was that I was Gio's sister and therefore safe from most of the boys' inebriated advances until much later. Had it not been for him, I'm sure I would have ended up as one of the sluts that flitted from boy to boy... or maybe I would have found my way into a church group of awkward kids and avoided the evil I was becoming a part of. Anyways, always, as it got darker and the good-ish kids went home, to bed and to parents, we came out in droves, ready for trouble.

Legend goes that The Hole was called The Hole because the fresh spring that nestled there was the only watering source old-time homesteaders could find for miles. I don't know if that was true or not, I certainly had seen evidence of old homes in the hills though, so maybe it was the truth. We didn't drink the water but we swam in it, usually naked under a dome of twinkling stars, or high-beam headlights, in the heat of summer when fire danger was too high to start bonfires. We fished in it. We floated in it. We loved The Hole. There was one main, rutted, and rocky road that led to that favorite place. The road was a grand promise, that if the jagged, jutting, jarring ride didn't prove too much, a reward would come. All I had to do was hold out long enough and always, the old, tired road gradually opened up into a big, bare space on the side of Slate Mountain.

The Hole was big enough to host two or three different groups of kids for mating, fighting or swapping drugs and alcohol at any given time. The Wenatchee valley was small and eerily interconnected and yet, there were plenty of cliques that paralleled but never intermixed with each other in the small towns that surrounded Wenatchee unless it was to fight. These fights played out away from pavement in the dirt around The Hole. Usually by the time a challenge was thrown down and the cars and kids had bumped and jumbled up the side of the mountain to The Hole, tempers were calmed with weed and boys ended up talking a lot of smack about the other kids with no balls but nothing really happened.

Those opposing groups of kids made up the other crowds that also assembled at our little lake hideaway. In any mountain scene there has to be granola crunching tree-huggers, right? Our hole had its version of free-loving, nature-worshiping kids from the Moss Clan. They were all related through actual blood connections or their parents' indoctrination into the Moss community. They were fairly innocent; a weed-loving commune of pacifist vegans situated outside of a barely-there town called Ardinvoir. The kids went to school, like regular kids from the area, but had surreal names like: Cumulus and Fern, Willow, Talon and Starry. Everyone knew they were big into weed, mushrooms and acid, and because their commune was also big into peace, there wasn't too much trouble from them, except for when some of the "peaceful" girls would get riled up and start fights between their boyfriends and brothers.

I can honestly say I never drank at The Hole. I rode up there drunk, wasted as a matter of fact, but never actually drank there. Gio and I had strict orders from Lester and Mom to only drink at home. They even bought our booze, but we had to drink it at home, and once we started we were supposed to stay home for the night (not that that always happened hence the drunk at The Hole times). I guess it never occurred to me to disobey them and drink the weak wine coolers or beer the kids had up there on the weekends. I could go home and have my choice of whiskey, vodka or tequila any night of the week or weekend. When I was done partying with the kids my party continued at home... but there was one night I ended up at The Hole, alone, and drunk off those cheap wine coolers I wasn't supposed to accept from friends.

CHAPTER 3

I'M NOT SURE exactly why. Maybe I wanted to go and Gio didn't, maybe we separated in town and that's where I flocked to, but for whatever reason I hitched a ride with Talon and Willow and for once, had no brother to hide behind. I felt awkward and out of place but I wanted to be my own person. I knew a few girls but I was more familiar with the boys because of Gio. Jackson and another of Gio's friends, Greg, were already there.

Every time I'd been with Gio, the group of mostly guys would go off without me to roast a bowl. At that time I was still innocent and had never been high. I guess there was some kind of stoner code of ethics that stated that if a girl who'd never smoked weed appeared at The Hole without her brother, she was not to be offered a toke, a vastly different philosophy than the church culture that wanted everyone to try a hit of the Holy Spirit. Everyone we hung out with, who at the time seemed like everyone that mattered in the world, treated me like a little baby sister and it bothered me to be looked at like I was this pure thing that should be kept that way. I wanted to get into some trouble. No matter what Gio said about me being a good church girl, I wasn't. I was tired of being perceived like that. I wanted to see how far these people would take me without my twin there to keep me off limits. I wanted to fit with the girls as a peer, not as a tag-along sister to one of the guys.

I clustered with "our" group and made some good conversation with a few of the girls. Willow was a sweetheart. She looked much older than she was without having to try. She flowed easily between groups because of her social graces and charm and she was kind to me too. That night, mostly because of her, I fit in without Gio. The "pure little church girl" stigma faded even as the daylight did. Then it happened, as it had every other time before, something about the darkness brought out the baggies. The bowls got filled, the lighters started flicking, the kids got high. I was used to them turning their backs away from me or forming a circle without me in it, out of respect of my innocence or something like that, but this time none of the girls left me out, none of the guys either. I was one of them. I stayed in the circle and when the pipe got to me, either Jackson, or another good friend of Gio's, Cumulus Moss, asked if I really wanted to do it. I wasn't afraid or nervous or anything. I had seen them do it day after day by then and knew no one got idiotic when they smoked marijuana. I said that I definitely did and, took my turn, imitating exactly what I'd seen them all do. And, yes, I inhaled. Held my breath and, when the time was right, exhaled a puff of pale blue smoke victoriously into the night. They were all proud of me! It was a celebration that called for more roasted bowls to honor a virgin's popped cherry. It was my one moment of fame, it was gone too quickly. By the next pass I was not new anymore and no one remembered it was still my first time.

I didn't feel different. I didn't feel high. For hours up there at The Hole I wondered if they were playing a joke on me. I didn't feel anything except normal. They all gradually faded into the marijuana oblivion I had come to expect. In short order they were sharing their mellow, meandering thoughts and memories so I knew it wasn't a joke. Their eyes turned glassy and red; if mine did I don't know, but I didn't feel any different. They were under the influence, the cadence of their talk changed, the hype relaxed, and they gave in to the high. I did not. I felt nothing, not the slightest bit different, my head felt the same, my body felt the same, everything felt the exact same. At least at home, when Mom let me drink whiskey and Coke or Fuzzy Navels I felt the alcohol affect my body and mind. I hated feeling too drunk, but loved the buzz so I tried to drink more to keep the buzz and usually ended up drinking too much and getting wasted. My point is, from the first whiskey and Coke I ever drank I felt something. I supposed cigarettes weren't powerful enough to affect me, but I really expected more from my first time smoking weed. As the night wore on, we smoked more, but there was still nothing.

Eventually Willow, another girl named Greta, and I wandered away from the boys and into the lake to skinny dip. That too was new to me and definitely made me feel something. It was daring and risque and dangerous. The boys all knew what we were doing and threatened to follow us in but never did. The cool water brushing against my bare flesh was foreign and strangely intoxicating. I hadn't taken a bath in ages and only swam in bathing suits. At The Hole, that night, and dozens of others that followed, bathing suits did not exist in the water. I was bare and exposed and the boys were only a few yards away. Boys like the ones Nonna and the church folk told me would come and get me any chance they got. They wanted to, we could tell that by their whooping and hollering, but they didn't. We laughed at them, they teased us and threatened to hide our clothes, but they stayed on shore, and left our clothes where we could get them. It was always the men that were evil, never the boys, in my life. It was truly a curious and enlightening revelation. I wondered for the first time that night how rowdy but respectful boys so careful and fairly timid around us could turn into dangerous devil-men.

The boys I knew were more concerned with intimidating other boys and proving they were tough, than mistreating girls. We called it "mad-dogging," but they were pissing matches to see who was stronger, louder, meaner. Sometimes they actually fought but mostly they talked a lot of smack back and forth, but they didn't mess with the girls. We batted our eyes and cheered for our favorite alpha males and received gratuitous attention from the boys but, at The Hole, when they were boys, it was our choice to accept or deny their attentions. I never heard of a boy mishandling a girl at The Hole. Maybe they did and it was never spoken of, or maybe, despite the drugs and alcohol, the boys I ran with, at their core, were somehow of a better, more noble caliber then the men my mother let into my life.

After we redressed and returned to the boys, I watched Willow and Greta closely. All a girl, who was even slightly attractive and shapely, need do to gain a male's attention was look at them confidently. It was that simple; the look. An invitation or challenge for a game of catch to begin. No matter the age, intoxication level, or group affiliation, one look and a guy was generally hooked. The only thing that could really affect a guys' attention was if he had a girl with him already or if he'd singled out a chick to make his girl, be it for the night or for the foreseeable future. All the girls needed to do was decide who to allow the time of day to.

Greta was a heavily made-up and slightly overweight foster girl. She was buxom, bold and the most boisterous of us and made sport of the boys'weakness. She had no problem sauntering right up to the boys and flirting; teasing them and taunting them with her feminine guile. No unattached boy would walk away. I assumed they thought things would lead to a hook-up, but inevitably, at least that night, she'd just laugh, call them drunk or high, smoosh their cheeks together with her hands and move on to the next one over the course of the minutes, toke hits and hours. They all wanted her, or at least her body, and if she offered it, which the rumor was she did regularly, they might call her a slut behind her back, but they would accept the offer.

In light of the night's activities, the revelation changed. It wasn't that men were pigs and boys were gentlemen until something changed them, it was that all males were highly sexual beings, and some males lacked, or never learned self-control, or self-respect. That made much better sense to me. I already knew all men weren't pigs. Gramps wasn't a pig. I knew male teachers who never fell for the looks girls tried out on them and certainly never touched. Another light dawned: I understood why touch was limited at church and school. Men had an insatiable sexual hunger even from youth, they wanted to be strong, brave hunters, and could be, if they fought for it; but most settled and were nothing more than desperate scavengers that fed on easy meals. All a pretty girl had to do was look and most of them would fall; if they touched, they were done for. Men with self-control or a close walk with God or their woman to keep them from falling, were the good men, but they weren't the only men out there. The rest would fall for a look, or imagine one that wasn't there.

I noticed that when the guys were under the influence they mistook some of our unintentional looks as suggestions too. It was easy enough to tell them to get lost, but I started to wonder if, as a child, maybe I looked at Brad wrong and that's why he came after me. I played and replayed interactions between Lester and I over in my head, trying to remember if I did anything to make him think I was open to him touching me. I knew I didn't, but watching how easily the boys were influenced, helped me realize it happened because I was easy prey and some men were vile and weak-willed, not because I was me.

Flirting was our game. The boys pretended to be men, acting tough and spraying their testosterone around for other boys to smell. The girls reminded them that all no matter how tough and strong they thought they were, they were no match for feminine charms. I didn't fully appreciate the power we held until later, but I wanted to learn the techniques of wielding it. Even with my shapeless, gangling form I could turn heads. It felt good. I liked the attention my look could draw. I loved the power I possessed.

Brad and Lester had stepped over a line and taken what was not offered. The boys at The Hole and most of the other males I'd ever interacted with dared not cross it. They were stronger than that, they were better than that. If a girl didn't initiate or stopped an encounter, it was over. Whether I said no with my eyes, my body, or my mouth, they stopped. My body had the power to attract guys to me and my "no" had power to let them come only as far as I allowed. Men had appetites, boys were growing into theirs. Females were generally the food they feasted on. If I offered an invitation they would come, if I rejected or rescinded, they would leave. It was an easy technique to pick up. Of course I didn't master it by the end of the night, but I was definitely catching on.

It got late and I went down the mountain with some kids and headed home to rejuvenate for another night the next day. I had no idea what I was in for when I got up.

CHAPTER 4

THE NEXT MORNING dawned like a birthday. I didn't look any different, I didn't feel any different either, but everything changed. While Mom slept and Trent played I told Gio that I smoked weed at The Hole. It wasn't necessary for him to know that we teased the boys, he had been teased himself plenty of times. There was no point in me making my brother feel weak by sharing with him how gullible males were to a feminine look.

What he did when he found out I smoked weed scared me to death.

"So," he asked, "How did you like it?"

I shrugged.

"What does that mean? Did you like getting high?"

"I didn't really feel anything, I thought I should have. I smoked a lot."

"It was like that for me too."

"Why?"

"I don't know?"

"Is it like that for everybody?"

"How should I know? Would you do it again?"

Again I shrugged. "Sure, I guess. I mean, it's whatever."

Then he got stone-cold serious, almost angry looking, and he said he was telling Mom as soon as she was awake. I was floored!

"What? You're gonna rat me out?! Why? You get high too! Oh, it's no big deal for you but you're going to tell on me? I'll tell on you, jerk!" and punched him in the shoulder.

"Hit me all you want Gia, I'm telling Mom!" he grinned. I was petrified with fear. I went to my room and did what I did when I had no control, I raged. I found a pillow and screamed until my throat burned. I guess my logic was that if I raged the trouble would be less because I'd already done some sort of penance. The rest of the morning I waited fretfully for Mom to wake up. Once he heard her putsing around behind the door, Gio knocked, looked back over his shoulder at me, and entered her bedroom. My heart squeezed inside my chest. I was busted, I knew it. That jerk brother of mine was nothing but a dirty snitch. Sure enough, Mom called me into her room. It was my turn to look over my shoulder. There was Trent, and I was sure his ear would be stuck to the door as soon as I shut it.

Eyes closed, deep breath and I went in to meet my fate, my first real trouble at Mom's. She was still lying in bed. Gio stood beside her occasionally making smart alleck faces at me, the way he used to behind Vickie-Jean's back, while Mom lectured me about the dangers of drugs. The stuff could be laced, it could be something other than what I expected it to be, bad drugs could kill me. She went on and on about how marijuana was a gateway drug. She told me I was in danger of trying other things since I tried weed. I'd heard all the things in school lectures before. I was hearing it again because my stupid ratfink brother told on me. I should have known Gio would tell, that's what he did. He lived to get me in trouble. I'd been so happy to reunite with him I almost forgot all the annoying things he did to me. They were forgotten no longer.

Then it happened... like Eve's life after she ate the fruit, my whole life changed. "Gio, hand me my bong," she said. I had no idea what a bong was, but I thought I was in for it. Gio bent down and retrieved a brown and orange kaleidoscope looking thing with a bulbous bottom from the other side of the bed and handed it to her. My mom took a plastic baggie full of weed out from under her gray down comforter and loaded up, what I would later learn was called the bowl with the pungent stuff. I watched in shock as she lit it then inhaled deeply. The apparatus they said was a bong slushed and gurgled as she breathed in. She smiled at me, vaudeville mischief twinkled in her beautiful green eyes, while she held her breath and passed the lighter and bong to Gio. She exhaled several seconds later without the slightest hint of a cough, and commenced to lecture me.

"Gia, listen to me, don't you dare get your drugs from anyone but me again, do you understand?"

"No... I mean, yes?" I was confused. My mother, my parental unit was telling me to use drugs as long as I got them from her.

She wasn't done, "If you want some weed to take out, I'll give you some, but don't take it from strangers."

"They weren't strangers," I defended through my shock over what was happening.

"I don't care who they were. It could have been laced, they could have brought other stuff out and you would have done that. Weed's one thing, there's a lot of bad stuff out there, honey, and I don't want you getting into a bad situation. Don't take drugs from other people again, or you'll be grounded, understand?" She was serious.

"So... I'm... not in trouble?" I looked from her to Gio who was making the bong gurgle.

"Not this time, but if it happens again, big trouble. Got it?"

I nodded as Gio exhaled and stuck it to me, "Gotcha!" he laughed. He knew the whole time I wasn't going to be in trouble but he built it up to make me suffer, typical Gio style. My head was reeling! My mom, my Chopin and Bach playing mother was in bed getting high in front of me. She passed her drug smoking thing to my brother and was telling me to get my drugs from her! In my whole life, never would I have suspected my mom would be telling me something like that. Moments before I thought I was going to be grounded for life for smoking weed and I came to find out I would only be in trouble for not getting my drugs from her.

"Yeah, OK. I'm sorry... I won't ever take weed from anyone but you?" It sounded wrong, surreal, and I wasn't even high. By that time Gio was done with his second turn and handed the paraphernalia to me instead of my mom. I held the bong in my hand like a new, unfamiliar tool. It was plastic and lighter than I expected even with water in the bottom of the rounded end. The tube that extended from the bowl dropped into the water, this caused the slushing and gurgling upon inhalation. There was a hole in the back of the long tube part too. Gio explained the procedure of smoking from a bong to me and then they watched while I took my first hit. I did what they did, held my breath, then choked on the blue smoke inside raging to get out. Yes, I inhaled. Mom handed me a pillow and told me to be quiet so Trent wouldn't hear me. Pillow before to scream, pillow during to cover my coughs. They both thought it was great fun to hear me cough and said things to each other, like, "She's going to feel that." I handed it back to Mom, she finished burning the last of the weed that was still in the bowl and loaded it up again with a fresh bowl. They let me hit it first. That's when I recognized the smell from before, not in the days before with Gio, but in the years before. It was the distinctive, sour, earthy smell that Mom and Lester's room sometimes smelled like. For as long as I could remember her room smelled that way and the smell all these years was marijuana. My mom was a pot head and I'd been totally clueless to it. I took a huge hit off the bong and left the lighter on too long. Both of them told me to let the lighter die and breathe in slowly. They said it would stay lit and sure enough, they knew what they were talking about, and I got that fiery hot cherry rolling. I was able to hold the hit without coughing and passed it to Gio. While I was holding my breath, I noticed that these bong hits were much longer than the pipe ones the kids were puffing on at The Hole. The smoke stung my throat more than it had too. Still though, I didn't get high. It was nothing but a moment of bonding with my mom and brother. Their eyes both went red and glassy, if mine did that time, again, I do not know, but I was not high, what they said I would feel never came.

To celebrate my first smoke out with my mom and Gio, whom I swore I'd payback, I got my very own baggie of weed. I didn't understand the value of its content at the time but what I received that day had a hefty cash value because of its size and quality. Gio called it a fatty-gram and Mom said that was my allotment for the day and told me not to smoke it all at once because I wouldn't get anymore that day. Gio got his stash too and I pushed him into the wall as we left the room in retaliation.

For the first time I fit somewhere. I wasn't locked out of the room, I wasn't excluded from the circle. Like I had been the night before, I was one of them and I liked it. Pot was the great equalizer. It felt good and right to be a part of a group. Obviously my church training was no match for the power of belonging. Sure I fit with the church kids, Max and Ruthie and the others, but only because I was always at church. I knew in my soul I was not like them. I wasn't a good kid. Too much bad had happened to me. I didn't have to tell

Mom and Gio about Brad and Lester, because they already knew. They chose not to believe it, but they knew. Gio knew about Lester's movies, no one knew about the rages, but with Mom I fit more easily than in Leavenworth. Finally I fit. I had a mother who was treating me like a peer and not a child she could order around like a slave. I was being treated like an equal and I respected my mom for that. It was short lived, but in that first little while after I started using weed it was nice.

I learned quickly that what Gio and I had for our daily allowance of weed was far and away better than the paltry supply most teenagers were able to scrounge from any dealers they could find. We had buds; big, fat, red-haired, juicy good buds and very little shake, which was the left over that most other high school kids were lucky enough to get. Mom had Cadillac-class stuff, and we got it for free. The other kids usually had shake with maybe a bud thrown in to make it worth their fifteen dollars and it was enough for them. Some time later, when school started and I had to try and fit in, and I knew what a high felt like, I met a grungy, curly haired, skater chick named Molly. She had a chip on her shoulder and was a known stoner and dealer. A lot of kids got their stuff from her. She smoked me out once, out of the kindness of her heart, and I didn't have the heart to say no, despite the severe warning about eternal grounding and parental wrath. Her weed was garbage compared to ours, or ours was far superior to what she was supplying. I think that's when I knew my family had to be in deep. It had become my life but Gio and I knew it was wrong. Trent and Hannah knew nothing different. All four of us were doing what our parents told us to, but for other kids...even the bad kids partying it up in the mountains, they had to sneak and lie to their family and worry about getting caught. All we had to do was lie to others about where we got our drugs.

After the first smoke-out, Gio told me to be careful with who I shared my weed with. Moochers wouldn't leave me alone and would clean me out once they found out, and loose-lipped "friends" could get me, or my family in a lot of trouble. Like the good student I was, I watched him and learned how to handle other kids. He shared but only very occasionally, like everyone else. What I found really interesting was that he actually put his money into the collection to buy one of the sad little grams floating around town, and he smoked with them even though we had all we wanted at home. What they were smoking wasn't enough to get him even a little bit stoned, but it was his way to fit in, and in high school everyone wanted to fit in. I followed suit.

Since we got "in trouble" for smoking anyone else's pot we never told Mom about that part. Gio usually kept most of his weed for himself, I was careful, but admittedly more generous than I should have been at first simply because I didn't realize the value of what I had. I wanted the companionship smoking someone out could offer. I was fitting in. I belonged. It was nice for once to feel like I mattered, even if it was because I happened to have weed. They didn't stop talking to me when I was out, or at least lied and said I was. They were still my friends, and I quite liked having them. I didn't care that moochers asked me if I had any weed every time I got to The Hole, they did that to Willow and Talon and the rest of the Moss clan too. I liked the attention especially from a particular boy.

Jackson knew the abundance that Gio and I were privy to because he'd lived in the house. He liked to ask me if I had any frequently. Since I especially liked his attention, I gave it to him often to keep him from straying elsewhere. I shared to be nice but mostly because I wanted him to pursue me. Sometimes I teased him with weed like I teased other boys with my body. He didn't look at me the way the creepy guys did or the way some of the other boys did. He really didn't look at me too much at all; like Gio, he treated me more like a sister. But, when he wanted to get high, he turned up his charm, and I fell for it every time. His eyes would melt me, his hands would undo all of my senses, but always in secret and never around anyone we knew. He knew how to use me and I guess I liked to be used even when I knew it wasn't real.

Jackson was, in a lot of ways, like Tyler. He had no emotional connection to me and I was too smart to not know that. In Tyler's case it was a purely physical connection from both of us, but I really liked Jackson. I wanted there to be more between us than drugs and making out. His face and hands and personality turned me on. I wanted to touch and taste every part of his body, he was everything I thought I wanted that summer and though I flirted and messed around with other boys, it was him my heart attached to. I would have given him anything he asked for if I knew it would keep him around, but I wasn't stupid enough to believe I had anything that would keep him interested in me, except the weed. The boy was hot and wanted by lots of less awkward and messed up girls. I scrambled and used the drug at my disposal to collect any attentions he would aim my way and knew my family's secret was safe with him.

Unlike Gio, I never smoked alone, because I never got high. I didn't tell anyone I didn't get high because I was afraid it would be another proof of my craziness, which I still felt, but was able to stuff under the weekend drinking binges that Lester and Rachel and their other friends started before Mom got home on the weekends. I played along, got a kick out of watching everyone else go from sober to intoxicated weekend after weekend like that's all their life was good for. It puzzled me and made me wonder what was wrong with me. Needless to say, my stash grew rather large.

By the middle of August I fully understood the power weed held over people. I used my ration to get attention, wrong attention, but attention from girls I wanted to be my friends and from boys I was hot for. I started to hang out with the girls a little more than tagging along all the time with Gio and the guys all the time. Willow, Cumulus and Greta were my main friends, and since Willow and Greta both had licenses, I could get rides into town or to The Hole pretty effortlessly after an offer to smoke them out. I followed Gio's advice and was careful not to share with any one person too terribly often (except for Jackson of course). Once I knew what shake would do for most people, I made my own little shake baggies for the day time and saved a big bud or two for special occasions. Something inside me liked knowing I had what everyone wanted, and I could use it to get what I wanted. If I needed to get away from Lester, weed was my ticket to town. If I was horny or lonely, it was a fantastic way to draw attention from Jackson for petty sexual favors.

I didn't want him to have sex with me, though he did try more than a few times to take me that far. I wasn't ready for it, and, even when that kid was high, he respected my no. For some reason I really wanted my first, by choice time, to be with a boy I loved. I'm sure it was the church in me, but I wanted to save that first real time. At least if I couldn't give my body away the first time to the person I chose, I was going to give it the second time to the person I loved. I was hot for Jackson, I liked him, but I did not love him. He didn't know music and I didn't think I could love anyone that couldn't make music with me. And I knew he didn't love me; he was just another horny kid and loved the weed in my pocket, and he was the one friend that knew why I always had some on me so I didn't have to be as careful with him.

CHAPTER 5

LIFE STARTED TO take on a familiar routine. There were the Sunday pick-ups and church with Nonna, the Tuesday trips to Grandma's so Lester could run the fruit stand, the monotonous mid-week, mid-summer days and then came Friday and Saturday night, also known as party time! If I'm honest Gio, Jackson and I probably spent as many weekends in as we did at The Hole or running around Wenatchee. Weekends at home were a combination of a hippy love-fest and frat party, always with plenty of piano and guitar, alcohol, weed... and porn if there were no ladies (apparently Hannah and I didn't count as female). Lester, and his two best friends, Mark and Jaime, also orchardists, smoked loads of Chronic and watched their soft-porn horror movies or jammed on a guitar or two to The Beatles, Bob Dylan, Jimmi Hendrix or Creedence Clearwater Revival. Sometimes when they jammed it was so good it was almost like listening to a live band. Luckily neither of the guys looked at me or Hannah like Lester did, he was the only creep, and coward... he only looked when he thought no one would catch him.

The music or movies drowned out the kid noise. We were as wild and unruly as ever, it occurred to me, Lester and the guys didn't take much note of us whatsoever. When I was younger, I always felt like Lester was acutely aware of me and Hannah when he watched the movies but as a teen, and after spending more time in the house getting familiar with him, I didn't think so. Porn was just his routine, he came home from work and unwound with a fatty bud and a dirty movie, which he promptly hid before his wife came home. On the weekends him and his boys watched it together... if the lady folk weren't there yet. I tried to convince myself he wasn't as creepy as I imagined him to be, he was a normal guy who wanted to watch porn in a house where young kids happened to live. He paid the bills and taxes... to the fascist man... he could come home to his sanctuary and watch whatever he wanted, yell at whomever he wanted and do whatever he wanted. I tried to convince myself he was not a threat of any kind; he was nothing more than a sniveling, washed up beatnik relaxing like a free man in the comfort of his own living room. I knew, though, that not all guys did that. Dad never pulled out porn when Vickie-Jean was gone, I would have heard it through my vent if he had. Gramps never did either. Tons of other men never looked at me the way Lester did, so the convincing never quite worked, but I tried to feel less anxious around him.

When Mom wasn't home, no one looked after the kids. More than once, Trent and Hannah had taken sips of someone's alcohol-laden drink. It was funny then, sad now, the time Trent chugged Gio's Coke and whiskey when he was nine. He didn't know it was full of alcohol, he was thirsty and drank it and then spent the rest of the night spinning on the couch while Mom was playing the piano in some far away casino lounge and Lester was strumming his six string. Trent was the mellow kid but me, Gio and little Hannah could get pretty crazy. Gio, Jackson (when he came over) and I often got into wrestling fights after we downed a few shots of whiskey. If Lester wasn't jamming to music or porning out, he could work himself up into one of his rants getting on our case. He'd call us drunken idiots and tell Gio and Jackson to be careful with me so I didn't get hurt. Usually he was too busy to care until we knocked something over. Then he had enough and we knew to stop or else. Or else meant one of his punctuated lectures. None of us wanted that so we usually stopped.

Every now and then Lester would allow us to have a couple of our closest friends over to drink, never to toke-up, at least not with him and his friends. He didn't want anyone knowing what he did. Before anyone could come over, he had to know them, meet them, and "get a feel for them" first. He would stand, arms crossed, a short, pony-tailed sentinel at the door, and gauge them. Lester kept the thick carved oak door bolted always and if anyone came over he never opened it before first peering through the brass peep hole. After the peek, he'd go out to meet them. He asked stupid questions … who are your parents, where do you go to school, do you play any sports… and he had to get acceptable answers before allowing them into his space. I always thought he was being a paranoid druggie, making sure no one was a cop's kid or would have to leave early (and likely still drunk) for a game or tournament, but at least I finally had friends to come over.

Usually, on Fridays, as soon as Lester got home with Hannah from daycare, he would shower off the pesticides and dirt of the day and get the drinks flowing. His buddies would come over, the guitars and bongos came out of the corner and into life and the night started. Lester, Mark, Jaime and sometimes me and Gio wafted between the bedroom and the living room Lester's mind-grating "ha!" at the end of each sentence, graciously drowned out by Mark's strumming. I swear that guy couldn't toke (that's inhale) even once without coughing. Sometimes I felt like he did it on purpose to annoy everyone else. When Gio and I were there, it was mostly for the alcohol and weed and because we didn't have a ride up to The Hole. Of course, I would find my way to the piano unless Rachel, my mom's best friend and Mark's wife, was there because she was a pianist too. Rachel was nowhere near as good as Mom, actually not even as good as me, but she was older so she won because of seniority. Me and Gio, if we weren't wrestling, would beat the bongos, what hippy party would be complete without them? It would go on like that, with the porn or horror or music until Mom came home, then the porn would get hidden and we'd party even harder with my mom at the piano and Lester on the edge of the bench accompanying her.

That summer, as she sat there hovering over the keys and he matched her beat with his well worn guitar, I finally realized what she saw in him. It was never about his looks, because he had none. It was his music-soul. He was to her what my old school-mate Paul had been to me. They didn't need to talk or communicate in any language other than melody and harmony. They truly did make beautiful music together. No matter how creepy he was, or how mean he could be to my mom when he was mad and drunk, they played like they were meant to be together. That's why she stayed, the music made up for the names he called her and times he hit her, and the beast he was to her beauty.

I admit I loved hearing them play together almost as much as I loved the buzz from drinking. I couldn't get high like everyone else for the life of me so I drank until I felt the buzz... but I couldn't quite stop there. I always drank more and would usually inebriate myself. There are more times than I can count that I forced my feet to shuffle unsteadily to the bathroom bumbling into the hall walls on my way down. I'd sit on the toilet for who knows how long telling myself to never drink that much again. I hated losing control of my body, but every weekend I was home I chased that buzz and got too drunk. It was easy to stay cool at The Hole because there wasn't as much alcohol as at home, or at least not as hard of alcohol and ... we had to come home sober-ish so the parental units didn't know we were drinking and drugging away from them. My head always lied and told me if I drank more the buzz would feel better, but it never did, the buzz always gave way to loss of bodily control until I couldn't even move my fingers on the piano keys. Sometimes when I drank way more than I should have, I had to make myself throw up to get rid of the feeling.

At some point during the nights I stumbled to my and Hannah's bedroom and passed out on my bed, or tried to. I hated laying on a spinning bed. It didn't matter how soft it was, cool it was, hard it was or hot it was, I know because I tried anything I could do to be able to close my eyes and not spin. Nothing worked until enough alcohol was worked out. When I closed my eyes, even for a second, the world would spin uncontrollably and I was sure I'd fall off the edge of it. I had to keep our light on, which Hannah hated, and find something to look at or something simple enough for my intoxicated body to do until the spin was gone or I was passed out and oblivious to it. I'd cover my ears with black, spongy headphones and blast grunge music from my worn-out Walkman. What drunk person doesn't love the background voices in Queensryche's "Silent Lucidity?" Eddy and Pear Jam, Nirvana, Red Hot Chili Peppers and Richard Marx and Jim Brickman. I scrawled melodies or words into my journal going off on drunken tangents of my own, I imagined grand pieces that in the morning were nothing more than chicken scratch on paper, I yearned for Jackson, fretted over hell, wondering if God would forgive someone like me and tried to figure out why I was so weird. The words and notes while intoxicated were only barely legible and yet even then I was compelled to build my sonata, me in music form, always hearing who I was better in chords than words and always it soothed me.

The following mornings must have been bad for the adults, but I never had a hangover. Not once do I remember feeling even the slightest bit sick, that confused me too because everyone else complained about their hangovers, nausea and headaches... too much noise, light, blah, blah, blah. Not me. They said I was lucky. I felt even more awkward. I couldn't even have hangovers like everyone else. There was nowhere I fit in, but the alcohol and Jackson helped me push my self-hate away temporarily.

And then the night came that I finally wanted to sleep with Jackson but decided to hate my mom instead.

That night was like any other hot, summer Friday night at home; weed and alcohol, sex and violence, guitar and bongos filled the house and wafted out the open windows too. I think Gio must have been at The Hole, or I've blanked him out of the memory. Jackson was there and we were partying it up with Lester and his cronies. He slipped us both some weed to smoke, clapped Jackson on the back and turned us down the hall, and told us not to come into the living room for a while. I didn't get what he meant, I still am not sure if he was giving Jackson his "blessing" to be with me or turning us away so that we didn't spoil the "guys' time" while the women were gone. All I know is with happy grams in each of our hands, we eagerly obliged and trotted down the hall like we were getting away with something. I still hadn't been high, and I'd smoked a lot of weed by then but we started roasting a bowl in Gio's room, because Hannah was in mine. Jackson and I had made out plenty of times. He wanted me, I knew that, and he always took what I would give, but he was safe and never took more than that. I was happy to be alone with him, even if it was kind of creepy having Lester send us off the way he did.

After we smoked we started kissing, our bodies close, finding the same rhythm and swaying to the music wafting down the hall. It was everything I liked in a hot steamy make out session. He showered me with sensuous kisses that didn't compare with Tyler's but had become so familiar I was forgetting what Tyler's kisses even felt like. He fondled my breasts, touching me inside and outside of my shirt and I loved every moment of it. No boy had ever given me orgasms like I could give myself, but even without the climax, things felt much more sensual when his hands touched me than when I touched myself. He was good at foreplay, a lot of boys jumped right to trying to get in a girl's pants, but not Jackson, he was a lover, he liked to move his hands all over my body in time to the music and pull me in close to grind on me while we let our passions build slowly.

By that mid-summer I had concluded that I could do pretty much whatever I wanted with boys and, as long as our clothes stayed on, I stayed out of the "slut" category. I can't say what made me decide that, and I don't know if it worked or not, but that's what I told myself. I know a couple boys accused me of being a tease, but I don't remember anyone ever calling me a slut, like they did other girls, so maybe my theory (and practice) did hold weight. Tease, in my mind, was lots better than slut, and guys still fell for it.

Anyway, Jackson and I were having a great time, in our own little world, until my stupid mom had to ruin it. I was drunk, but not high, he was both, and we were rolling around on a fuzzy blanket on my brother's floor reveling in the hot, heavy, lusty moment. She knocked and we tried to ignore it. We honestly almost couldn't hear it over the music, but she was persistent and knocked and called us each by name, over and over again. Reluctantly we gave up the passion, he winked at me and smoothed my hair. I knew that meant we were done. We adjusted our clothes, pulled ourselves away from each other and I took a seat casually on Trent's bed like nothing had ever happened while he opened the door to both Mom and Rachel. They came in, bong in Rachel's hand, and were going to load up a bowl when Mom looked at us both. She lost it and started crying. She looked gaunt and fragile, maybe even a little crestfallen. She wanted more for me than this. She begged Jackson not to take advantage of me. She went on and on about how she'd lost her innocence to my dad and didn't want that for me.

CHAPTER 6

I HATED MY mom. Not like I hated Vickie-Jean, but similar enough to recognize it for what it was. She was ruining the good time I was having with a boy my age, a handsome boy, a boy who knew how to make me feel good, and she was trying to squash it. Her tactics worked because who wants to make out after hearing a mother cry like that? But damage far beyond ruining that night was done. I had told that woman about two men, two MEN she'd introduced into my life, who touched me wrong, who molested me, who took advantage of me and she didn't believe me. The woman who was begging a boy not to take away my innocence had called me a liar and attention getter when I spoke up about dirty men. Then, when it was a boy touching me, with my permission, she tried to stop it? She allowed the perverts into my life, she ruined my childhood and didn't believe me, but all of a sudden was coming to my defense? She was pathetic.

Then I noticed how she looked at Jackson, how she had always looked at him. It wasn't about me at all. She didn't care about me; she liked him. She had some kind of freaky crush on him and was doing what she could to keep me away from him, or him away from me. As soon as the thought came to me, I pushed it away. It was absurd to think that my mother was crushing on the boy I liked. It couldn't be. I told myself I was wrong, I was mad at her for ruining my night and making up irrational conclusions. I tried to pretend like that wasn't even a possibility, but as time went on it was clear that my mom had a thing for my boyfriends and Gio's buddies. I'm not saying she was Mary Kay Letourneau, just that maybe the boys made her feel young and she liked to feel that way again. No matter how hard I tried to shake the notion, it was stuck after that night. As it turns out, it wasn't just me, Gio noticed too, so did some of our friends. But that's another story for another time, that night all I knew for certain was that she spoiled my fun.

There were plenty of other opportunities for Jackson and I to find each other after my mother all but forbid us from being together. I snuck out to be with him once. I'm sure it was the lamest sneak out of all history, but I did it. The plan was hatched in town the night before. Jackson knew I had weed and knew how to get it from me. He asked for it and I told him I didn't have any. I teased and flirted to get him to beg me for it, which he did in all the ways I liked him to. I smiled, batted my eyes and told him I'd be happy to share in a more intimate setting. He told me he and a brawny, ball-capped buddy, Alejandro, had a fantastic star gazing spot up a mountain road I'd never heard of before. He told me when they'd be coming for me and that I should hike down the road a bit and meet them.

Even though I knew Mom and Lester would pretty much let Gio and I do whatever we wanted as long as the cops stayed out of our lives, I knew this would not be OK. The meet-up time was way past midnight, on a week night, with a boy Mom specifically didn't want me alone with. I waited until a little before the time, grabbed my stash, about an eighth of a pound of high quality marijuana and hopped out of my window. I walked toward town and before too long Alejandro and Jackson appeared in Alejandro's beat-up old Chevy that smelled like oil and dirt. I climbed into the middle seat and away we went. It only took us ten minutes to get to the mountain road they had in mind and we climbed up slowly, the city lights always in view. We parked but for the longest time sat in a cluster of trees, me doling out my stuff, us all talking about dumb stuff. They were getting high, and I was getting bored,

"What's all this talk about stars you were giving me Jackson? I don't see any stars, do you Alejandro?"

"Nope, not me. I can take you to the stars if you want me to."

"Yeah I do! Get on it!" I slapped him playfully on the knee to encourage a change. It worked, he started up the truck and we climbed higher, past the tree line, and parked under the most beautiful night sky I had probably ever seen. We all got into the bed of the truck and laid down on a thick piece of foam that was smooshed into the bottom that had come from Jackson's dad's upholstery shop. We laid on our backs, looking at the stars and talking even more nonsense than we had in the cab. I was again between the boys, when it hit me that Alejandro was flirting with me. It was a cool realization because even though I was way too into Jackson, two boys' attentions were even better than one. I was after all a tease and there was no law against playing with two boys at the same time.

Physically speaking, I didn't necessarily know yet what I liked but I knew enough to decide that Alejandro was not my type. He was a big young man but a little chubby and had a fuzzy wanna-be mustache that was not at all attractive to me, but he talked a lot, and complimented me a lot. I noticed the compliments because, with the exception of teachers, no one said nice things to me. I was a tag-along sister, a burdensome drama queen, the tease who never put out, but never one to be complimented by anyone in any group... ever. I was laughed at and I laughed along with them to avoid admitting my awkwardness but here he was, this boy I didn't find attractive at all, saying nice things about me. It completely changed the way I looked at him. Maybe in the half-moonlight I imagined him to be more attractive than he was or maybe his kindness did truly make him more handsome.

I started to flirt with him the way I played with cute boys. I touched him a little too often (not that I could help it with our close proximity) and leaned into him when I didn't have to. I made it seem natural, like I did with Jackson, but my intention was to draw him to me, boys were suckers for that kind of stuff. After roasting who knows how many bowls, the boys were beyond high. I asked if they wanted to smoke another round when conversation lulled. Alejandro looked at me, the silvery light casting a glow on the top of his hat, "You don't even feel anything do you?" He was the first person to ever call me out about not being high. Jackson stepped in before I could answer, "That's what I've been saying, dude! The stuff Gio and her get is chronic. Dude, she's used to it!" But I wasn't, Jackson didn't know me. Alejandro knew I wasn't high. That intrigued me, that meant he was paying attention to me, not just my body and my weed, but me. Maybe it was because he was not a cute boy and he had to make an extra effort to catch a girl's attention that he did it, but he noticed me.

When Jackson slipped out of the truck to pee, Alejandro and I got more personal. We touched more, he put his arm around me, but wouldn't lean in for a kiss and I was glad he was a slow, nervous guy, not like Tyler. I was all of a sudden confused and conflicted; I thought I wanted Jackson, but I liked Alejandro's attentions very much. I wondered if maybe Jackson had brought Alejandro along for me, so he could finally be rid of me. Maybe all he really wanted was to get high, and he knew Alejandro liked me. But most of the time Jackson was the one approaching me, sure it was because I had weed and he wanted it, but he didn't have to. He could have gone to Gio. I certainly didn't throw myself at him any more than anyone else, I favored him was all. I didn't really think he was trying to set me up with Alejandro... he was a boy and they didn't think that way. While Jackson was gone, I snuggled up to Alejandro and he welcomed me, but when we heard Jackson coming back, we separated and played it cool again. He was conflicted too.

Jackson came back to the truck in a panic, so afraid of something he saw that I think he missed the new chemistry between Alejandro and I. He swore he heard something in the woods, a man's footsteps to be precise. Alejandro picked up the fear too. I told him he was hallucinating it, I'd seen enough kids and grown-ups high by then to know that paranoia is a real and often times funny side effect of the drug; at least it was funny for me to watch. These otherwise normal people would start imagining the craziest conspiracies and paranoid plots. Alejandro was asking for details, mostly about where the man was and if he was certain it was a person and not a cougar or bear. Jackson assured us that we were not alone in the darkness that night. Their paranoia infected me too. While we were talking about where the guy was, Jackson pointed to the edge of the road and, there he was, wrapped in a blanket, leaning against a tree, watching us. We all froze for what seemed like years, our talking hushed even quieter than the whisper voices we'd been using. We were up on a mountain and we were definitely not alone.

The original plan, not that we put a lot of thought into the details, was to get out of the bed and into the cab of the truck as stealthily as possible; as if a man a hundred feet away might miss us in the bright moonlight if we were sneaky about it. Like sleuthy secret agents we stayed low and scaled the bed walls and landed silently on the dirt. We crept to the driver's side door and cringed when the creaky, squeaky, rusty hinges betrayed our location. But we were in and he, whoever he was, was behind us. We tried to figure out what to do, I thought it best to drive away, in a forward direction and completely avoid the scary man. Jackson and Alejandro both disagreed. They knew the area well. Driving away from the man would lead to a dead end, and that, in their minds would make us dead meat. Our only choice was to turn around and drive past him, which we did. He was an odd looking, scraggly man. He stood and watched as we drove by. A mile or so later we veered onto a different mountain road where we would hopefully avoid any more zombies in the pines. Those were probably the longest miles I ever rode on dirt roads, but in short order, the creepy stranger man on the mountain was all but forgotten.

We goofed off the whole drive, me in the middle loving the attention. Eventually we stopped at another locally known party site and the boys smoked more weed. I kept catching Alejandro's eyes on me and gave him coy grins of encouragement because I was so pleased by the attention. Then as it was dark with little else to do I smoked up again after we all climbed back into the truck bed. We were back in the tree line and it was completely black, and in the darkness both of the boys made their attentions known. Jackson on one side, Alejandro on the other. Alejandro and I played an innocent game of 'keep-away' with a lighter he had, touching hands too much and too often, fingers interlacing, teasing turned into caresses. Then Jackson went in for a kiss. For the briefest of moments I entertained the thought of both of them. Could I make out with two boys at once? Would they be into that? How would that even work? But it wasn't for me; physical intimacy was too much like music making, it was virtually impossible to play two pianos at once. There was no way I could manage both of them, nor, as I decided in that moment, would I want to. It would have been sensationalism, it didn't suit me and anyway, I was Jackson's; that was it.

He was the cute one, the lips I knew, the one I had history with. It was a no brainer for my body to choose him. I tried to continue a one-handed game with Alejandro for a little while longer but Jackson demanded more attention; even if I had wanted both boys, it was obvious in that moment, Jackson would not have had it. He laid down in the truck bed and pulled me on top of him. Alejandro got the hint and was sleeping in no time. Jackson and I made out until the dawn broke. Both of us kept our clothes on, the only skin to skin contact were his hands fondling my breasts, stomach and back. He really must have liked kissing because I've never known another boy or man to spend that much time aroused with me who kept it at that level for that long. I would have given myself to him that night if he'd have asked, the adventure of sneaking out, the rush of being the center of attention and having two boys save me from a scary stranger would have gotten the better of me. I would have, but he didn't ask and he didn't take, and I, so used to men taking what they wanted, had yet to learn how to give myself away. I may not have given my body to Jackson that night, but I undoubtedly turned over my heart. I thought I loved him and all of a sudden wanted more than making out and smoking weed. I wanted him to like me, to treat me in town like he was treating me there in the truck bed; like I was his. Alas, it wasn't to be and I'm still not sure why.

They dropped me off a quarter of a mile from my house and I walked home that morning in a sunrise bliss of wonderful emotion. I knew Lester would already be at work and Mom should still be sleeping. I planned to knock quietly when I heard Trent or Hannah shuffling around and get away with the whole escapade scot free. But Gio had different plans.

"What are you doing out there?" He swung the heavy door open, stepped to the side and as I walked past, into the warm, cozy house the exhaustion of being up all night suddenly hit me. All I wanted to do was find my bed. I'm not sure why I didn't tell him the truth except that maybe I didn't think he'd like knowing I was out with his friends without him. I came up with the stupidest lie ever told by a teenager sneaking out.

"I went out to smoke and got caught up watching the moon...must have fallen asleep and then when I woke up the door was locked. I didn't want to wake Mom up."

"You were out here all night?"

I knew in that moment I messed up. I shouldn't have said anything about the moon. I should have left it at 'went out to smoke,' but I embellished and it bit me. Gio let me in, like it was no big thing and seemed to buy my story.

I shuffled down the hall to my room, plopped on my mattress and slept most of the day away with my head under the pillow. I woke up to a piano rendition of *Ice, Ice Baby* sometime after noon. Mom was practicing for one of her "Pop on Piano" performances. She hated those the most, but made the best tips so she was always playing around with popular chart toppers. I didn't bother to tell her what had happened when I woke up, but Gio already had. Mom told Lester when he came home and off he went on a crazy rant about how smart and superior he was compared to ignorant me and how he knew full well what really happened.

"Nothing happened. I locked myself out and Gio let me in." He couldn't or wouldn't produce any facts about what I did because he hadn't even been home when I knocked on the door. It didn't matter, he was fired up! On and on he droned in his spazzy beatnik meets southern Baptist pastor way. He made me want to throw up. I was feeling feisty so I argued back instead of keeping silent to get it over faster. I already knew trouble in their house wasn't much trouble at all. I knew I'd live, and I knew beyond a shadow of a doubt that the night with Jackson was totally worth the beady-eyed man's thirty minute lecture.

"If you're so sure something else was going on, tell me what I did then. Where did I go? I'll tell you where I went, I was out there the WHOLE night asleep on the grass!" The only possible way anyone would know what I was up to was if that creepy old man in the woods ratted me out, and that didn't seem likely to me. Shocking as it was, my attitude backfired on me. After the lecture, they decided that I was grounded from going out for two weeks. That meant I could only party with the grown-ups. My weed supply was still provided, weekend alcohol was still poured, Willow and Greta still came over. I really hadn't lost anything and never felt a serious sting of punishment, only a twinge of remorse when Gio left without me.

CHAPTER 7

THERE WAS ONLY one other story from that summer worth telling, and I suppose the only reason why is to make the point about how stupid I was and even then, having totally shunned the idea of God, how I realize He must have protected me. I was so hungry and thirsty for attention, and it felt so good to have boys notice me, that I put myself in a lot of precarious situations.

I hung with my new girlfriends, like the Moss girls, but I didn't quite fit in. They were all either a bit too desperate, too cool, or too feminine for me to really connect with. I didn't have history with any of them like I did with all the girls I left behind, and history alone, I was learning, was a significant connection. I knew I was weird; I either talked too little or talked too much and had a hard time listening to others when they were talking, so I was not good at conversation at all. A girl would be in the middle of a desperate story about how much she loved this or that guy and all of the rest of them would commiserate with her about how she should "go for it" and tell him, and share how they could tell he liked her, or, in the case of Greta, they'd tell her to not throw herself at him. I'd tune out and get lost thinking about what the boy looked like, or the last time I'd seen him, which would make me think about where I'd been and what I'd been doing the last time I'd seen said boy. Before I knew it, while they were switching gears, like girls do, and changing topics I was in a far away la-la land of somewhere else in my head. I'd totally miss the conversation switch and then spend several silent minutes trying to get back into what they were saying.

It was work to be with the girls, not to mention I didn't wear make-up and had come from a different, more prudish, culture. I didn't know a lot of what they were talking about so they had to teach me. It was awkward, I felt it and was sure everyone else thought I was weird too so I stuck mostly with the outcast girls when possible; the bigger ones, uglier ones or ones with worse reputation. Like in Leavenworth, I knew if I blended in amongst them, I wouldn't be the lowest on the ladder; or more correctly I should say I felt better about myself with the other odd ducks, and usually the ugly, fat or desperate girls were nicer and more patient with my quirkiness than pretty girls too.

I digress... back to the story, it was easier for me to be with boys, they didn't talk too much. I could follow what they said better, and they were usually always nice because I was Gio's sister. After that night in the mountains things with Jackson got kind of weird. He must have told his hot and horny friend Greg because Greg became overly interested in me. If Greta was known for throwing herself at any boy, Greg was her male counterpart, and I had become a target.

He was cute, a little on the slight side, but cute enough. There were rumors about him with every 'easy' girl in town and there were jokes too. Most of the jokes revolved around his penis size and it intrigued me because it seemed that guys were far more sensitive about their parts than girls were about whether they had breasts or not, but I was developing and quite endowed so maybe I didn't notice breast envy as much. The rumors were prolific in our group of people. He wasn't ostracized, he was one of the more regular guys in our group, but it was a common rumor. I never heard him really deny it, if any girls said anything about it he'd make some flippant comment about how that wasn't what they said the other night, or that wasn't what their mom said. If any of the guys said anything about it, which rarely happened, he punched them.

Greg was on the scrawny side, but something about his physique promised he wouldn't always be so small. And Greg was a charmer. His advances were sickly sweet and overused. Every girl knew he was just buttering her up to be another notch in his belt. Usually the guys would tell him to knock it off, like the girls did to Greta. But I was a girl hungry for attention. I loved his lavish lines and didn't reject his advances so he pursued harder when the mood suited him. That was the thing, he'd be nice, say what girls wanted to hear while the mood suited him, then, like a bee pollinating the planet he'd fly off to the next flower. Maybe he didn't have endurance to chase one girl too long, maybe no one girl ever caught his fancy, or maybe he liked trying out all the flowers. Whatever the case, his ardent affection was fun, teasing him was a blast, turning down his incessant advances only to have him return over and over again turned into our little summer game. And, yes, I did sleep with him, but not that summer.

One night that summer, again I don't think Gio was there, I found myself with the group at a pizza place somewhere in East Wenatchee, a sister town to Wenatchee, across the mighty Columbia River. Amongst the others were Jackson and Greg. They were both especially flirty, almost, but not quite aggressively so. True to my attention-loving self, I played right along with them, twirling my straight hair between my fingers and batting my eyes even though their attentions were a little too thick to be attractive. I knew the affect pretty girls had over boys, and I knew my flirting was getting them both riled up, hot and hard, I might say if I'm being honest. I didn't yet know how singularly focused a boy could become when the prospect of making a conquest was in front of him. Usually in groups the guys would joke with all of the girls and vice versa, it was a familiar seduction game all teenagers played back and forth except for the fact that we were the baser class of society so we carried our games a little further than what was socially acceptable.

That night, as the sun set against the backdrop of Cascade mountains, Jackson and Greg more than implied that they both wanted me. Again the idea of making out with two boys at once struck me as a definite possibility and kind of turned me on. I wasn't the only one the fancy struck, they wanted to share me and made it clear in no uncertain terms. I knew what a threesome was, I'd seen far too many of Lester's movies to not, and I thought I loved Jackson so I thought would go anywhere and do anything for him. I'd always felt safe with him, and Greg was, well, Greg, so it didn't surprise me. Anyway, the joking was always crass among us all so I sort of didn't actually think they were serious; neither did I think it was a joke, I honestly didn't know what to think of their comments except that I was turned on, and attracted to both of them, and caught up in the moment. I stopped thinking, they wanted to go out and have fun, the three of us, together. They asked me to take them both out for a ride in Greg's dad's truck. I played along, sort of knowing their intentions, but never imagining it would really happen in real life. The boys always talked about what they wanted to do to the girls and the girls always played along, it was a game. We all played it, we talked a lot of talk and touched playfully but, at least for me, there was generally no physical consummation. Heavy petting was plenty.

In our circle of friends, except for Greg and Greta, no one got involved with anyone close. We were all "just" friends and besides that, most of the girls were somehow protectively attached to one or the other of the boys; close family friends since birth, cousins, or siblings, like Gio and I were. To complicate our gang with sex would have made things different than what it was, even as teenagers we knew that and kept the tomfoolery for other people. The girls got dates from other hot guys, the guys slept with other pretty girls, usually one of the many Moss girls; but our dirty, foul-mouthed group bantered playfully tossing flirtations back and forth like a volleyball. It always stopped at banter, until that evening.

I didn't believe them when they said they had a truck. We were all younger-aged teens in the first place, we got rides from our parents or older kids to go anywhere. I honestly figured the truck was a joke, but there it was in the parking lot when the three of us got out there. Sure enough, Greg's dad's banged and rusted, well used white Ford F150 was waiting for us. His alcoholic father was out for the count that night and Greg knew the truck was his until dawn. We all climbed in. The seats were littered with trash and beer cans, most of which had been emptied already, but there were a few still to go that Greg's dad wouldn't miss. If they'd wanted to set a more romantic mood they should have stolen or "borrowed" a convertible, or something sexy, but an old rusted out farm truck with dirt everywhere was what we had to work with.

The less than ideal wheels didn't help to make me feel horny, it made me feel yucky, I didn't want my skin touching that fabric, let alone making out in there. Who knew what germs I could get? I didn't drink beer, hated the taste, actually, and had more potent stuff at my fingertips at home, not to mention I wasn't so stupid as to get inebriated with two boys who were horny as bucks in rut. I was a tease, not a slut and what they were propositioning could push me into the slut category really fast. As Jackson drove out of city limits onto dirt roads I didn't know, Greg and I made out. Between shifting the beastly diesel and guzzling beer, Jackson stroked my leg, played with my breasts and encouraged Greg to get me wet. They took me out to a secluded place I'd never been to before and asked who I wanted to go with first. That's when I realized they weren't playing like we always did. Clearly it should have occurred to me before, but it didn't until then. I guess it was something about that night, maybe I teased too much, maybe it was the freedom and boldness the truck gave them, maybe it was the beer, maybe it was the two of them, OK fine, the three of us, feeding off each other, but they were serious. They both wanted me.

The reality of my first real sexual choice was before me... if, in fact, I actually had a choice anymore. I had taken them too far, and they me. If I wanted, if I had a choice anymore, I could decide that that night, in that nasty, farm truck was going to be the first time I had sex on my terms. It wasn't what I wanted. I didn't know what I wanted, but two boys at once, in a gross vehicle, on a whim, in the middle of nowhere was not what I envisioned. Then I started to think, maybe it wouldn't be my choice; maybe I'd teased them too far and for too long that they would do whatever they wanted and I wouldn't be able to do anything about it. Gio couldn't save me, no one could. Maybe I was going to be gang raped by the boy I thought I loved and the male whore of our group. I told them there was NO way I was going to sleep with either of them in that truck. Jackson threw his beer can out of the window in a frustrated burst of pent up sexual pressure. Greg spared no expletive when he called me a tease, a dirty, rotten tease. With all the courage I could summon, I told them I wanted a ride in the truck, an actual, ride not a sexual one, and played it like I didn't know that the ride they'd implied was something different. There would be no meet up with friends, there would be continuation of the flirtations. The game had come to an awkward end. It was over. We drove back to town, this time Greg drove. They didn't push anymore, and I didn't offer.

They dropped me off at my house hours later, after we'd smoked and drank plenty more. It was a lifetime later that I realized how truly stupid I'd been that night. That night could have provided two more bad guys in my life; Brad and Lester could simply have been the first two in a succession of weak-willed men driven by lust. I could have questioned my worth, and what I was for and lost the instinctive restraint that lived somewhere inside my chest to reserve sex for someone special. But I got lucky, those heathen boys, Jackson and Greg, even flooded in all their teenage testosterone knew there were some lines that ought not be crossed because of a sense of honor that lived somewhere inside their chests. They did not defile me. Sure, I had Gio, one of their boys, as a brother, so maybe that played into it. But I was lucky that they were decent enough to not force me and strong enough to suppress their urges. Punks that they were, they respected my "no." I am forever grateful to them for that. A lot of girls and women don't get off so lucky in situations like that. It could have turned out so much worse. But there are men of honor and young men, even rough ones, who possess within themselves self-control. Something about that was sexy to me. It changed the game a little. The flirting was all fine and good, but the self-control appealed to me too.

Not long after that infamous truck ride, summer, like the setting sun over Saddle Rock mountain, slowly slipped away. Its close, much like its passage, accompanied by my mom, or me, on the piano. Another new normal was about to take over. Toward the end of August Mom took me to the monstrosity known as Wenatchee High School, in the shadow of that Saddle Rock mountain, and registered me for my tenth-grade year. My life had completely changed in three months. I saved any idea of God I had for Sundays with Nonna, I left what was left of my innocence there too. By the time school began, other than my secret rages and mutilations that still manifested when I was upset, I was utterly unrecognizable.

CHAPTER 8

THE NEXT SEVERAL years are a sorted mess of highs, lows, and desperate grasps at thin air. I was a bigger mess than I'd ever been in Leavenworth. The family I moved in with, my own flesh and blood, and him, was a mess. My life reflected it. Cliques were different in that big school and I found my niche fast, or it found me. Because of Gio, because of my family and my summertime friends, whether I liked it or not, I walked in the doors and knew I was one of "those" kids, so did every other student as well as the teachers. I can't tell the story of my addiction in a straight line because that's not how drugs work. Their whole point is to alter reality and nothing made sense for a long time after that. Hopefully the jagged path accurately conveys, as much as it can, the utter confusion and lostness any addict feels, but especially how I felt.

Wenatchee High School, institutional, brick, and gigantic was filled with hundreds of kids I'd never seen on the streets that summer. There was nothing sacred about the stark learning space. Erected in 1971, it was barely older than I was and lacked the history or timelessness that comes with age, the kind of thing a musician soul could fall in love with. It was nothing more than an austere rectangular holding cell. I was from American Bavaria, which in truth, the Bavarian theme not much older than the high school, but it was a place packed full of history and stories and tradition. Wenatchee was big and modern... utterly unattractive to me. Old, for some reason felt safe and good to me. The floors in the main building shined so brightly I could almost see my reflection, the bathrooms, where I smoked, if I thought I could get away with it, boasted the finest in plumbing advances. Like everything else in my life, it was a huge disappointment. But there was some safety there inside those walls of children's academia.

I knew school. Buildings could change, teachers too, but school was the same. All I had to do was follow the directions, turn out the assignments and I'd shine. Only for the first time, it didn't matter to me so much whether I got A's or F's, it didn't even matter if I went to school. My mom would pre-write tardy and absent slips for Gio and I six at a time on a sheet of crisp college ruled paper. All I had to do was tear one off, turn it in to the attendance teacher any time I felt like skipping, and ask Mom for more when I was out of excuses to stay out of school. Mom thought it was a great idea because then she didn't get called every time Gio or I skipped and we thought it was great because...well, really what kid wouldn't love an unlimited supply of get out of school free cards?

I always seemed to find my way to my music classes on time but other than that, I skipped a lot that year; forty glorious days of the one hundred and eighty day school year. My grades showed it, for the first time ever, I saw C's on papers. Something inside me couldn't allow them to slip lower than that, but a C was as good as failure. One of the strictest teachers at school, Mrs. Simpson, somehow saw through my lifestyle. I feel like she saw who I would have been under different circumstances and gave me a break on attendance too. She told me to show up and turn in my work weekly and I'd be good in her class. So I did, and I finished with a good grade.

Even with my poor attitude toward school attendance I hated punks that goofed off during class. When I went to school, I actually wanted to be there, the least they could do was shut up and let the teacher talk. But the stupid popular girls ran their mouths and batted their eyes, suckering even the teachers into their ploy to get out of work. Stupid slackers. I knew that trick too but I was no match for their appeal. I suppose I was jealous of them in some "wannabe liked" way, but when I showed up, I wanted to learn in class, expand my mind, and not have to listen to a cheerleader talk about how she was soooooooooo in love with a football player. I didn't need any goofy boys making noise in class either. I did my work in most of my classes and carried on my social life outside of school.

It was my first chance to branch out from Gio's circle of friends, some of whom had become my own, but they were his friends first. I was the tag-along sister only allowed deep into their ranks because of him not my own standing. They were some of the biggest little trouble makers in town with their minor thievery, fights and vandalism and I was party to much of it. The few other girls deep in their little group were tag-alongs too but high school socialization provided me the opportunity to get to know people on my own terms. I tended to gravitate to the outcasts and eccentric musicians like I was becoming. Inside the institution I found my own set of friends. Several of the new girls I was hanging with lived in the little sleepy neighborhoods of Wenatchee that I had never been in before but most were within the boys' thieving and vandalizing territory. I thought to myself that they were lucky I knew them, that made their houses safe from being stolen from because the boys were pretty adamant against stealing from people they knew. It was easier to get away with it if there was no connection.

Emily was quite possibly the most popular and generally liked friend I had in all of my high school years. Her house was blocks from the school and though her parents took some interest in her and her brother's lives, they largely left them to their own devices, sucked in by their own vices, so her house became a frequent hang out. It would be a lie if I said it was all about Emily. It was her baby grand I loved too, reminded me of sneaky nights in the good old AG of LV church when my former classmate Paul and I would spend hours playing and making music.

Emily's stick straight hair is what first bonded us. Hers dirty blonde, mine, unsure if it wanted to be brown or auburn, both thin, straight and utterly useless. It's a strange way to make a friend, I suppose, but it worked for us. Her bubbly, gregarious nature carried us from straight hair straight into a fast, fond friendship. She was easy to like, talk to and listen to. She and I shared a math class in one of the stale newly remodeled classrooms. She talked a lot and I shushed her more than a time or two during math lessons, but more often then not, I'd listen to her gab on and on about who was who and what was what. Her talking didn't bother me like the attention hungry girls' did, she was not all about herself, she was open and friendly and had lots to say.

Emily came over to my house a few times but she and I both got the feeling my parents didn't like her much. Her dad was a local prosecutor that made a living putting bad people in jail, so her knowledge of what went on in my house could very well have landed both Mom and Lester in prison and us kids in state custody… sometimes I'd think it was too bad that never happened. She didn't mind that they didn't make her feel welcome, Lester creeped her out too so she preferred not to stay at my place. I was secretly glad about her confession, it felt validating to hear someone else say that something wasn't right about him.

Ironically, my other new friend, Abby, a quirky pimple-faced softball player, saw Emily as a rival for the affections of one boy in particular. I thought the whole affair was downright sad because the girls had apparently been good friends for a long time, and then a boy ruined it all. Though I was friends with both it made my relationship with them awkward. I think that's when I learned to really hate gossip. I genuinely liked both Abby and Emily. They were both my friends and I hated the cattiness of their fighting and bad mouthing each other. So many of their, I mean, our friends would fuel their fire, egging them on in their anger of each other. Some people, usually Gio's lot, even encouraged them to fight it out. I kept my mouth shut. I didn't try to defend one to the other either, that would have been a losing battle. Abby too lived only blocks from the school. I spent many languid days before winter with either her or Emily. Of course, I shared my weed, and of course a little shake (the garbage weed in my house) went a long way with two light-weight girls and me never getting high.

One morning before school, Mom called me in for another bedroom talk. "You're getting awfully friendly with people from your school," she accused from her bed, covers up to her chin and only half awake from the night's work. Usually she was still sleeping when Trent, Gio and I got ready for school but something must have kept her awake that morning, or woke her up.

"Yeah, I've made some friends. Is there a problem?"

"No, I just want to be sure you're not telling anyone about our weekends or the buds you get."

At that I bristled a bit, "Why is it OK if Gio's friends know but my friends can't? Jackson knows."

"Jackson's different, he lived here. We don't need the world knowing our business Gia."

"Wow, thanks mom. Obviously I know not to say anything, but thanks for your vote of confidence."

"Oh knock it off, I'm a mother, it's my job to make sure my family's OK, and if people found out, we wouldn't be OK Gia. You understand?"

"Yeah I already know Mom. I haven't told anyone. I promise. I gotta go, or I'm going to miss the bus." I cinched up my backpack straps and left her. It was the honest truth. I never told anyone where my weed came from. I was old enough to know the trouble that we all could be in if they got caught. I didn't care so much about what would happen to Gio and me. If anyone ever found out that my mom and Lester were dealers we'd go back to Leavenworth. Trent and Hannah wouldn't. I guessed they'd go live with their far away, fruit-stand grandma way over the mountains in Arlington. I couldn't begin to guess if I'd ever see them again. I don't know if that's the reason I was so tight lipped, or if it was just how I had become. I let no one in. If anyone wanted to know me, my secrets, all they had to do was listen to my sonata. It was all there.

The novelty of being away from Vickie-Jean was gone before my first semester at Wenatchee High School was over. Things at my mom's were as bad as they had ever been in Leavenworth. When I really thought about it, except for being able to do whatever I wanted, whenever I wanted, it was way worse at my mom's. Any time a thought like that popped up, I'd drink it away and wonder why I couldn't get high and smoke it away. Everyone in the house picked at everyone, I wasn't singled out, I was lucky enough to be one of four kids who were ridiculed. Everyone antagonized each other. We didn't cheer each other on, we made fun of anything we could think of, stripping the humanity from one another. I was as guilty as the rest of them, but when Mom or Lester or Gio picked on me, I'd rage to deal with it.

My rages, the scratching and hitting and screaming, started to include alcohol. I was desperate to find a way to make their words and digs and insults stop spinning around and around in my head. Drunkenness helped get them out. I'd sneak a bottle of weekend whiskey back to my room and drink while I screamed their insults into my pillow or carved scars into parts of my body no one would see. They even turned my natural ability to learn into a joke. They laughed that I was book smart and brain dead. How could someone as smart as me, they'd say, be so stinking dumb? How could a girl that could get all A's and B's without trying say something as idiotic as that? It never let up and if I tried to defend myself, that only made it worse. Lester would sneer that I was being overly dramatic. I was used to Gio teasing me but Trent started to do it too. Then when I lost my cool Mom would tell me to straighten up and learn how to take a joke. They insisted I was too sensitive. Once, on my way to my room to drink in secret and get away from their picking, I screamed for everyone to shut up and leave me alone. I turned toward the textured wall full of our school pictures and slammed my head so hard on the wall that I nearly knocked myself out. I fell to my knees, and saw stars, had a nice knot and shiner for a few days too. They laughed all the more, Mom told me to pick up the picture that had fallen in the melee. It took me a few minutes to recover and gain my bearings again then I went to my room to drink my fifth of whiskey or as much of it as I could alone.

I wanted to get away from the pain of it all, my whole life was a sick joke and I hated it. I drank a lot to dull the pain of my existence. I hated me, my pitiful self. I didn't want to go back to my dad's and Vickie-Jean. I didn't want to be there with all of them picking on me. I really, seriously wished I was dead. But I couldn't pull a trigger or cut deep enough to bleed to death. Jumping held no appeal to me, something about being all sprawled out and my guts or brains oozing freaked me out, pills were easy, too easy but Wenatchee had a hospital and if anyone found me too soon I'd just have my stomach pumped and everyone in the house would have one more thing to laugh at me about.

School was my savior. It was the only thing I had to hang on to; not the new friends I met there, not my loser friends I inherited because of Gio who were sometimes as desperate as I was to get away from their lives, certainly not the teachers. Just school. Just music. Just learning. I liked to learn and make music, they were the only things I was good at anymore. School, even if I skipped a lot, was an escape from the reality that was my sad, sick little life. School and raging, partying on the weekends and cramming in all my homework on Sundays became my habit. It was easier to harm my body, beat myself, shake my brain, scratch and cut and do the weirdest things to rage away the pain that was manifesting inside me more and more every day. It was like the alcohol and the weed that didn't get me high at least got me bold enough to take my self-mutilation to the next level. Then the high came...

CHAPTER 9

AHHHH MARIJUANA! IT didn't completely stop the rages or all of the drinking, but it made it so much easier to handle the bad and finally I understood what my mother's music moods were after all the years of watching her have them.

The first high I ever experienced, months after I started smoking (and inhaling) was on a crisp, cool late-fall morning. I'd smoked weed socially all summer long, with never a hint of high. Gio was in the habit of smoking up before catching the bus to school and I did it with him in the morning to, I don't know, bond or something. We were twins, it didn't feel right to say no when he asked me to do something. That particular morning, school wasn't the only thing on my mind, I had a mission, and a boy to deal with. I was nervous about the encounter; maybe the adrenaline I was dealing with was the reason the THC finally hit me, I still don't know what made that day, the day.

The boy, of course, was Jackson. I was still infatuated with him but by that November day, hanging out in the mountains, or at all, was restricted because of school and weather. Apart from a bonfire here and there, I saw less and less of Jackson outside of the school halls. At school when I saw him, he barely acknowledged me, but I dreamed of him with me, his lips on mine, of all the times we'd spent together making out. I wanted more of him, but I heard rumors that he was getting sweet on a girl in his own freshman grade. The night before, I wrote him a note, an ultimatum and confession of sorts. I told him I truly liked him and was tired of playing the make out games we'd been playing. I wanted him to be done with me, or for us to be more. I didn't like the ambiguity and needed to know what direction things were headed.

The morning that would become the first time I got high, was also the morning I planned out the route I'd walk to deliver the single-sided, fancy-folded note I'd stuffed into my back pocket so it was ready to hand to Jackson when I saw him. I wanted it to seem like I randomly happened to bump into him on my way to Math. Clearly, with a note in my pocket, the encounter would be more than mere chance, but he was a boy and I was sure he wouldn't catch on to that. My idea was to walk through the heavy metal doors and beeline down to the freshman hall and find him. The words I was going to say were burned into my brain, the letter was ready to go. All I had to do was pull it from my pocket and slip it to him.

Gio and I smoked a few hits apiece, enough, he said, to get to lunch, he always took more to smoke later, I never did because it was no fun to risk getting caught when there was no pay off. Trent, who was old enough to ride the bus too, though he continued on to the elementary school after the high school and middle-school kids were let off, had mom's red Ford Taurus sedan warming up for us in the drive-way. On the days when she went straight to bed, and that was one of them, we were allowed to warm up her Taurus, that she never drove after November without studs, and park it at the end of the driveway about a hundred yards from the house to wait for the bus. We had to keep it far enough to the side of the driveway or Lester would have a fit if he couldn't get his truck around it. I smoked my morning cigarette, like every other day, because by then, I was most definitely addicted to my smokes! I grabbed my backpack and tapped my back pocket, ensuring I had Jackson's letter and headed down the quiet hall, past mom's door, to the waiting boys in the car.

I was so nervous about giving the letter to Jackson, about exposing my dramatic self to him and risk losing what I thought we had that I didn't notice the creeping high at first. I started to feel a little different in the car as we waited, no longer nervousness, it was something I'd never known before. It became difficult to focus on what Trent and Gio were talking about. My mind was fading into a different dimension. I don't know that anyone can effectively describe a high because the experience is so mental, but I was high, like I'd never been before and I knew it. All of a sudden, everything everyone talked about made sense... and I had to go to school. Somewhere in the haze that was still creeping up on me, expanding and unfolding like a scene behind a curtain slowly opening, it occurred to me that I could get out of the car and walk home. I wasn't totally high all at once, it was slow but steadily getting stronger and I had no idea how big a real high could get. When the bus pulled up, I got out of the car and headed towards it. Unlike when drunk, I had full control of my body—it, quite frankly, amazed me. My body knew exactly what to do and did it remarkably well. At least I thought it did. I thought about moving my arms and legs...and they moved like I wanted them to, I couldn't do that when I was drunk. Since I had my words and route and course of morning's events already set in my mind, I got on the bus and tried to be cool.

Everything was different; the teeny-tiny rocks smooshed into the road that I never noticed before seemed so noticeable and notable even at the bus's fast pace. When the bus let us off, the cracks in the stone banisters outside, the streaks on the waxed floor inside, the thread dangling from the flag hung in the foyer, all so interesting and mesmerizing. I wanted to look at everything and see it, because I felt like I'd never really looked at anything before. More than that, I wanted to hear it on the piano. My mother's music moods made perfect sense. But I couldn't be like her and lose myself in the movement. I had a mission nagging in my mind, my mission was in fact, the reason I walked through the foyer in the first place instead of taking my usual route to the sophomore hall. I had to find Jackson.

Finding Jackson made me think of the letter. I had to get the letter. My hand reached back, slid into my jean's pocket, the sensation, was, well, sexy. I suddenly wanted to touch my bare skin and imagined how wonderful it would feel. It took the panic that had been threatening to take over away. I was intrigued, I decided then and there, my next high would be alone, just me and my body, but for that moment I was looking through the faces for Jackson and I was reaching into my pocket, and thinking of how I'd touch myself when I was alone all at the same time. The things my body could do surprised me and impressed me. Then, unexpectedly, my field of vision narrowed, like someone put blinders on my eyes and covers over my ears. It was not comfortable, I couldn't connect with the world around me. Whatever was directly in front of my eyes I could see and hear perfectly, but I couldn't filter anything else. The world became a blur. All I could think was, "letter to Jackson, letter to Jackson, letter to Jackson..." I found him in the hall, handed him the letter, I don't know what my face looked like, or what we could have talked about, because since the mission was accomplished, I switched my focus to the next thing to do, "get to class, get to class, get to class..." Jackson and I never even talked again after that, I don't think...oh well, I'd met my new lover...weed, I had no need for any other relationships.

Math that day was more of an opportunity to get my bearings than a chance to learn exciting new arithmetic principals that always, for some reason, sounded like music inside me. Had I not been high, I might have used my nervousness over the letter as an excuse to ditch class, but all I could think about was getting to class, so that's what I did. Sadly, but not surprisingly, I couldn't concentrate a lick on what Mr. Polanski was saying, but it struck me then how walrus-like his thick, coarse, salt and pepper mustache made him look. He was a walrus that knew math, but a walrus nonetheless. Emily kept whispering, trying to talk to me. I don't remember what she was saying or asking, but her freckles were adorable! I was high and I needed to stay cool. I felt like everyone in there must have known but kept my secret, because they must have been like the Gianellis too and kept everything a secret. In the middle of the mental rush of feeling and seeing and hearing everything differently, paranoia took over. I knew that at any moment Mr. Polanski would confront me. I knew that I was about to be busted. All of Mom and Lester's paranoia about getting caught made sense now. I tried to appear cool but I was freaking out inside. I understood why stoners got so quiet, changed so dramatically, it was the high. It was a rush on the senses, but also I was terrified I'd get caught. And I wanted more of that feeling that was consuming me, but didn't know how 'more' would really make me feel. I wished though, I would have been as smart as Gio and brought some weed to school with me. I spent most every day of the next year and a half getting high morning, noon and night with very few exceptions.

The exceptions were the worst times because that meant we were out of our supply, or rather, Mom and Lester were. I hated the lean times when we all waited impatiently for more, biding our time with vicious fights, or dangerously explosive silence.

Our family could be out of weed, I mean totally out, up to a week. No one would share anything they scrounged in the lean times either because we were all fiending too bad to care about anyone else. Lester soothed himself the way he always did, with porn and sniveling lectures about anything under his skin. At least by then, I was old enough, or smart enough, to escape to my room and bring Hannah with me, even when her incessant childish banter drove me crazy. It was still better to have her with me than leave her to him.

When we were out of weed, Lester and Mom's fights were out of control, often ending with some kind of physical altercation. The only thing good about seeing and hearing them fight was the piece of childhood it fit into place. Withdrawal was what all those childhood fights I saw had been about, that's why Mom wouldn't quit going after him, they were both crazy because they were out of weed. It didn't help my anxiety but it did help explain it. The lean times explained Mom's "not talking trips" too; those silent tirades that could last FOREVER or end in a frantic, frenzied rage about all her missed opportunities. I think she went like three days once without talking to anyone in the house, except maybe Hannah and that was only to tell her to get ready for day care.

When Lester finally had enough of her silent treatments, or music moods, he signaled the finale with a classic piece of rock music. Like the lightning and thunder stirring before a southern thunderstorm, he'd blast "Cold as Ice" by Foreigner, from the over loud speakers. No one ever knew when the cloud would burst, sometimes it started in the daytime when everyone was already on edge because she sat there at her piano never noticing the life around her. Sometimes we were jarred awake in the middle of the night. Sometimes, if she was at her bench, she'd bang and bang the intro notes along with the band while the song repeated and replayed over, and over, and over again until their fight, like the torrent, came down on the house.

Always, when it played, we knew the house was in for trouble! The four of us kids would find shelter, down the hall in one of our rooms. We would huddle together... or, sometimes as peculiar as it was, we'd play together like nothing was happening out there. We avoided recognition of what was happening. We pretended that it never happened. Trent tended to peek out the door more than the rest of us, he liked to see what was happening, but never interfered. Hannah would curl up in my lap and cry.

They crashed and banged and sneered and growled. They ranted and raved and the song played, and played, and played. Lester screamed and Mom yelled right back. Inevitably one of us would mutter "Shut up," when Mom wouldn't shut up. I think we all thought that if she shut up, he would leave her alone. But she never would, she kept flapping and flapping her mouth until he had no alternative but to slap her, the clap, like thunder reverberating down the hall right into our ears. It usually shut her up but sometimes only long enough for her to catch her breath and get right back in his face. That's when it would really escalate! He was a wife beater and she was going to make him pay. All she had to do, now that she had proof, was call 9-1-1. "Go ahead!" he challenged, full well knowing she never would because she never had.

The high covered up their hatred for each other, but it came out when they were out. I dreamed about taking a gun to Lester's head when he was sleeping; how sweet it would be to see his brains on the pillow...to end his endless raving about stupid pointless stuff. I dreamed of the day his mouth would be silenced, his sneering would be over and he would be out of my life. But he never was, Mom never left or called the cops or did anything about it but get in his face and make him mad. He kept on yelling and she kept on taking it. Then, the storm broke, the song wouldn't repeat anymore and sunshine came to the house once again. We emerged to assess the damage of our parent's hurricane, sometimes things were broken, other times Mom had bruises or Lester scratches, but when the fights were over they no longer existed in our familial history, only our collective memories. No one spoke of them again. Like the Gianelli whispers and secrets, they didn't exist.

Usually after a fight, Lester fixed a nice dinner to feed to his children and children of the woman he yelled such awful things to.

He'd leave, that's why the music stopped, and go, not to the bar, or another woman, as far as I knew, but to the grocery store to shop for our favorite kinds of foods. He came back with more than enough sacks to fill the cabinets. Instead of a torrent of shouting, savory food smells wafted down the hall to us, and when dinner was done, he'd call to us, like a good dad should. He made our plates and we all sat on the couch, or living room floor, watching sitcoms and eating like any normal family would. It was enough to throw me off. I'd wonder how a guy that could prepare a meal for his family, be so vile at other times. How could he do that? Wasn't bad supposed to always be bad? In my head, the child molester of my toddler years, Brad, was always bad, but seeing how Lester could be a good provider made me wonder if Brad might have not been all bad too. The fights mixed with the "normal" made their way into my collective consciousness. I kept it all secret but pondered it often and prayed for more weed before they fought again.

When we were out, the little kids grated on my nerves and Gio and I fought like Mom and Lester. When we were out, it was hell on earth. After I tasted and felt what high was, I couldn't stand not to be high. Sometimes it got so bad Mom would even give Gio money to go into town and get a hook up of the crappy weed we usually mocked so we could at least smoke something. They were a pathetic bunch of fiends and from that first high on, I was as bad as them.

CHAPTER 10

I KNEW BY then that Mom and Lester weren't just smokers, they were dealers, that's why our weed was so good compared to the other kids' shake in town. Though they were nothing more than loser addicts, they were close to the top of the supply chain because Lester the molester, creep that he was, was a talented grower. It was a pretty exclusive club because the whole operation was, at that time, very illegal in Washington state. Never in a million years would I have guessed who their supplier turned out to be. The Musselmans were the most unsuspecting, wealthy and family oriented people among my mom and Lester's bunch of "friends." In hindsight, that should have been a clear indicator to me, because why would a family like *that* be associated with a family like ours? They never came to our house parties, ever, but we went to their house every month or so. The guise was family dinner and movie night but in actuality Lester was checking the crops or it was a harvest or crop delivery night.

I liked the Musselman's place. Their two-story house was spacious, furnishings were sparse but bold, rustic and substantial. Jazz, or some other easy listening music, always played from the surround sound during dinner and, best of all, their ceilings were made of knotty pine. Most of the houses I spent any amount of time in were unassuming and quaint, maybe the Leavenworth loft was a little more trendy and contemporary, but I knew nothing so posh and opulent as the Musselman's. Their house was full of the best name brands and fine art and though they never did or said anything to imply it, as far as I can tell, I always felt "lower" than them somehow.

I vaguely remember when I first really took notice of Stephanie Musselman, the wife, about a year or two before I moved in with my mom. She was a summertime friend of Mom's who talked on and on about any little thing beside the pool when we were kids and ran wild. She impressed me, though in my opinion she was nowhere near as beautiful as my usually sleeping mother. She had an air about her, friendly and welcoming but somehow... better than, richer than, more than the likes of my mom. I can't explain it, but it there was something about her. Sometimes, I tried to make like a grown-up and join in on their conversations but most of the time I was playfully pre-occupied in the pool.

When I moved in and started to attend family dinner nights, there were several occasions, as Mom and Stephanie prepared the meal, that I remember Stephanie talking to my mom about how to get control of the kids, how to calm them down, and how to discipline them. I always assumed she meant the little kids, Trent and Hannah, who never failed to get into things they weren't supposed to or act up in some embarrassing way. I wondered then, if maybe Stephanie was on to the dysfunctions in our family and was, in some way, trying to help. It only took a few family dinner and movie nights to realize it wasn't parental coaching or friendship that brought us there, there was more to it but the kids weren't privy to it. It didn't make sense to go over there otherwise.

One time, I found myself alone in the kitchen with Stephanie and asked her how she came to know my mom and Lester. She looked at me funny, nodded, almost indiscernibly, and craftily wove a tale so rich with truth and colored with lies that I bought it completely until the day, years later, when she and Carl were arrested for one of the state's biggest marijuana growing stings in history. Stephanie told me that Carl, her husband, had been a long time friend of Lester's, from way back in high-school.

"Our families don't really fit together, do they?" she admitted, then must have seen some kind of distress on my face, "Oh sweetie, I hope that didn't offend you," she hugged me then gently pushed me out to arm's length and added with a wink, "You don't fit into your mother's family much either. Let me tell you something, Gia, believe me now, OK? You are meant for far more that the life your mother is giving you. You stay focused in school and get out of her house. Make a name for yourself, take the talent you have and do something with it. Don't let it be wasted like your mom's has been." Like a mallet on a gong, her statement struck me; my mom had her rants about her wasted talent, but never anyone else ever did, certainly not anyone of consequence. Not only did Stephanie affirm my mother's incredible talent, she put it on me too and wanted me to do something with it. I always loved her for that.

Her story was woven thick with interrupted compliments like that, she made me feel special; I had to believe everything she said, because I wanted those compliments to be real. She said she'd only known my family a handful of years, since she married Carl, it was the second time around for both of them. She admitted to treating Mom like a little sister of sorts, because she said she "wanted to help" with a shrug. I suspected Stephanie must have known about her moods or isolation tendencies and that's what she was referring to. I imagined she was trying to help my mom get better, that's why the invited us over, to see a better way of life. But no, that wasn't it, Carl and Stephanie were the main distributors of the weed my parents got. They were the hook-up. And they had the good stuff! I mean good, with a capital G!

The comfort and relief of 'plenty' after a time of drought and famine was as welcome as a perfect spring rain. For some reason I never linked dinners with Stephanie and Carl to re-supply nights, but always the weed came into the house at night. Late, late at night, when Hannah and I were supposed to be sleeping in our room and the boys in theirs. Lester would creep into our room, his sneaking always shook me awake and sparked that hot, horrid dread that crawled up my body. I waited breathless, fearing the touch, but never for me anymore, always Hannah. He lingered by her bedside. I couldn't tell in the dark what for but knew without knowing, and yet, I stayed still and frozen, afraid that he would come for me. And he did, and he lingered, but I never remembered hands on me in my room after I moved in permanently. I think he was only checking to make sure I was sleeping. I don't know how often it happened but the night time check-ins always seemed to be followed by a muted ruckus; shuffling and transferring, from somewhere outside, I assumed the cab of Lester's truck or his big diamond-plate tool box, to their bedroom. It was sort of like Christmas Eve, a dreadful Bob Marley Christmas Eve night but Christmas Eve nonetheless. The next morning Gio and I were sure to get a plump, pungent stash from mom, never Lester.

As long as the weed was fresh and the red haired buds were plentiful, my life could carry on. That's a lie. I hated me, I hated life, I hated everything. I hated my mom for letting Brad defile me and letting Lester beat her and touch me. I especially hated her for calling me a liar about both guys. I hated my dad for working too much and being a hero to everyone else but never talking about what I said happened to me. I hated that Vickie-Jean didn't like me and Gio and that we would never be kids she'd love like her own. I hated how she pretended, like the rest of the Gianellis, that life was great when it was anything but good and we all knew it. I hated that I was never good enough for her or Dad or Mom or Nonna. I hated that I was only good enough for sick perverts to touch and force to do whatever they wanted to me. I hated my thin, flat hair and nasty, pale skin, I hated that I was a girl. I hated that I couldn't think of good things to say in groups and always screwed up conversations and inevitably pissed someone off, or bullied someone else to hide my personal embarrassment. I hated that Gio was the favored twin and I was never as good in anyone's eyes as he was…and I was the one with good grades and no suspensions!

I was full of hate and rage and learned, after bullying always left me with guilt and regret in my stomach that made me feel even worse about who I was, the best person to take it out on, with the least amount of guilt, was me. I wouldn't get in trouble for beating myself. I wouldn't tell on myself. I was an easy target. I was the one everyone else hated, so it made perfect sense to put aside picking on others and move on to full out punishment on my flesh. I deserved it for being who I was.

I was the one that was never good enough. I was the one that never measured up to Gio. I was worthless, so what did it matter if I hurt myself? No one would notice and no one would care. And so with or without alcohol or weed, or the pills I had started to pop at pill parties, I would rage on my body worse than ever before. Like masturbation, it was compulsive and uncontrollable. When the urge struck, I had to get somewhere away from people to satisfy it. I had to feel the pain, to release it from inside me, to get it out. I hated myself for doing that too. I felt there had to be some way to control it, but I could find none until I saw blood bubble or bruises appear.

The God that I "prayed" to, what seemed like forever ago when I lived with Dad, wasn't there anymore. Not that He ever was there, but if He ever had been, I knew He certainly didn't live in a drug house with unruly children and fighting adults. The only church I got anymore was on the weekends I'd go see Nonna and Gramps. I don't know how often I visited because I can't remember much of that time but I'd visit them, usually when Nonna made the trip to get us. We blew her off most of the time, but sometimes she wouldn't have it, and would insist that she come get us, Trent and Hannah too. Gio and I mobbed into Sunday school like small town gangsters, in our brand new parkas. The kids were the same but I didn't fit in anymore, they knew it and so did I. I never preferred Gio to the company of my church friends until I moved to Mom's. After that they seemed too good for the likes of one so dirty as me. It was odd, I could sing the same songs and do the same things and I thought no one suspected I had been high the day before. If they did, no one ever said anything. Those were the only other times, other than when we'd smoked our stash before the new shipment was in, in that span of my life that I wasn't high.

I found myself laughing at the character of the church members, the old parishioners of my grandparents from my childhood, so long ago, even though it was only really months ago. For some reason I decided that they were losers and pathetic low-lives that used God as a crutch and had to talk to Gramps about their horrible lives. I realized then, like I hadn't in earlier years, that most of Gramps church folk weren't the high class business owners that Vickie-Jean preferred, but the old, and discarded and working class, trying to float their store-front dreams, or simply make it to next payday on a minimum wage cashier's paycheck. I didn't despise the church members, and rather relished their welcoming hugs, but I tried to feel sorry for them. How sad it must have been, I thought, to live a life where you "needed" Jesus to get through the day. I knew their smiles were as plastic as mine. I remembered their secret heartaches and resentments. I felt sorry for them... but safe, but I knew it wouldn't last so it was easier to stick to feeling sorry for their sad, needy souls.

My brothers and cousin went there too. Billy and Andy, from their perfect life with their perfect parents who got them whatever they wanted. The boys, the brothers I once cared so much for, thrived now that their family was rid of the refuse of my dad's mistakes before Vickie-Jean. I hated them and envied them and wished I could have been born to Auntie Maria instead of my dad and mom. She would have loved me, but I was not meant to be hers. Within the church walls we tried to pretend things were like they'd been when we were all little and Nonna watched us, but Gio and I were too different by then. We didn't get to enjoy the luxuries they had in life, we got dumped on and both of us had begun to rot while they lived the lives of kids of privilege.

Every time I went to church with Gramps and Nonna and the cousins, everyone was all smiles and hallelujahs, but I couldn't get into it anymore. Gramps had this habit of sucking air through his teeth and fiddling with the candy in his pocket. I liked to watch the little kids come up to him for their piece of candy. He'd hand it out with his smile and carry on with his conversation with a church member with a smile. Nonna and the ladies would smile and laugh and talk about superficial stuff like the position of the drums or the tables for the pot luck. The cousins and their friends talked about going to the movies and hoping their parents would let them stay out past their 10 pm curfew. Other churchy people talked about the dumbest stuff like the world hinged on it; the peace of God and the "nudging" of the Holy Spirit. It was all bull and I knew it. I was living a life of reality. I knew what was real and what wasn't. I grew up in church and knew every one of them and their plastic smiles hid the truth of their lives. They all had their secrets, they hid them behind their ugly, fake smiles and pretended that everything was fine. I did the same thing every Sunday I was with Nonna and Gramps. Smile and nod, tell people what they want to hear or some type of spiritual garbage and they'd smile back and do the same to me. I never saw any of those people in 3D. I only knew one dimension of them on Sunday mornings. I only saw their best dresses and attitudes, but knew it was all fake.

Then church on Sunday would be over. If there wasn't a potluck meal after service, Gramps usually treated us to lunch or dessert at Krystal's, a nice restaurant on Highway Two. We sat at the biggest table because we were sure to be greeted by other parishioners. We ate our food. Then we'd make the long drive into Wenatchee, to feast on Costco samples before they dropped us off at the house in the middle of the orchard. We hugged and waved good-bye like good children, then ran for our pipes and our smoke. Sometimes, if she was playing for a church in the upper valley on a Sunday, Mom would pick me and Gio up and we'd clam bake in the car on the way home. I never understood that expression, clam bake; I did not know how getting high with the windows of a car rolled up could at all be likened to cooking mollusks on a grill but it was a frequently pondered musing of mine during those clam bake rides home.

The funny thing was, despite the fact that I totally bashed the people at the church, and made fun of the experience of church itself, church felt good somehow. I always went whenever I could, even though I made fun of it. That church always smelled like clean carpet, coffee and perfume, the air wrapped around me warm as a blanket on a cold, dark night. Gramps and Nonna's church was almost like a high in itself to me, I always went back to it. An age old clock hung on the wall and ticked a unique cadence, never heard until every head was bowed and every eye was closed and God Himself was there amongst those people and I waited for the lightning. The alter and that beautiful piano I'd snuck in to play oh so many times in what seemed like a lifetime past calmed my unsteady soul. The musky basement rooms and fixtures and door knobs; day after day, month after month, year after year always the same. The whispers may have floated around inside those church walls with never a bad thing getting addressed but there was no bad, other than denial, that happened in those walls. It was safe, the closest thing to peace I had in my life; church, whether I liked it or now, was home.

I wished for childhood, innocence again—not that I'd ever had it, but at least before I knew what I did after moving to Mom's.

Innocence was gone and the only good I knew was in that church. It was the only time when I wasn't high that I didn't want to be high. That church was the only place I never raged in. Not once, not ever. Not upstairs and defile the sanctuary, the alter and the sacred piano, not downstairs where the children memorized Bible verses and stories came to life on a flannel graph board. Their church was safe, and I was safe when I was there—safe even from myself. That church was a good place. Nonna might have been full of words that made me feel like I wasn't good enough and never would be, but despite that in Nonna's church I was safe. Gramps might long in helping this or that person, but he always came in whistling as he locked the front door and never once yelled or misused his authority as a man. I loved church even though I couldn't admit it.

Then after that safety, I would go to the place I called home.

CHAPTER 11

WEED, WHISKEY, THE needle of a compass and algebra, waited for me there. It's what made me. A monotony of highs, stupors, vomit fests, hanging out, and improv jam sessions filled my pathetic life. There was nothing good, save the music, but if felt so good to be high! I loved the high, I chased it, I fed on it. Sun, moon, stars and school it all began and ended with a little green bud and red wiry hairs. How I got hooked, I don't know. I felt stupid to be so desperate for something like that. When we were out and I fiend for it so badly, I knew how dumb that was. It was a little green plant and it controlled my life. At least the whiskey didn't run out. It was always there, shot by shot, fifth by fifth, as much as I wanted. I started not to care that I couldn't walk or feel. I started not to care that I wanted to drink so much.

No one cared what I did or drank any way. I was a problem, a nuisance. To both my dad and his photogenic life with Pacific Northwest Photographer of the year, Vickie-Jean; and to my mom and her freaky messed up psycho life with cowardly pedophile of the year, Lester, I was garbage. I was rubbish. I was merely half of the twin set of left-over mistaken high school love gone wrong. I knew it, Gio knew it, they knew it, it was just improper for anyone to say it out loud, so it hovered over my life like the whispers and the weed smoke. I wasn't stupid, I knew we were unwanted.

I felt completely useless. I even began to question my own mind. The mind that could memorize pages of sheet music with hardly any effort, the mind that could get high, drunk, skip class, and still produce honor roll grades with no problem. I questioned if I'd made up Brad making me suck his penis. I wondered if I'd

actually dreamed Lester putting his fingers into my vagina and
fondling me. Then in the middle of my high I'd hear Lester and
mom fighting and know I hadn't imagined any of it. My life sucked
and all I could do was get high or rage on my body to try to forget
how pathetic I was. Everyone in the house told me I was crazy,
dramatic, overly sensitive. Everyone insisted it was me with the
problems and I believed them. It had to be me, it couldn't possibly
be that in every house I'd lived in, with all the different parents, I
was the ONLY one that was not messed-up. It clearly made more
sense to me that I was the one with the problems, not all of those
grown-ups. It had to be me, because they told me so. All of them
said it was me, something was wrong with me.

One man didn't say it was me. The second semester at my new
school, I met the person who would become my favorite person in the
world. I found a dad I'd always wanted. He couldn't stop my life from
being so bad either, but he tried and he loved me… and he was safe.

His name was Mr. Patrick Kearny, high school music teacher.
He was a nondescript man, slightly stalky build, average height,
middle age, if there was gray in his blonde hair it was impossible to
perceive at his age. He had old acne scars on his never bearded
face, and kind eyes with wrinkles at the corners from all the
laughing I imagined he did with his three children who sat framed
in a family photo on his desk. He was supposed to teach kids
music, not really solve emotional problems, but he solved lots of
mine. I was lucky that I liked guys, so many girls who've been
molested distrust all men. I was fine with them because Gramps
and Dad, when they were there, were great men and most of the
guys at church were admirable. I knew good men existed, even if
my mom seemed to have a knack for finding the bad guys. Mr.
Kearny was a good guy, but he wasn't a lady and that's why I
think I bonded with him so well. It was all about the music, not my
problems. Ladies have to feel everything, had he been female and
wanted me to talk about things, it never would have worked. I
already felt enough. He was honest, he was steady and he became
my god, my savior, my only light in a dark place in my life.

I don't know why I started going to see him outside of class;
maybe because he invited me, but his little office, off the music

room, turned into a frequent haunt for me. At first it was a way to dodge class if I hadn't left campus. I could sneak a smoke in the bathroom and then go to his office to shoot the breeze with him. He had a student teacher that did most of the lessons that first semester and was often in his office. I imagined he was waiting for me. Looking back, I remember he was usually in the middle of a stack of papers, probably trying to get them graded and I was intruding, but he never made me feel like that. Everything stopped. He gave me time. No one had ever done that before.

He tried to use the music to find out what all was going on with me, "Hey Gia, Marriage of Figaro or Moonlight Sonata kind of day today?" He'd ask after beckoning me into the little office when I waved from the other side of the diamond shaped, wire-lined glass wall. Had he asked how I was feeling, it would have been easy to evade, but I couldn't lie about the kind of piece the day was. If it'd been especially bad at home, if Mom was silent and emotionally absent, it was a Moonlight Sonata o Gnossienne number one, its dark, chaotic cadence gave more away than words ever could have anyway. If I was crushing on some boy, I always seemed to pick the Vaudeville tunes, but I'm not sure if he ever caught on to that. I thought I was careful what I let out, but that man, a fellow connoisseur of music, could see right through the notes. He'd drop hints on how to handle life, like he was giving me advice on how to play the pieces we listened to. Sometimes he asked subtle questions while the music played; gently, patiently easing under my tough skin to teach me better ways to manage the feelings I couldn't speak of.

Then after our time was over, however short or long the piece was, he'd give me a pass back to class and I had an excused absence or tardy slip for the teacher. The longer I knew him, the more I was sure he was safe, the more I let him know. He didn't make me feel stupid or invisible. He believed me and I slowly started to open up to him. I started in the distant past, to keep the focus off of my drinking and smoking because I didn't want to give it up and knew a teacher would tell me it was bad for me. Turned out that there was enough bad stuff from way back to keep us talking. I never had to address that my mom was presently my drug dealer or how often I got high.

There was a time that year when I threw up everything I was eating. It was probably some type of minor bulimia related to my weight and to my hatred of myself. I pretended like it was some kind of sickness, that kept me from keep anything down, and I was incredibly weak from the lack of nutrients. I didn't have to gag to induce the vomiting in any way, it came out of me any time I had food in my stomach. I must have vomited a handful of times daily. Mr. Kearny could always tell when I'd thrown-up at school and would use "the sickness" as a bouncing board to see if I did any other self-injurious things, to probe my family life, to deposit little nuggets of encouragement that I could rise above it all.

My "sickness" was treated with lots of razzing at home. They all were sure it was fake and made sure I knew it. They were right, it wasn't a real sickness, it was me choosing to vomit; but I'm not sure that it started out fake. I think I may have genuinely been sick at the beginning and then there was something I liked about the feeling of absolute weakness and control over my body. I chose whether to keep or reject food. I didn't rage a whole lot over those several months of sickness, the vomit was my rage. I kept it up for a long time, eating then quickly regurgitating whatever I put down, it turned into a game with Hannah in our bedroom. She'd bring me food to eat and see how long it took for me to throw it up. Mom actually bought me flowers and balloons, I guess even with their razzing, they might have thought I was really sick.

A couple months into it, Mom took me to the doctor. He told her there was no reason why I couldn't keep food down so he sent us home with no reason why I was ill. I lost interest in going into town with Gio on the weekends and get hands laid on me at Gramps and Nonna's church for a special anointing kind of prayer. I'd come home from school, get high and lie down on the couch. I'd sleep until dinner. I'd eat, throw it up, do homework, then get high and sleep more. I'd wake up when it was dark, go down the hall to my room and sleep until morning. I managed to find time for my school work and always rallied to get my work done and turned in. It was a familiar routine, one that allowed me to rage while everyone watched.

Day time at school and night time on the weekends changed the monotony of my life. The weekends, if I felt like going out, were pretty much the same as they'd been in the summer only faces and the temperature changed. I partied at home a little more often because of the weather and my sickness, but still found time for my friends. I slummed with Gio and his friends in town if I chose that route for a night. We were trouble, we all knew it, the police knew it. Once a police officer saw me smoking outside the old brick Liberty Theater and I was sure he was going to bust me and take away my smokes but instead he talked to me like I wasn't a menace to society and told me he'd buy me a pizza if I could quit for six months. It was Emily's uncle so I figured he was being nice to me because he knew her, but that's the kind of guy he was; he was in his profession to help the community.

There were other cops though that would bust us, pull us over in one of the group's familiar trucks or cars, take our weed, pills, pipes and smokes and then let us go. It was the same cops that did that that ever time; Officer Smedley, Officer Smith and Officer Burnham. I'm sure those guys never filed reports. I doubt they were in it to help us but rather to get a free high they'd never have to report. Who knows though, maybe they wanted us to not have bad things and not get in trouble. I'll never know because I never asked them. We were punk kids, back then there was nothing we could do about it. It's not like we intended to narc out a cop and get ourselves in trouble for possession in the process. We just handed over our contraband when they pulled us over and made our own assumptions.

As the school year progressed I hung less and less with Gio's crowd. They started to get too violent for my sensibilities, if truth be told their antics scared me so badly I preferred Lester's porn and pedophilic tendencies to their company. We stayed out late at night and the colder it got the closer to the city we stayed. Usually we'd ride around in trucks and look for trouble. They liked to stalk people coming out of bars, drunk, staggering and alone. They would ambush them, beat them senselessly and take any money they had on them. They'd carry battery laden black and white bandannas and wait for the drunks or anyone walking by our side of the street. The bloody and barbaric shows of force and violence were far worse than the acted out violence Lester watched on his scary movies because it was real-life. The random beatings of innocent drunks wasn't a game to me, it was flesh and bone. I feared for anyone walking alone, and I feared to cross any one of them myself; so like I did all the years of my childhood, I stood by in silence and watched horror happen in front of me. There were often other girls there too, sisters or girlfriends of the boys, but I think they were all too afraid to say anything to stop them either. It was a little better when they'd fight with each other because it was mutual, but their fights were still brutal.

The leader of the violence, Jose Menendez, kind of owned the group. He was sixteen, new to the valley and crazy enough to turn on anyone, and had, so no one crossed him. Jose said he was a gang member from some group in California. I never liked him enough to try to bother to figure out his whole story or why he started slumming with us. I think he got in too much trouble in California and his family sent him north in hopes of straightening him out. Clearly it didn't work. All I know is everyone changed when Jose was around. The usual group of dumb, chummy boys morphed into violent, heartless thugs. Without Jose's influence, they all had some level of respect for humanity in general but it all together disappeared when Jose was around. Except for the ridiculous scraggly patch of black hair that covered his dimpled chin, he was a handsome young man; tall, broad, muscular, strong jaw line, but his eyes were dark and evil. I hated it when he looked at me; he didn't look to see, but to intimidate like a dog does. If he saw weakness he attacked, finding ways be it physically, psychologically or socially to assert his dominance over all of us while demanding "we" be strong. I learned not to look away nor to look in such a way as to give him, or his girlfriend Trina, the impression I was attracted to him, because his girl would pummel any girl she perceived as a threat. Mostly, I tried not to put myself in his way. I avoided him whenever possible which meant avoiding Gio's gang when I knew he was around. He was a bad, bad young man and nothing good came from being in his presence.

I went to the homecoming dance with a group of girls Abby introduced me to and made acquaintance with a boy, Phil. He was cute enough and had the body type I liked, thick, chiseled and muscular and he didn't shy away like most boys did, held my eye contact and had the goofiest grin. We hit it off and made out. His kiss was ferocious! I assumed he must not have kissed too many girls because his tongue was all over the place in my mouth. It was not hot. He couldn't have seduced me with that kiss for a $1,000,000 but I already led him on. I figured I'd give him that night and avoid him at school after that. He would get the hint and I'd be nothing more than a memory in his brain of a homecoming dance fling. It was a warm autumn night so we left the dance and drove downtown together. I knew where Gio was hanging out, I didn't bother to think it might not be safe to introduce a new boy to them; they were punks but they were also my friends. Other than Jackson and the innocent flirting with a few other boys I had no romantic attachment to any of them. I didn't figure any of them would care about me finding a guy. I was wrong.

CHAPTER 12

TURNS OUT, I wasn't just Gio's sister, somehow, I had become property and Phil was evidently trespassing. It probably would have been fine if Jose wasn't there, at least that's what I told myself, but he was and I led that poor boy into a trap. They were all huddled around the hoods of their vehicles when we pulled up. I should have known when I saw the bandanna in Jose's pocket that they'd been thumping drunks. I should have known, seeing them all crowded together and pacing like jackals that they had locked on another target, but I didn't get it. I never figured they would attack someone we knew. Before Phil could shut his door, Gio and Will, one of the boys my mom flirted with way too much, approached him. They started wailing on Phil without any provocation, the fact that it was only their fists didn't make it any better; they were attacking him, and he couldn't defend himself. That boy stood through it all, but he did not fight back. His focus was getting in his car and getting out of there.

"Why?!" Phil asked as he got back in his car nose bloody from the beating.

"She's our girl, not yours, that's why!" Will yelled, slamming Phil's door shut. "You got no rights to her, man." Phil sped off without so much as a single look in my direction.

Once I knew he was safe the adrenaline kicked in and I was pissed!

I did not care that Jose was there. I started going off, screaming at Gio and Will at the top of my lungs. "What is your problem? I can't believe you did that!" I pushed Gio, I wasn't so sure Will would let me get away with it, but Gio would. I started to walk away, high heels in my hands, when Jose told me I better get a ride home with Trina. I didn't want to do anything he said, but I didn't want to stay there either, and was too far from home to realistically walk barefooted. She didn't say much on the ride back, only that they were in a fighting mood. Not an apology, just an answer to Phil's why. Needless to say, I didn't have to ghost the boy. We never spoke after that, but he kissed weird so I was ok with it.

I was disgusted that Gio and his friends could be that vile. I let it go when it had been strangers but after that night, I hated their violence. There wasn't anything sexy about it, they were preying on the weak. It was vile. It never bothered me when they started and finished fights with other groups who were flexing their muscles too, but their anger didn't sit right with me after that. It was wrong to attack the innocent; not that drunks on the street in the middle of the night were completely innocent, nor were Phil's intentions, I'm sure, but their violence was unprovoked, and senseless, a waste of strength and honor. It turned my stomach and gave me a sharp distaste for the group I'd come to associate with. They were not people I wanted to be hang out with anymore, but I decided cutting ties would have to be slow and strategic to keep from angering anyone and facing their wrath myself... and I'd seen Jose sick Trina on other girls so I knew I was as vulnerable as any drunk on the side of the road.

Bettie Crawford was my bait and switch. I brought her in to the circle with hopes that I could exit quietly unnoticed and under the gang's radar because of the ruckus she was sure to make. I had my own friends at school by then and liked Emily and Abby best, but, truthfully, I loved them too much to expose them to Jose. I wanted to keep them safe from the group and innocent from that kind of violence. There were other girls I knew, with less steady families, who were more akin to the kind of shady lifestyle our group embraced. I targeted them and hoped their slow easy merge into the group would fill any emptiness my absence might bring if I stopped hanging out cold turkey. I really clicked with a girl named Megan. She was a slightly unattractive upperclassman; her eyes too closely set, her nose too large for her small head, and her thin, thin hair she insisted on dying raven-wing black worked together against her. She was musically inclined though and that was enough to bond us. She had a friend, Ali, a thick native girl whose shyness hid the trouble she was capable of getting into, and Ali was my ticket to Bettie. Ali was best friends with the younger girl, and they each had one half of a dollar store "Best Friends" necklace to prove it. Bettie was disgustingly infatuated with Jose and would do anything to put herself in a position to get closer to him.

All Bettie could do was talk about how much she loved Jose and how much she hated Trina because if it wasn't for her they could be together. Inside I thought she was lucky to have Trina as an 'out' and would be wise to steer clear, but she wouldn't so I was more than happy to facilitate her wishes. She always wanted to know where Jose would be and wanted us to be there too. She couldn't understand why I wasn't into Jose; he was, after all a strikingly attractive young man that many girls threw themselves at. I'd seen the viciousness he was capable of first hand and I feared his influential power. He was hideous in my eyes, I could no longer see past that vile shell. Looking at him made me regret all the horrible things I'd done to girls in Leavenworth and also made me wonder why my move, into a darker home-life, had somehow softened me, while his to a presumably better home-life made him worse. Or maybe he was better in Wenatchee than he had been before, and that thought chilled me to the bone. Jose was bad news but Bettie couldn't see it and was determined to be at-least his side-chick, if she couldn't bump Trina from being his girl.

I don't know what he saw in her, but Bettie eventually got her man. I guess they ended up being together for quite a while, years actually, before she finally saw him for what he was and made her own escape while he rotted in prison for an attempted murder charge. I never really did too much with Bettie because I didn't want to do too much with Jose but she was a good offering and distraction. Maybe I didn't need anyone to "take my place" and only imagined how much my absence would be noticed but it was easier for me to tell Gio I was going to be busy when he invited me to do stuff, but that Bettie might up for a night out.

Ali and Megan were often the answer to why I could tell him I was "busy." Sometimes they came to my house, Megan and I would take turns at the piano or hide out in my room, she knew Lester's type and understood why bedroom doors got barricaded at night. More often I'd go to friend's homes and in so doing, escape both Jose and Lester. For my fifteenth birthday Megan showed me how to put on make-up, she liked hers dark and Gothic but showed me how to apply just enough to look good without looking trashy. It was amazing to me how many more looks I got with eyeliner and red lips!

I never spent much time with Megan at her house, she was more typically staying at some one else's house. There were two reasons why certain houses were avoided in our group; either because the parents were good and we couldn't get away with anything, or the parents were so bad it wasn't safe to go there. Megan's were really bad, so bad she never spoke of life at home, but the frequent hand-print bruises on the back of her neck and upper arms said enough, even made me thankful for "just" Lester and question how bad he really was in light of other evils that could happen to a girl. She was not very good in school and had she been my age I would have helped her. I think the self-confidence of doing well in school could have changed her life, but she was older and I couldn't help much, but I tried.

I didn't get into a lot of trouble with Megan or Ali, we were all mostly about the high, chasing it with whatever we could find, pills from medicine cabinets, weed from my parents or elsewhere, booze from anyone who would get it for us. Then we'd fall asleep and do it all over the next day. Sometimes we'd hole up in Ali's room at her house, her Native parents, both with their own alcohol addictions to feed, seemingly oblivious to what we were doing. Sometimes we hung with the boys, but since my plan was to slowly fade away from Gio's especially violent friends, and Ali and Megan weren't automatically accepted into the group by blood like I was, and neither girl was what any boy in the group was physically looking to hook up with, our time with them as the months passed diminished.

Megan and I stayed pretty close to home... or pianos, but Ali would wander wherever the car she hopped in took her. She hitchhiked a lot because she didn't have a car like Megan, and lived about as far south out of town as one could get and still be technically within Wenatchee city limits. Her parents, severe alcoholics, never kept tabs on her, had it not been for her younger brother and sister she felt obligated to care for, she'd have been totally lost. It was common to get calls from her in a neighboring city asking for a ride back into Wenatchee or inviting me to the cool new party house she found. Megan and I would go get her or I'd hop on a bus and find her myself. She usually found the best, and warmest, places to party as the season turned cold and winter blew in. I'd long since lost my secret stashes because I smoked all the time by then, no one used me for my weed anymore, I was just another fiend looking for some kind of a fix, I didn't have any to share.

I didn't abandon my friendships with Abby and Emily, in fact, I stayed as close to them as I could while sheltering them from who I was at other times. They probably thought of me the way I thought of Megan and assumed my home life was really bad and that's why I always stayed with them. They were friends of a different sort. Their parents were more stable, more in tuned with their children. Not surprisingly they were the most popular of my friends. It wasn't acceptable in their homes to stay out, or up, into all hours of the night. They had curfews and quiet times. Occasionally they'd get to go to the late movie playing at the old fashioned Liberty Theater or stay out past midnight for a special dance, but late nights were exceptional in their houses. Their places reminded me of Dad and Vickie-Jean's without the hoity-toity airs I couldn't fit into. I don't remember staying often at Emily's, but we did talk a lot on our cordless phones and had even fallen asleep with each other only to wake to the beeping of a dying battery.

Abby was boy crazy and it was easy to get caught up in infatuations when I spent time with her, and I spent a fair amount of time with her because of that beautiful baby grand. For the longest time her primary crush was a boy far outside my circle, a much higher class of kid. She spent hours on the phone with him, flirting, listening to him babble about cars and whatever else he was into and I'd sit next to her wondering why she invested so much time in someone she wasn't sure liked her. I'd done that with Jackson and it turned out bad. I'd decided it was better to let the boys come to me because it never turned out good for the girls who pursued. They got hurt every time. Boys didn't like it and lost interest and moved on in short order. Abby's attention faded from the high class boy who turned out to be nothing but druggie. She didn't particularly care for the drug scene, so I kept my family secret from her. But he was a huffer, liked to sniff gas, so his lack of intellect was what eventually made her attentions fade.

I spent a lot of time at her house, in her room, listening to her on the phone with the boys she thought she loved, weaving her seduction games on the phone. She played boys well even though she chased them; she twisted it to make them feel like they were the pursuer. The problem for her was, she also gave her heart to them if they played along. I wanted to keep my heart, it hurt too bad to be rejected by my family when they called me a liar, my dad when he let me go to Mom's without so much as a real fight and the last time by Jackson, who I found out almost every girl I knew had been "in love" with at one time or another, he had that face and body any girl would want. The rejection that came after handing my heart over hurt too bad. I didn't want to feel the pain. I felt sorry for Abby because I could tell when she'd fall for someone new even before she knew it. Then when it didn't work out, I watched her crumble into a mess of sadness, and she may not have liked druggies but she like to drown her sadness in a bottle of Black Velvet.

I didn't want to be desperate like that, but I decided I wanted to have sex. I was tired of being a technical virgin. I was tired of knowing Brad had taken me the furthest I'd ever gone and my step-dad's were the only fingers, other than mine, that had penetrated me. I wanted sex on my terms. I just had to find a guy willing to do me.

CHAPTER 13

IN MY NEW circle, without the God factor, sex was just another thing to do. Whereas before, the guilt of being defiled and impure made me feel like Brad and Lester had ruined me, my new culture and friends' behaviors made me feel like those men had robbed me of the fun sex could be. They took my choice from me; I wanted to choose, to be pure or a whore, I wanted to choose, like my new friends did to have sex or hold back, and I chose to have sex. On my terms. I wanted to experience the hype for myself and know what it was like when it was my choice. I wanted to prove to myself that I had been defiled, even if no one else affirmed me. I thought I could prove it by doing it and see if my body reacted the same way. But it was my choice and I wanted to be really picky. I didn't want just anyone, and I didn't want to get a reputation of being a slut either. I knew I had to choose carefully.

I really only have myself and whiskey to blame for the enormous letdown my first real time was. It was the biggest joke of a sexual encounter anyone could expect. After all was said and done, and there wasn't much said and certainly not much doing, I felt as cheated as before only I was the one who allowed the boy to cheat me.

I wish I could 'uncount' the whole event, reduce my sexual partners by him, put it in the back of my mind where Brad and Lester's tally marks lingered but were never counted as "real." It was pathetic. The boy was Greg, yeah, that Greg, the man slut of those boys of summer. The place was Abby's cold, creaky front porch. The season was winter, a much milder winter thirty miles west of Leavenworth and the cold Cascade mountain corridor, but winter nonetheless. It was still my sophomore year and nothing had changed much with Greg or I since the summer except that we spent a lot more time inside.

Abby was a little eccentric, that's probably why she accepted me even though I didn't quite fit into her social circle. One of her quirks was building forts, the kind most kids grew out of in elementary school. She liked to frequently rearrange her room with an upturned mattress and box spring draped with blankets. She made mazes with her furniture and other peculiar things. She was never happy leaving things the same. It came as no surprise to me one weekend night when she wanted to build a fort outside on her porch and sleep out there. We hauled out something like fifty thousand blankets and pillows and made the most magnificent palatial fort of sheets and comforters that any front porch had ever seen. She pulled out a bottle of whiskey from her parents' liquor stash. I pretended like I found Gio's weed and pipe in my backpack. We drank up and smoked up out there, blowing through a toilet paper tube with fabric softener stuffed inside it to hide the smell. We were as goofy and giggly as two inebriated teenage girls could be and shared secrets and dreams and crushes into the wee hours of the night.

To this day I have no idea what Greg and another high class cronie friend named Matt were doing slumming those residential streets that night. We saw them through a slit in the sheets from our perch on the porch and we called them to us. Sex and Candy played on Abby's little boom box and set the mood. Matt and her started making out right away, Greg and I...not so much. We had a summertime history of teasing and flirting and frequently humiliating one another in public, but we'd never spent much time alone actually talking. Greg was a cute boy, and knew how to charm ladies, but I had a hard time getting past the rumors of his man-whoring. He was a horny little boy that's all and nothing more. It never occurred to me to choose him.

While Abby and Matt made out under the covers next to us, Greg and I talked on her porch swing about stupid things that meant nothing to either of us. He turned on his charm the first time I laughed at his joke. I guess he thought he had a shot. We talked about the ill-fated truck ride and how badly he'd wanted me way back then. His arm slid around my shoulders and he pulled me close to him.

"I'm glad you didn't," he said.

"You're glad? You seemed pretty … ummmm… mad…"

"Meh...I don't know. I mean, the two of us? I probably still would have, but I was kind of nervous about it too. What if it was just you and me?" He asked and nuzzled my nose. A shiver, a tingle of passion and excitement shot through me, right to my lady parts and I wanted him.

"I suppose," I played along leaning into him. Then it hit me that this was my opportunity to see what sex was like. There would be no strings with Greg because Greg was just in it for sex too. Abby and Matt were busy so I could easily say we just made out if he started spreading rumors and they wouldn't really know. I took the opportunity, told him we should get under the covers too. He was such a child, so young and overly excited. He couldn't believe I'd go for it. He kept on trying to sweet talk me and I started to get nervous, not about the sex but about the boy, the choice. He hadn't even kissed me, he wanted to get down to business.

I wanted it like it was with Tyler or Jackson only to go further. I wondered what had kept me from going further with either of them. I supposed, while I was teasing Greg and waiting for him to fondle me or put the moves on me, with Tyler it was lack of opportunity; it was virtually impossible to have sex on a bus, with other boys right there to get away with it. I didn't know why I hadn't with Jackson; I wanted Greg to be Jackson, I wanted Jackson to be my first, I wanted his washboard stomach pushed up against my soft flat one. I wanted him to hold me and touch me the way he had so many times and I wanted to give all of me to him. But I was under covers with Greg, not Jackson, and he was too excited.

I changed my mind and didn't want to do it anymore but felt sorry for him because his buddy was getting some and I'd totally led him on, and under the covers, for that very reason. I was too far down the path to deny him or change my mind. We didn't use protection, he didn't have a condom, and I wasn't in the habit of carrying them around. It should have been my way out and I should have taken it, but I didn't. I said OK. We barely had our pants off, he worked and wiggled and finally inserted himself inside me, and he was finished. I thought he whispered, "I just can't," and had changed his mind and for the slightest moment all of my suspicions about being totally different from any other girl were confirmed. Then I speculated it was loyalty to Gio getting in his way. I told him, it was OK, I wouldn't tell Gio and he said, "I can't believe I just came!"

No foreplay, nothing afterward to try and help me climax too, but it was fine because I was not aroused at all after that. It was utterly disappointing. Greg knew it too and was whispering apologies, trying to say I was too hot for him to hold it. I got up, embarrassed, and went into Abby's bathroom to clean his quickness off of me and knock my head a few good ones for letting that be my first time. I was so mad at myself! It was my choice and that was what I got?! It was the biggest joke, the dumbest decision, and was one more resounding reason to hate myself all the more.

Then I went to go pee and felt the pain. I knew that pain! I had no pleasure, but at least I had proof with that pain that I had most definitely been defiled before that night. I knew without a doubt for myself that Brad had put something inside me at least large enough to cause me that pain. I knew it had to be bad to leave me screaming and crying on my bed and having to put Vaseline on my vagina. The whole world could call me a lying drama queen, but I knew from that second, I hadn't imagined or made any of it up. I was right, I'd been abused, and they could all shut up about me lying! I don't know how long I stayed in the bathroom crying, scratching and hitting myself but it was long enough for the boys to have left when I came back out to the porch. It was probably a low blow leaving Greg like I did, but he really ruined my first real time and he was gone so I didn't need to apologize.

Boys sucked, men sucked worse, I hated them all, but I set in my mind that I'd find someone to have sex with who would do it right.

The rest of the winter passed, though Gio and I visited the family at Nonna and Gramps during Christmas break, there was no mention of staying at Dad's for any part of the holiday which was fine with us, we knew he didn't need us in his perfect little life. Lester gave me a gift I'd never forget that Christmas Eve day.

As far as I could remember, way back to the first time Santa made his terrifying entrance and I ran away fearing he was Brad coming to get me, Christmas Eve belonged to Nonna. She graciously allowed everyone to do what we wanted on Christmas but the night before was the matriarch's. We were obligated to go to Nonna and Gramps, there was no alternative choice.

By that time in my life I was so deep into my personal pain and humiliation...so far gone down a path of getting high and drinking that to think about spending one whole night without anything, not even a cigarette, was like torture. Of course in a house of addicts, I couldn't admit I didn't want to go somewhere because I couldn't get high for a while; we worked hard to pretend we weren't hooked on weed, and we had articles to prove it was impossible to get hooked. I argued that it was because of all the religion stuff I didn't want to go. I was tired of Nonna forcing Jesus down my throat and scaring me with the rapture talk. I had known for years I'd never make her god's cut and I was positive by then that I was most definitely too tarnished for her bright shining god. My excuses did not matter, Mom pretty much forced Gio and I to call and arrange a time to be there. She even drove us. We left for Nonna's sometime that afternoon but the rest of the day is a blur...here's what I know.

While it was still daylight, mid to late morning probably, but I can't be sure, Lester came into Gio's room with his bong. It was really weird because Lester NEVER came into our rooms...except in the dark of night when he thought everyone was sleeping. His glass bong, a swirling array of rainbow colors that glowed in black light, was off limits to us. He'd never let us smoke out of it before, but that day he brought it to us along with some of the hugest, fattiest, hairiest buds I'd ever seen. He didn't stay to smoke with us, he said something like, "Merry Christmas," or "Enjoy," and was gone. Gio and I examined the sweet gift, awestruck. The juicy buds were plump, tart and tangy smelling. Dew droplets of what I mistakenly assumed was THC sap seeped from the leaves like condensation on a soda can in the heat of summer. We were giddy with excitement. We oohhed and ahhed with each other about the droplets and all the thick, wiry red hairs and then we loaded the bong. I should have known...Lester was a snake, not a good man. As soon as that bong and gift weed came in the door I should have known, but I didn't.

We packed the bowl full but neither of us wanted to get too high because we had Christmas Eve at Nonna's that night. I don't think we smoked more than one big bud though he'd given us three or four. When Gio and I got high together, I usually toked up and then played video games. I got as far as switching on the TV before things went haywire. Snowy static bounced on the screen and I sat transfixed, falling into it. I hadn't even switched on the game before whatever he laced the weed with hit me. I laid or sat on the floor and fell endlessly into the static. I was a Salvador Dali painting; melting, dripping, fading into oblivion. From somewhere behind me, through the tunnel of my auditory canal, I heard Gio, "I can't make it stop! Somebody help me. Make it stop!" he begged in a panic. I couldn't get my mouth to move to respond, I couldn't muster enough emotion to be afraid. My head, like a lead feather, drifted slowly onto, and into, the carpet and I was lost in the beige fibers…for hours.

Hours later, Mom was at Gio's door telling us it was time to get ready to go to Gramps and Nonna's. My brain slowly flicked back to life. It was dark, it was evening, it was hours later and I had no idea what had happened. My eyes barely worked. I could only see directly in front of me, I don't know if it's because my eyes had been fixed for so long or if it was an effect of whatever we'd smoked. I don't think I could say much, but I think I tried. I can't remember what happened to the rest of the weed but I think Mom took the bong, at least, out of the room in a huff. She may have been mad that Lester had brought it up, or maybe was mad that we were high. We got in Mom's car, traveled west for an hour to Nonna's house and I still couldn't shake the fog from my brain.

Gradually, as the night wore on, I was able to see more from my peripheral and focus on what people were saying and even slightly participate in some simple banter, like saying thank-you after opening a gift. I tried to act normal. The family saw so little of us by then that maybe they figured nothing was wrong, or maybe they did, and kept it to themselves like a new Gianelli secret.

Obviously, Lester laced the weed. My best guess from what I researched was that it was probably PCP and that most all of the weed we got from him and Mom had at least some in it. It explains why we all freaked out so badly when we were out and why our weed was so much better than everyone else's. If we regularly had weed laced with PCP it would account for Lester's unpredictable surges of anger. It even helps to explain why my first high hit me so hard, maybe that batch had a more potent concentration and it was enough to jolt my system into responding. I still get sick thinking about it; I'd blacked out a few times by then and I hated it, but that Christmas Eve high was different than a black out. I think I was semi-conscious but stuck and melting.

It was one of the worst feelings in the world to come out of that realizing I had no idea what happened to me for all those hours, or if anyone touched me. I started freaking out that maybe Lester came back into Gio's room and messed with me, full well knowing I couldn't do anything. I checked my body for proof of any violation. No marks, no feeling of penetration or tenderness from him touching any of my private areas. I don't think he touched me…I don't think. He never brought his bong up before or after that, I guess in his sick and twisted head, it might have been an early Christmas gift, or maybe it was a sick and twisted joke, I don't know.

CHAPTER 14

WINTER PHASED INTO spring and my life persisted as it had, every day, a little worse than the one before. I dusted off that old sonata I used to work on in Leavenworth to try and cope with the ever growing pain inside me. I decided to add something new to the current movement I was working on. The tones were low and foreboding, I thought it gave the piece quite a masculine personality which I captured in C sharp minor chords of forlorn misery like my favorite Moonlight Sonata and I called him…Pain. I thought it was clever because I could say his name and no one would know I was referring to anything more than a part of the movement, but I was. Pain had become my best friend. I wasn't into all of that hocus-pocus demon possession stuff, but maybe, just maybe Pain was a demon because after I brought him to life on the piano, he was as real as the Velveteen Rabbit grew up to be, only darker and far more ugly.

Pain was my friend and I could count on him anytime things got too rough. The weirdest thing was the more personal I made him, the less it hurt to hurt myself. There was no pain when I was with Pain. I could scratch or cut or carve my skin without unpleasant sensation. I could scream and rage and his rhythmic lull repeated over and over in my mind like the childhood ruminations I couldn't shake. He held me like I wanted Jackson to hold me. I hated and loved Pain and, though I created him, he scared me sometimes. My rages were out of control, my black eyeliner got thicker and Nirvana and Pearl Jam found their way into my headphones. I hated my life but couldn't fathom escape, it was enough that I was free from Gio's violent gang. Sulking, sullen teenage depression suited me, everyone at home accepted my mood, like they accepted my mother's is what made me me.

"That's just Gia," they'd say.

And that was me. I was angry, addicted, depressed and wildly creative.

I went to see Mr. Kearny more than ever. He tried to talk to me about stuff, help me sort it out on the piano. I always felt like he could look right through me, because he knew music. He heard Pain, and noticed I always wore long dark sleeves and asked when the light left my music. He suggested I add some high notes and runs and would offer suggestions on the keyboard for example, then, carefully, oh so carefully that I hardly even noticed, he'd throw in helpful life tools.

"Hear this?..." he'd ask as he played a spritely melody, "You need some of that in there to balance it out. Otherwise it's too dark for anyone to handle. You gotta put in some hope, Gia, everyone needs hope. Take a walk by the river..." and he transitioned to play something strong and bold, "Or a hike up Saddlerock..." He added vigorous, victorious, triumphant runs and seared those local images in my head. I could walk at the river for inspiration, and escape, and I started to. I could sweat and pant and heave my way up the scree and windy Saddlerock mountain trails, now free of snow. I could stand over the Wenatchee valley from the top of the iconic summit and see the mighty Columbia carve its way to the ocean. I could look down on the city below and feel strong and successful, and inspired. I could do those things and add those melodies, and never have to admit that my parents gave me drugs. That would have been like taking away my heartbeat; I needed the weed and alcohol they gave me like other kids needed allowance.

No one knew what to do with me. At home they laughed, picked on me, or yelled at me to shape up. Leavenworth visits were rare by then but Gramps tried to psychologize me behind his oak door and Nonna cast the devil out of me whenever I saw them. Pain remained, so whatever he was, he wasn't the devil or something I could think my way out of. I hardly ever talked to Dad. Mr. Kearny was my steady. He was the only one who said nice things about me. He saw good in me and made me acknowledge my strengths, not my weaknesses. I loved being with him because he saw me different. He wasn't creepy like Lester, he wasn't detached like Dad, he didn't try to fix me like Gramps, he was all about wanting the best for me, and he believed in me. He said I had to believe in myself too. I just didn't, I felt like I was a lost cause, but I kept going to see him, to share my music and hear someone say nice things about me. I liked him almost as much as I liked toking up in the morning before school. I needed his words in my life. Even if I couldn't believe in myself, I needed to know someone did, I needed to know someone saw something good in me and he was my someone.

The pain and the raging got so bad my arms were always marked, half the time I didn't bother to cover them anymore. Lester used my raging as an excuse to search my room and took all my razors and knives...but he left the compass point, which is what I liked best anyway. I wasn't really suicidal, like a lot of cutters, I was medicating with Pain. To cut to my arteries would be the end, and I had enough fear of hell in me to not want to go there intentionally. I wanted to be noticed, to be accepted and loved. I wanted my life to change and someone to care so I used the compass to draw attention to my pain. Straight letters were easiest to carve, so I carved, "KILL" into my left forearm and refreshed the scraping regularly until it was permanently scarred on my arm.

Mr. Kearny made my parents notice, whether they wanted to or not. He called a meeting with my mom and dad and they worked up a plan to get me help. Gramps offered to psychologize me, but Mr. Kearny thought it would probably be best to have someone else be my primary counselor. They hooked me up with a local clinician, a very large, elderly female clinician, and I was diagnosed as depressed. She was a sorry excuse for a counselor, or I was too much of a mess for her to help. She was nothing like Mr. Kearny, or Gramps for that matter but everyone hoped I'd get better with her.

We only met a few times before my parents stopped wasting their money. The first time, I saw her alone and spilled the beans about Brad. I kept Lester out of it because I figured I could get the help I needed focusing on Brad...besides the last time I'd told anyone about Lester it totally blew up in my face. Then the old lady wanted to meet with my parents. Dad was too busy to make it. Mom thought it would be relaxing to get high before we went in. I really wanted progress, and knew I'd be stressed so I agreed. The counselor told her I was convinced I'd been molested by Brad and that my injurious behavior was due to the trauma.

Mom smiled and nodded, I thought maybe this time she'd verify it, but she politely told the lady counselor she didn't believe it. She admitted to Brad beating her horribly but said she'd never left us alone with him long enough for it to have happened like I remembered.

"Gia, you played with him, honey, you laughed with him. You weren't afraid to be around him. How can you say he abused you?"

The counselor asked her to at least be open to the idea that I was traumatized. I thought maybe she'd sway my mom, but then she proceeded to say that I was so young at the time I claimed the rape happened that it would be virtually impossible for me to remember things with any reasonable clarity. Maybe it was her way of bridging the gap between what I knew happened and my mom's denial, but I felt like the stupid, dumb counselor believed my mood-swinging, high-as-a-kite, freaking mom over me! Even the counselor that was supposed to help me didn't believe me!

I couldn't win; I raged all the more, some of the things I did were ludicrous. I'd ball myself up in a corner and rock for hours, I'd put on layer upon layer of clothing until I could hardly move, I'd shake and throw myself on my bed. I couldn't handle the pain of life, so I went to Pain for help. He soothed me, one cut, one hit, sweet droplets of blood running down my arm and I could at least breathe.

In one of the sessions the worthless counselor had me write out what I'd do to Brad. The mutilation I put him through on paper was so bloody and violent, even Jose would have blushed. She didn't flinch; no reaction at all. She looked up from the paper and asked, "How do you know he molested you? You were so young."

I told her AGAIN what I remembered about the closet and the vegetable and the big penis in my mouth. I didn't tell her about the fluid because it was embarrassing to me to think I might have been peed on. I told her what I remembered about the hospital bed or vet table with Aunt Maria hovering over me. I told her about the vaginal pain as a little girl and how similar it felt to when I'd had sex with Greg. Then she focused on the fact that I was having unprotected sex and the risk I was taking.

"Had! I had sex once! That's it... wanna guess how many times Brad did me? How about that number?!" I screamed inside, pleading desperately with her to believe me. Why couldn't anyone even possibly believe that I might actually have been molested by a sick pedophile who also beat my mother? I couldn't win. I told my mom I wanted to quit seeing her.

The only good thing that came out of the sessions was a deep breathing technique and her encouragement to find a "safe place." She told my mom too, who told the rest of the family. After that, when I'd lose it, they told me to go find my safe place in laughing, mocking voices. I did though, I found a safe place along a concrete irrigation trough down the road. It was beautiful there, in a dusty, slightly shaded kind of way. It was quiet and free from everyone. I could listen to recordings of my sonata without a little sibling breaking my concentration. I didn't have to hear Lester share another conspiracy theory, like a freak, or Mom sing along to her songs, or Gio mooch my weed because his was gone again already. I could be all alone; just me, nature, my music book and a pen. Most all of my "Painful" movements came from those times at the river. The harmonics I envisioned and refined were dark and inspired by Pain, but I was at peace there. Something about flowing water, running through the canal, bringing life and refreshment, carrying away leaves like rubbish soothed me. I'd watch leaves spin and twirl and float away from me; I wished I could take what I knew Brad had done and throw it down the river too. I wished I could float what Lester had done down. I wished my life were different, I was tired of the fighting, tired of the yelling, the smoking the lying. I was tired. I had no one and nothing and realized that I never would if I kept up what I was doing. There had to be another way to rage, another way to hurt without looking so bad all the time. I almost had an idea, but nothing fixed in my mind.

Spring morphed into a school-less jobless summer much like the one before it. Party with my friends, party at home, party, party, party. Smoke it up, drink it up, toke it up! Life was good if I was high, actually no, it wasn't good even when I was high, but at least when I was high Pain was less obvious. I was embarrassed with the person I'd become. My self-esteem was in the toilet, just like my vomit. I drank so much on the weekends by then that puking out my window or in the toilet was the norm, not the exception. I drank so much Mom and Lester would cut me off! I hated it, that they cut me off and that I drank so much in the first place. I hated getting stupid drunk but I could never stop at buzzed, so I hated myself even more.

I couldn't stop, I always wanted more high than what I was so I'd take or buy whatever else everyone was doing. Inspired by Teen spirit, the Moss clan I'd somewhat reacquainted with, were all depressed like me and preferred the downers; pills, alcohol, weed and hallucinogens. I was a hopeless druggie. My friends were all druggies, when I shared weed with the group, I pretended like I bought it from some super-secret source I couldn't tell anyone else about, which was nearly the truth, except I never had to buy it. Everyone knew my mom would buy whatever liquor they wanted so I took cash and orders all the time. When I stayed with Abby or Emily, we snuck their parents alcohol and toked what I had. Some of my friends seemed happy sometimes, but we were all desperate and depressed and lost. It was an endless circle of a miserable life.

Dad actually invited Gio and I to come "home" for the summer. The proposition shocked me! I hardly even remember talking to him during the last school year, and he wanted me to come over? It didn't add up for me. I really didn't want to go. By that time I was so hooked on weed and whatever else may or may not have been added to it, drinking, and smoking that I couldn't imagine a day without a fix let alone a summer. Then again the thought occurred to me that getting away from it, going back to my sweet Bavarian town, might be what I needed to start over. I couldn't imagine living with Dad again full-time because of Vickie-Jean and the favoritism and the hatred I felt… but maybe a summer was what I needed. I knew Gio would never go back permanently and he was part of me, but maybe he too would consider a summer. I couldn't live without him. I told him I wasn't going back if he wasn't. He agreed to go and so we went.

CHAPTER 15

IT WAS EXACTLY like before, Dad didn't want us, he wanted our free labor. Not only were we withdrawing we were right back where we ran from. Vickie-Jean hated us and we both knew it. Dad was always at work, nothing new there. Martin and Alex were so different from us. I realized that summer that they weren't rich because of Vickie-Jean's photography, but simply humble shop owners and dream chasers. In all honesty, Mom and Lester probably had more, and the decision to let us go was probably largely financial. Still, I felt like their boys lived a more privileged life than what Gio and I had when we lived there. The boys got summer school art-in-the-park lessons, the very lessons I asked for every summer and never got. The boys went to the Christian school away from the evil kids in public school like I begged to go to. I'd even offered to pay for part of it with my own work money and got a resounding "no," the boys though were allowed to go all on the parent's dime. Vickie-Jean bought the boys name brand clothes and talked about them like they were jewels. It highlighted the garbage she thought Gio and I were. It was like salt in an open wound. It hurt worse visiting than when we lived there. But the summer belonged to Dad, and he did actually pay us twenty dollars a day, so the money kept me from leaving.

When we weren't working, Gio and I would go out and visit old friends, I wished to see my old wrestler fling, Tyler, now that I knew more about sex and making out, maybe that would make my summer, but we never saw him. I hadn't stayed close enough to anyone to make special arrangements to see them. They were all in their own little churchy world anyway and church was the last place

I wanted to be, even though we had no choice but to go every Sunday. I saw them there and that was enough. We visited shops in town too, like we used to. The taffy store where we cleaned out the bins for free taffy was still there as were most all of the stores I ran errands for. We shared our secret stash of smokes Mom had packed for us as we walked through the trails on Blackbird Island. It felt surreal. I couldn't believe I'd lived so long there, and now it was nothing to me but bad memories. Home was Wenatchee, not Mom's house, but Wenatchee. Leavenworth was an overcrowded, hot, sticky, dismal, polka-playing place.

The shop and loft weren't like we left them. We looked around at all the undone things we used to have to do. There were hand prints on the walls, dust on bottles and shelves, droplet marks on the faucets. I even noticed a dirt ring in their tub. When we lived there that never would have been tolerated. We joked that now that they had no slaves their house was a mess. We both couldn't believe how Vickie-Jean let the little things she insisted we do for her go in our absence. I felt even more unwanted. Both Gio and I stayed up in the attic, my old room, that summer. We looked in the crawl space and found remnants of our old life there in chewed up cardboard boxes. The mice, at least made use of our memorabilia. Not only did they let their places go to waste without us there to scrub it for them, they let the vermin trash the place. Honestly I don't think they knew we stashed stuff in the crawl space but we blamed Vickie-Jean for the mess.

We called Mom almost every day. Gio was going crazy with no weed, I think I was too, but we made it all about Vickie-Jean. She was cold and mean, we didn't feel welcome by her and felt used by Dad. We told Mom we wanted to come home early. She insisted we stick it out the rest of our time, but stopped by on their trips to the Fruit stand in Arlington and gave us some weed to get us by. It worked for about a month but we insisted she get us out of there. She did. Dad was so disappointed that we wanted to leave early...but he'd made no plans to do anything but work or go anywhere fun. We didn't even play games in the shop, we were cheap labor. I was over disappointing him by then. I knew my very existence and femaleness disappointed him. There was no point in staying and he let us go early. We were garbage; best packed up and barged away, never mind we might be in some serious trouble with addiction or small town gang violence or cutting. He packed us up, hired minimum wage help, and once again, forgot about us. We were Mom's problem again.

Mom didn't bring any weed to the pick-up, figuring that we could wait the forty-five minute ride home. Gio and I were pretty pissed about that. I must have smoked a pack of cigarettes on the way home. We didn't even get our suitcases in the house before we started toking up. I was starving for weed and smoked like I hadn't gone half the summer without it. Relief flooded through me as the high set in. I went out to the car to bring my things in and realized my mouth felt dry. I knew I was going to pass out, so I dropped my bags and made for inside as quickly as I could. Daylight was fading around me, but I made it up the unusually long outside steps. Someone's voice echoed from far away, "Gia, you don't look good." I couldn't answer but I made it to the couch. I dropped onto it face first. It hurt a lot worse than I imagined a cushioned landing to feel. The next thing I knew Hannah was crying asking if I was dead. Gio and Trent were laughing at the spit hanging from my mouth and Mom was hysterical because I'd passed out. Turns out, I didn't make it to the couch like I hallucinated I did. I was about ten feet from it when I fell like a chopped tree onto the moss green carpet. My knees bruised instantly and my two front teeth had cut into lower lip mixing blood with the slobber still frothing from my mouth. After she regained her composure, Mom got me a glass of water and a cold rag. I told Gio and Trent to shove it and shut up. Not even one day back and they were teasing me again. Hated in one home, humiliated in the other. I didn't fit anywhere. It sucked to be me, something had to change.

I decided the change would be me.

I wanted my junior year to be different. I told Gio my plans over a slow rolling bowl about a week later. He liked it and together we planned to rule the world. It's crazy the wacky things we came up with when we were high. Our plan required that we be mentally and physically fit. We both acknowledged we smoked way too much weed. We were smoking through an eighth of a pound every few days, It was entirely too much. We gave ourselves a 3 bud a day limit. We always ended up smoking more but made excuses for it. We were addicts and that's what addicts do. But it did reduce our intake and we did get up early before school and work out together. We ran together, for a while, then he phased out of the running, but I enjoyed it very much and carried on alone. I ran two miles each day, usually in the morning. After the weather turned crisp the run was always in my purple sweat pants and Wenatchee High School gym shirt. The canyon road was quiet that time of day. I loved hearing my feet slap the asphalt in the fading darkness. I reveled in the fresh air. I felt invincible when I ran, like I knew my body was doing something good for itself, and yet there was space for Pain to live too. Those painful runs, angry and furious, frenzied and chaotic, often up the side of the canyon mountains instead of along the predictable road, helped to heal my skin. My feet and knees and lungs paid the price while the scabs on my skin, for the first time in years, disappeared.

Though Gio preferred weights to miles, together as summer ended, we transformed ourselves into a very fit, very attractive set of siblings. Trent, bless his little heart, wanted to run with me sometimes and would cry and cry if he couldn't come. Sometimes, when I wasn't running off angry, I'd let him ride his bike along. Sometimes Gio let him lift weights. We let him feel like he was in on the transformation with us, and in some ways he was becoming one of us as he approached adolescence.

We plastered the boys' room with maps, we had Washington, the US, the World and finally even a scaled solar system kite string tacked around their ceiling. We really thought we could rule the world. I have no idea how we planned to do it, but that was our idea. Our brilliance, we decided, was in our spoken word. We had to be the best looking, the most charming, the fittest and the smartest; and if we were, then we could rule whatever we wanted. Our first mission was to take over the house. We decided to control our parents, which was easier than I expected. Once, Lester asked Gio to take out the trash and he said, "No, I'm not going to but I think you'll do it for me." And...Lester-the-loud-mouth actually did without complaining or freaking or anything! As he was exiting with the trash Gio and I were euphoric with our "power." He looked at me and I nodded back, silently acknowledging his victory. I don't ever remember anything more significant than having them give us money or do our work chores, but we had good times dreaming about how the world would be if we ran it.

I really started to love my siblings. I don't know that it was in Gio's plan to be affectionate toward our siblings but it was definitely part of my plan. I wanted to do special things with them to make them feel cared for and loved, so they never had to feel like I did. They loved me back and didn't pick on me as much when Mom, Lester or Gio would. It was easy to find things to do with Trent as he got older because he could hang with Gio and I; but I tried to make sure Hannah didn't feel left out either. I would use allowance money to buy her simple flash cards with colors and numbers so she could be smart and rule the world too. I took her on walks up the mountain path I'd walked so long ago with that long forgotten friend of Gio's who had made me feel so safe. Coddling them woke something inside me. I guess I felt purpose. I could make them feel safe and loved.

For me, taking over the world involved raising my social status; not so much for Gio. I surmised that hanging out with stoners and violent criminals wouldn't help my credibility. I needed new, popular friends, and it seemed to me they were in the advanced classes and on the sports teams. Despite my bad luck in Leavenworth with the popular kids, I wanted to try to fit in with them, if I could, in Wenatchee. Abby and Emily were higher up on the social ladder, I decided I could befriend some of the girls and boys they knew in the advanced classes. I thought the familiar connection would be an easy in. I didn't really want to lose Ali or Megan, but it was an easy separation because Megan was older and neither she nor Ali could get the advanced classes I could; they didn't need to know I asked for the advanced placements. I found Mr. Kearny on registration day and told him I wanted to go for some of the advanced classes. He took me to the office and introduced me to Ms. Schram, the guidance counselor, and she fixed my schedule with advanced classes, and best of all, I got to be Mr. Kearny's teacher's assistant for second period.

This time, I didn't show fear, I oozed confidence. It started out really good for me, eye contact, I learned, was key. If I locked eyes

with any boy playfully or suggestively enough, he'd talk to me. If I
made friendly eye contact with the cool girls in an interested enough
way, they'd talk to me. Holding the teacher's eyes let them know I
was serious, interested, worth their attention. And, I could finally
look Mr. Kearny in the eyes. He was so proud to see how I'd
improved and put my focus on my grades. I loved being around him
and making him proud. I wished I was an orphan and that he'd say
he wanted to adopt me, to be my dad. I felt like I'd do anything to
please him. I mattered to him, and that, more than taking over the
world, made me want to be better.

I stopped publicly toking and drinking, though I still ingested
plenty. I still got high every morning before school, and with the
tolerance I had it took two or three bowls to get a good buzz rolling.
I usually brought a small stash to use in the bathroom around lunch,
but since I was more cautious about who knew I used, I tried not to
toke up daily at school, tried. I told everyone I quit using; I even
wrote a paper about how I didn't anymore, but I still was and it
delighted me that I could pull off nearly all A's high every day and
drunk every weekend.

CHAPTER 16

I WAS STILL boy crazy and decided I definitely wanted to have sex, real, good sex that I could be proud to count. Brad and Greg didn't count and Lester only crept and touched. I flirted with anyone who'd give me the time of day and plenty of boys did. There was an overly active curly-haired boy named Adam who took an unusual liking to me. He was attractive, piercing blue eyes, thin but muscular. But his personality was a little too over the top for me. He was older than me by a year but in a lower grade. I didn't like that he didn't apply himself. I checked his GPA on Mr. Kearny's computer and was shocked to see it was .067...who gets a .067 and still shows up for school? Apparently Adam did. He wasn't in the social class I was looking for but I was drawn to him for some reason.

Adam was smart despite his laughable GPA, and his intellect enchanted me. He knew so much about so many things, even a healthy bit about music and music theory though he didn't play any instruments. He wrote wonderful letters; flirtatious, introspective, enlightening, well written letters. A dumb boy couldn't do that. He bared his soul about the things that mattered to him and his difficult home life; both of his parents were alcoholics. I understood broken parents, it bonded me to him. He started to meet me outside my classes and walked to the next with me. We'd have fantastic conversations about everything that could possibly matter to two stoners along the way. He was cute and funny and undeterred, but he was too scrawny to be the one I wanted for my official first.

There were a couple of new immigrant Mexican boys that were apparently attracted to me because of my eye contact. In their culture holding a gaze was a proposition and I was always unknowingly propositioning them. The least attractive of the two, Angel, tried to seduce me one day after school. We were walking down the hall toward the exit when he slowed his pace. His hands wrapped around my waist and he pulled me back... into him. It was hot because he was so forward about it and so intense. His lips found my ear and he said something Spanish and sexy into it. Goosebumps! I didn't know how to answer back something sexy so I used the best vocabulary and sentence structure from my second year of Spanish to tell him I had to catch my bus. With a backward glance, I winked after wiggling free of his grasp. That face, was not what I was into. I stopped making eye contact to deter his affections.

Angel's cousin, Mario, on the other hand, was fairly attractive; dark skin, even darker eyes. I entertained his attention. He was a little scrawny like Adam, but so handsome under his ever present ball cap. I let him kiss me once between classes by my locker. He followed me like a puppy and we kissed a couple more times. Whether he pretended like he didn't understand a word I said, or really didn't know, I'll never know but he acted like everything I said to him translated to, "Besame." It was fun to be courted so overtly, to be pursued, to know their intentions straight-up even if we couldn't speak the same language. Had I spoken better Spanish or Mario better English, he might have been the official first, but I couldn't have sex with someone I couldn't talk to. It wasn't... sexy.

I shifted my focus to other, more popular class prospects. Jocks didn't really go for me because I didn't get their lingo and wasn't a cheerleader but the smart boys and band boys did. It was kind of frustrating to me that the nerds didn't carry themselves like the jocks but I liked their minds and appreciated their humility. I felt like the jocks all had egos and too much arrogance. They reminded me of Gio. Making out with someone like Gio would be like making out with my brother, so I guessed it was OK none of them asked me out. At least that's what I told myself to feel better about them not being into me.

I was a smart girl, a musical girl, loud and opinionated in class and overly proud of my talent. Smart, secure boys took notice in me most. Unfortunately, for some reason it seemed like nerds and band geeks weren't unconcerned about their physical image or muscular build. I wasn't attracted to sloppy hygiene or weaklings. I wished for a smart boy who could play or sing or write music and bench a hundred and fifty pounds. Disheveled or not, I definitely preferred hanging with the geeks in band to the boys on the ball field. They spoke my language; melody, tempo, harmonics, tone, it wasn't about what brand of clothes was in and what kind of car they drove, it was about making music.

Even though I wasn't really into the style, the Jazz band was the group I felt most comfortable with. As luck would have it, one of their two piano players graduated the year before, as did five other band members, and they had tryouts. With the exception of Steph, one of the five saxophone players, Kate on a trumpet and Amy the other piano player, the group of seventeen upperclassmen was all male. I was a pretty girl (I made sure I wore long sleeves to cover my healing scars) so of course they chose me over the other five hopefuls. I don't even think Mr. Kearny had to influence them. The best part was, Jazz band seemed to care more about their image than average band geeks. They looked good, I could talk about more complex theories or musical pieces with them and their eyes didn't glaze over like other kids did…and they made music! We connected in a special way. I could count on one hand the people that understood the music that stirred inside me; my mom, Mr. Kearny, and that long forgotten boy from Leavenworth, Paul. I wondered what my new friends would be like high or wasted, but then again, I appreciated their purity so much. Like the jocks, we practiced until five or five-thirty every day and prepared for our big performances.

It was bound to happen with as much time as we all spent together that crushes evolved. Steph was secretly into Brandon, the drummer, but he liked Kate, and she alternated her affections between Les and Enrique, two other trumpeters. The baritone sax, Dustin, asked me out after a month or so. He was tall and stalky, had the body I was in to and had lots of family money. He also had talent, charisma, ambition and he wanted me! I didn't think twice about saying, "yes" when he asked me out. I was thrown off when he and his dad rolled into the driveway to pick me up. I didn't think to be embarrassed of my small, humble, orchard house until I saw how big his family home and white fenced horse pasture in the affluent Sunny Slope area was. I ran out to him as soon as they pulled up to keep him from the pungent proof of the clambake in my parents' bedroom. He introduced his dad as Bill and then referred to his dad as Bill from there out. I couldn't wrap my brain around calling my parents by their first name. When we got to his magnificent Tudor inspired home on the hill, he introduced his plump, pleasant mom by her first name, Linda, as well. It was weird.

Of course they had horses, three as a matter of fact, he called them chestnut Gelderlands. He took me to the stable, or barn, or whatever their shelter was called and got one ready for us.

"This," he said, reaching his hand up to cradle the head of one in the crook of his neck, "is Buster. He's five and wily but rides pretty good. Do you ride?" I shook my head in the negative.

"Oh… OK," he shrugged, "We'll go together, then, but probably Bea will be better. You can ride behind me."

"Fair enough, who's Bea?" I asked pointing to the two other horses nosing around.

"This one," he answered as he walked to the next closest shiny, big eyed beast. "She's a good old mare. You like horses?"

I didn't want to be rude, but I couldn't help the apathetic shrug, "I don't know, I've never been a horse lady. I feel like a lot of girls dream of having a horse one day, but I never have. They're beautiful, though."

He prepared Bea for the ride while I watched. I was a little intimidated by the whole process, but we'd already talked about it during phone conversations so I kind of knew what was coming. The thing that struck me most, was that he was really rough with his horses. He hit Bea and pushed her and pulled her to get the saddle fitted properly. He told me to kick Buster hard when he nuzzled too much. It felt wrong, cruel even, but he insisted they were big and needed more force applied to them. Still, there was something about how he treated them that bugged me, he was too aggressive, it reminded me of Jose. I can't lie though, the ride, with my arms wrapped around his waist, up the sloping hills, was pretty spectacular.

After the horses were put away, we switched to bathing suits for hot-tubbing in the frosty fall air. I opted to change in the powder room though he welcomed me to change in his room. It was really cool sitting next to him, the warm bubbly water swirling around us. He pulled me up onto his lap and started massaging my back. My focus at the time was to find a guy to have sex with, not so much a relationship with. His aggression with the horses turned me off too much. No amount of smooth massage moves could take it away. I decided I didn't want him to be my partner; had I toked up or taken a few shots before the hot tub, I might have decided differently. Without anything to numb me to his persona, I couldn't give in. He just wasn't going to be it. He bent forward to kiss my neck and I slid off his lap. I told him I just wanted to be friends and it got quite awkward. We changed, we ate an uncomfortable meal at the table with his parents and his dad took me home. I waved good-bye then ran into the house and got wasted.

A young man named Toby who lived further down my road asked me out a time or two. He wasn't the most attractive boy, but he was built nice. I finally said yes, but the more I thought about it, the more nervous I got. At the time I didn't know why I was so anxious. I joked, as did my family, that it was because he had a hippy van, he could be like Ted Bundy or something, but that wasn't really it. I couldn't put my finger on why he made me so nervous. I got ready to go out with him, dressed nice, smelled nice, looked as nice as I could. But when he showed up, I didn't go with him. It was out of my character but I just couldn't. I felt bad for his feelings, it wasn't easy for boys to ask girls out and he did and I said yes, and then I dissed him. Something inside me was afraid of him but I didn't know why and I wasn't going to go out there and tell him that. I made Gio do it and sometime between way back then and now I figured out my fear. Toby resembled Lester. He had a similar nose and narrow beady eyes. Subconsciously I think I'd projected Lester's personality onto that poor boy just because he resembled him. No matter, I wasn't at a loss for suitors.

There were plenty boys of more unsavory character that asked me out, or took me out around town too. I hadn't totally cut off my ties with the thugs and so I'd make out at random with any boy that said he loved me. I hated how quickly they said whatever they thought I wanted to hear to get in my pants. The tactic was too predictable, and I didn't want love anyway, I wanted a guy who'd make my "Official First Time" something worth remembering. One boy, Ben, went way too far, though. We flirted at school and made out in a library aisle, it was totally casual for me. I was dating and making out with anyone who proved available...except for Toby. I was on a mission and was shopping for the right boy. Making out with Ben meant nothing to me emotionally. I loved getting boys all hot and horny just by how I touched and looked at them. It made me feel powerful to have that control over them. Then I shut them down just when they thought they were going to get lucky. The weak ones couldn't handle it and I wanted to make sure my real first time didn't turn out like my technical first time by choice with Greg. I tested the boys' stamina, their kissing, their personalities; I wanted a good first time.

Ben had potential to be my guy at first. He was handsome and reminded me of the Mexican boys; very forward and direct, I liked that, but then he started stalking me and it got freaky. Once in the hall, he saw me talking to Adam, and came up to me and pulled me away by the arm after Adam left. He pulled me hard. I told him to let me go, and he went off about how I was too close to Adam. I told him he had no business being in my business and could shove off. His eagle grip dug in just above my elbow, he tried to walk me down the hall. I kicked him in the crotch and threatened to sick Gio and his boys on him if he ever touched me again. And I told Gio about it that night and my twin took care of things. Ben never so much as looked at me again.

Another boy, Vince, well on his way to becoming a career criminal, was just what I was looking for physically. He was thick on the top, supremely muscular and defined, a piece of art, eye candy if ever there was any. He was stacked and I had a healthy respect for the work it took to look like that. He didn't talk much about working out, but he must have. The lines and definition in his abs and arms weren't there by accident, or even genetics. The problem was he was Lightning Jack when it came to being aroused. He spent himself too fast every time we made out and he didn't care; he wanted what he wanted and didn't really worry if I got off.

I gave him several weeks of fooling around to see how long he could wait or if his attentions would move from his pleasure to mine. He would always cum before I even had one orgasm. He was, like most of the boys, all about himself, and I was just a means to that end. He told me what to do to get him off, but didn't take any interest in what got me off. He was still attractive, but I lost interest in him because he was so selfish. I wanted a first time to count and I wasn't going into it lightly this time. So, as luck would have it, he went to juvy and I used it as an opportunity to move on.

CHAPTER 17

BOY AFTER BOY passed by. One boy, a trombone player in Jazz Band, Mikey, was little—not at all like the type I went for, but very fit and fun. He knew Tae Kwon Do. I always liked the martial arts stuff so his supreme knowledge of the art attracted me to him. Though a junior, he was younger than me, which was weird because I was usually always the youngest. He genuinely took an interest in who I was not just my body; I could tell the difference and that made him attractive to me. He would have been a handsome boy except that his face was marred with acne. Really, if any girl could get past the red and oozy pock marks, they had to admit he was a very cute boy. His eyes were piercing, smooth coffee brown. His face was symmetrical and, well, quite honestly, perfect except for the acne, maybe God gave it to him to make him the guy he was, strong, humble and genuine...not all arrogant and cocky like most boys.

I really did like Mikey. He took me out on dates. We went to Leavenworth a few times to walk around my old favorite places, and visit favorite shopkeepers, and an old but friendly church. I'd never dream of taking some of the boys I knew anywhere near church but it didn't phase me with Mikey. He never claimed to be a Christian but he fit in easily, and my oh my was Nonna ever happy to see not only me, but that a boy brought me. It was nice to have a boy I could take home to my grandparents. He was innocent enough that I was his first kiss, at a dance he broke out in a sweat to ask me. It was perfection, the song was right, the moment was right, it was totally like a movie, down to the last detail, a beautiful thing. His lips on mine, so soft, tentative but easily lead, instinctively catching on to the little lover's game. I know why guys like to be a girl's first, there's something about taking someone's innocence. It made me feel powerful to be the one who had it figured out.

If the opportunity would have presented itself I would have let Mikey have me, if he was too quick or not, it wouldn't have mattered. It would have been satisfaction enough that my official first time was his first time too. We never had the opportunity though, he was not in a hurry to get in my pants, and I wasn't used to pressuring a guy for sex. We did plenty together, though. We made it official and were officially "going out" for about two months. Then his dad got a promotion and he had to move to Spokane. The three hour drive's distance tore us apart slowly. We lived in different towns, went to different schools and it got old for me, and him, to carry on the relationship in letters and phone calls. Our hormones raged and we each had other prospects, so we broke up a month after he moved and Troy took over his spot with the other trombones.

It was an acceptable end, he was too good for me. Years later, in the thick of my addiction and depravity, Nonna commented to me that she'd seen Mikey at a revival meeting she went to in Spokane. She said he came up to her and asked if she remembered him. She said, he said the words he heard at church with me stuck with him. He found a church in Spokane and had given his life to the LORD and was a Christian. Nonna told me he wanted her to pass on a thanks to me for inviting him to church. I couldn't believe it! The only thing God had ever done for me, if He'd done anything at all, was spit in my face and hand me a bad deck of cards, and one of the nicest boys I'd ever been out with ended up leaving me and choosing to believe in God because I took him to church? I was indignant, but didn't even so much as shake my fist at God. It was easier to ignore God's existence at all than believe a god would allow the cruelty that happened in life.

I got over Mikey fast, and the chosen boy, like a packed away box of keepsakes, came out from the recesses of my past to decorate my present with a new wonderful memory. Until I became a Christian years later, I never regretted for one second our time together, and I'm still not sure how much I regret what happened; not very much, it was a good experience. No, it was a great experience, with Paul, my long forgotten musical cohort.

Our re-connection was quite interesting. Mom had lots of friends and co-workers with kids that needed babysitting and I was a teenage girl with time on my hands and no money in my pockets so I was always taking babysitting jobs from them. One of the ladies was not only a co-worker but a client of Lester and Mom's as well. Elaine had two little kids and she and her husband lived in a house about two miles from my school. I rode the bus over to her house to watch the kids after school several days a week until her husband came home. It was a sweet job and I never had to worry about getting busted if I got caught toking up in the bathroom. I doubt Elaine and her husband knew Mom was my drug dealer too, but the worst that would have happened was that they would tell on me. I was in the habit of riding the bus every day; and then one day Paul was on the bus too, and my life would never be the same.

I knew him immediately, those eyes, deep, quiet, thoughtful were unforgettable. Our circles had never once crossed since I left, but there he was, grown, filled-out, still grungy, but much more handsome. He smelled like mountain fresh deodorant and looked strikingly similar to River Phoenix. He said I wasn't the first person to remark on the resemblance. He looked strong, no longer the kid I remembered. He was thick, not as defined as boys who worked out to make their bodies that way, it was just how he developed. I couldn't take my eyes off of him and imagined what he looked like without a shirt on. The days passed and it was just like old times on the short bus ride. Turns out, his parents had divorced. He remained at school in Leavenworth with his dad, but visited his mom every other week. He was getting his license before school was out for the summer, but until then, he bus hopped from one town to the other to get to get back and forth.

I asked him once if he'd show me his stomach, I fantasized it was washboard hard and longed to touch it. He obliged, obviously flattered but remained humble. It wasn't a toned six-pack, but it was a nice healthy set of abs to be sure. From that moment on I started playing my fishing games to see if he would be the one. He didn't have a car so that kind of sucked. Since the divorce his family life was messed up. He lived with his dad and it seemed that while he loved his mom she was a bit unstable. This kid got me because he lived a similar life between two different types of homes. He already knew me, more of me because of those sonata nights in the church than most. He looked at me like he wanted me, but told me he had a girlfriend back home. It was OK. It was good to know he was attracted to me but wasn't interested in possessing me. When he looked at me, it was like before, he saw the music in me and I was a beautiful piece of... art. He didn't devour me with his eyes but clearly appreciated the changes time had made in me as well. I caught him look down at my breasts, that had developed into a pair of firm, perky B cups. His quick, almost unconscious peeks made me feel way more beautiful than I knew I was. I loved feeling that way. I was beautiful in his eyes, yet as before, he never tried to force anything, and frequently spoke of his affection for his girl. He went only as far as I took conversations about anything sexual and we were never short on conversation about any number other topics.

He was my choice but he was taken. I wanted him to be my real first time, to make the experience count and clean. I wanted a time full of sensuality and foreplay and love making, not just lusty, dirty sex. The fact that he had a girlfriend actually encouraged me. It could be just about sex, nothing more. We weren't connected in any other way, it could be our secret. No one in my circle of society would know that I slept with a guy, so I didn't have to worry about getting labeled as a slut. And no one in Leavenworth, especially his girlfriend, ever had to know. Also, if it was at all disappointing for either of us, it would be no problem to run to Elaine's house after school and not have to see him again. But how could I ask him to cheat on his girl, that he loved so much, to give me a first time I could be proud of?

We exchanged numbers and I brought the proposition up to him over a course of long poignant conversations. Maybe if I hadn't been so singularly focused on making him the one to erase all the bad memories before; I would have let my heart attach to him, or considered the girl I was asking him to cheat on. Regretfully, I don't ever remember really caring about him, or her. I wanted what I wanted from him. He was safe, he was good, he was known and yet anonymous. I was direct on the phone and told him about the abuse that had happened to me by two different men. I expected him to blow it off or not believe me, but his reaction was completely different than what I anticipated. He got mad…at them! He believed me! He was furious over what they did to me.

I could have left it there, but that wasn't the whole reason for asking him to have sex with me. I told him about Greg, how quickly he came and how disappointing it was. I propositioned him, asked him if he'd be interested in being my first official time. I made it clear I didn't want to break him and his girl up, I didn't want a boyfriend, I just wanted a good first time. I can't imagine a boy in the world that would have said no to that. Of course he said yes. More than that, he accepted it like a mission. He said it would be an honor to make sex something memorable and good for me instead of something I was afraid of or disappointed in. He promised it would be good, he would go slowly and he'd make it all about my pleasure. I knew I'd picked well and I eagerly anticipated the day.

Our phone conversations, for the most part, ended and during our every-other-week bus visits we focused on where and when we could make it happen. We both wanted it to be right, not hasty. He'd only been with one other girl, Kendra, his girlfriend, so this was going to be pretty significant for him too. No one on the bus knew either of us, so there, in that publicly secret place he reached for my hand one day and looked at me. It was a silent acknowledgment of his belief in all that had been done to me and his willingness to fix it. The special day was all about the timing. We both wanted a perfect day, which meant not having to ride a bus or hide or sneak to get away with it. By the time of my proposition and his acceptance he was only a month away from getting his license. We figured it'd be best to wait for that.

The day came; a sunny Saturday in spring. He had his license and a little, dingy black car he was still learning to operate manually. He had first and second for the most part, but the transition to third frustrated him most. His mom was going to be working until evening, so his house would be vacant. We talked past midnight that Friday. He was checking to make sure I really wanted it; I was high on weed and from the thrill of how the whole thing was working out.

"Yes! I'm sure, I've wanted this for so long and it's you! I'm so sure!"

"OK well, I promise I'll make it special Gia." His words excited me but I still didn't feel a romantic connection to him whatsoever. For me, he was a platonic friend I was going to have sex with; it never occurred to me that was odd.

Paul showed up early the next day, and we took off to his mom's house. I was excited and anxious. All my family knew is that I'd rekindled my friendship with Paul on the bus rides and we were going to spend the day together since he wouldn't be riding anymore. I never had a curfew but that day Mom and Lester decided to become parental. They told me to be home by midnight. I said OK, but I knew if I was late, nothing would happen so I knew I would get home when I felt like it, not when they told me to.

I agonized over what to wear in front of my cheap full-length mirror. I settled on a simple purple tee-shirt that made my emerald eyes pop, an over-sized green and black flannel wrapped at the waist of holey, tight fitting size four jeans, and of course, good old basic black Docs. My room looked like the lost and found after a Pearl Jam concert. I picked through the melee, stuffing other possibilities in my backpack: fishnet tights, another flannel, cutoff jeans.

8:00 AM and he was right on time. The drive to his house was strangely quiet, he focused on shifting, and I focused on the fact that I was going to have sex! I barely remember his house. His room, though, looked like his insides; full of music. Guitars, two acoustics and a red and black electric one plugged into a big old amp, were propped here and there. Billie Joe Armstrong stared, tongue outstretched, from a poster-sized concert shot tacked to his wall, along with multiple other grungy idols.

I pulled out my pipe and weed. I'd already toked up that morning and figured I'd share with him. He politely declined. He said this day was about me, not him and he wanted to be sure not to disappoint. I felt like I was dreaming or in a Brat Pack movie from the 80s. I took a couple tokes and saved the rest of it for later. I was ready! I breathed in deeply, looked up into his steely eyes and nodded, almost imperceptibly.

"You're sure?" He asked, stepping closer to me.

"I'm sure."

CHAPTER 18

HE TOOK MY clothes off, slowly, deliberately; shirt over my head, bra unclasped while he kissed me and walked me back until my knees grazed the foot of his bed. He slid the straps over my shoulders and as it fell to the floor between us, his hands found the flannel, untied it so it could fall too, then unbuttoned my pants. I knew my body well enough to know, I was already wet. I could tell he was aroused too, the proof was in his pants. I wanted to reciprocate, and reached for him but he insisted I let him take me slowly; the time would come for me to do what I wanted with him.

It was turning out better than I expected. I was with this guy who was doing it exactly like I pictured it happening. When he finally had me completely naked, he took my hand and walked me over to the mirror above his dresser. After he popped in an All For One CD, he stood behind me and told me to look at myself, that I was beautiful, while his hands and lips and long hair caressed me. No one had ever spoken to me so boldly and gently at the same time. I tried to look away from my nakedness or into the reflection of his eyes in the mirror but he insisted I look at me. He touched me, softly and gently, cupping my breast and kissing my neck. I felt him hard behind me and after a few moments he stripped himself down to nothing too. We stood there for a long time looking at each other in the mirror.

Then he picked me up, like I was as light as air, and took me to his bed. Though I did not love him, Paul made love to me. He teased and taunted my nipples, kissed trails down my belly and slid off the bed. He spread my legs, found the slippery proof of my arousal with his fingers and played with my clit. It was delicious and maddening and wonderful. He was careful to be sure I was ready before rolling the condom on and penetrating me. I was nervous because he was larger than Greg, and I didn't know what Brad had used on me, but I remembered how I hurt afterward. He shushed me with a kiss when I talked about them, pulled what he had of himself in me out. He started all over again, kissing my neck, sucking my nipples, trailing down my belly.

"You're with me, Gia. I'm not going to hurt you." He spread open the outer folds of my labia with his thumbs and licked me after the promise, then a finger penetrated me. He moved it in and out slowly, still licking and suckling my clit. He looked up and caught my eyes, finger still moving,

"You can stop any time you want, but be here with me. Don't go back there." I knew what he meant and couldn't help the smile, or tears. I stayed with him in that moment, eyes fixed on his as he mounted and inserted himself slowly and completely. I focused on our bodies, how he felt on me, how he was touching and kissing and moving on me. I'd spent so long dwelling on how bad it was to be taken by a man that I never imagined how good it could feel. The little I'd smoked that morning hardly affected me and yet I was high. He made me feel like I'd never felt before. After he insured I reached my climax, he grunted and shuddered and spasmed inside me before relaxing his full weight onto me and nuzzling my neck. We lay wrapped in each other's arms and he still made love to me, caressing me all over, telling me how amazing I was and how good I felt and how much fun it had been.

That was just the beginning. We spent the day making crazy love all over the county… it did get a little out of hand, but it was good and fun and at the time it felt so, so right. We showered together and had sex in the hot water. He played his guitar for me and marveled at how good he was. We left his house, had lunch, shopped together and had sex in the dressing room at Nordstrom. Then he took me home. Once he took me home, I was no longer safe. I was back in Lester's lair, it was over. I took Paul for a walk up the mountain side and he tried to give me one last time to remember; but it wasn't right that close to Lester, it felt dirty. He stopped. We were finished, I didn't love him, I honestly didn't know if I'd ever see him again. I'd gotten what I wanted and I was done with him. I don't know what his feelings were for me, if he did like me or want more from me, but he had a girlfriend to worry about and our time had come to its end and we both knew it. I thanked him when touched his forehead to mine. We didn't even do a last kiss. That was it.

I didn't call him, he didn't call me, we had what we had, did what we did and it was finished. In my mind it was the best scenario that could have played out. Other than saying no to him by my house, it was all about goodness and pleasure, and even that, an opportunity to say 'no' and be respected, had a flavor of goodness to it. We never had a chance to get mad at each other, to get tired or bored with the relationship. There was never any fighting or bothersome emotions we had to deal with because we had no relationship to go with the sexual acts. It was exactly what I needed; what it was for Paul, I did not know.

He had served me well, he'd taken me where no one else ever had. Paul single handedly redeemed the sexual experience in my mind. My hope was that my first official time would take away the pain and shame of the times before. It didn't make it go away but, after spending that day having all kinds of sex with Paul, I came away with a healthy respect and appreciation for good sex and a real good lover. I had a hard time believing it was wrong, like Nonna said, because it wasn't God's way. The Christian propaganda said to wait for a spouse and then love each other like crazy. I didn't have the chance to wait, I didn't get that opportunity to give a husband my pure and innocent self, my choice to wait was taken from me not once but twice. I'm not saying what Paul and I did was right, but neither do I think it was wrong. I'm indebted to that young man for purifying the sexual experience for me. After that, my desire to date and make out and find a boy to have sex with was satiated. I had fun flirting, but didn't need or want to date anymore. Truthfully, I figured any guy would have a hard time topping Paul. I just wanted to be me, to prove to everyone a daily Will could make straight A's, even though I pretended I wasn't getting high anymore at school.

The fear of getting pregnant hit me a few days or maybe weeks later. I don't know what the trigger was, I can't remember being sick, but I started to get really worried about it. Paul and I must have had sex five or more times that day and once, in the shower, without a condom. It was very possible I was prego and I couldn't stop thinking about it. I smoked half a pack to a full pack of cigarettes a day, I got high multiple times a day and got stupid drunk every weekend, sometimes during the week too. If I turned up pregnant the kid was going to be seriously messed up. Not to mention the fact that I was sixteen and any kid born to a sixteen year old druggie with psycho parents was bound for a life of sorrow. In order to have an abortion I had to know for sure I was pregnant, but I didn't know for sure and knowing for sure would probably make me reconsider actually aborting a baby, even one I knew would be seriously messed up from all my drinking and drugging. I didn't want to know, I just didn't want to be pregnant.

I invited Megan over and I asked mom for a fifth of whiskey, vodka and peach schnapps but the two of us only used the vodka and peach schnapps. I saved the whiskey for the next night. I worked out like crazy for hours, until the sweat was dripping off of me. I ran as much and as far as I'd ever run, then, when I couldn't work out anymore I started drinking and smoking. It wasn't dark, maybe only noon or even earlier. I figured if I could get down a whole fifth and then some maybe, if I were pregnant it would probably force a spontaneous abortion with the working out and alcohol. In my head, not knowing made it justifiable. I didn't want to know and I didn't want to deal with a pregnancy. So I drank and drank and drank some more. I remember Gio and I having a slap down wrestling match in the living room. I was so wasted I didn't feel a thing and when he body-slammed me onto the carpet, Lester put a stop to our rough housing because someone was going to get hurt. I think I went out running again, but I can't remember. It took a while but I got the whole bottle down. I'm not sure if I remember any unusual bleeding after that or not, but I remember thinking if I was pregnant before that day, I couldn't possibly be after it. I never missed a period.

Lester the lunatic searched my room all the time. I knew he invaded my space I and hated it. He claimed he was looking for things I could cut with, but I figured he was just a sick freak who liked to creep up in my room. I made sure to write things in my diary about how ugly and scary and sick and twisted he was. I wrote that I had no idea how my mom could live with a man as butt ugly as him with such a disgusting manner who liked to touch little girls. I left it where he was sure to find it. I don't know if he ever read it, but one day after school, and the whole drinking thing he met me at the door almost as soon as I got in. He told me to get in his truck I was going somewhere with him. I looked at my mom and she looked stern like I had to go with him. I had no idea what was going on.

My first thought was that they knew about Paul and I, and now that I'd officially had sex he was going to rape me and take me all over again...the whole way this time. I was freaking out inside, totally paranoid about what would happen when I got in the truck. He didn't speak to me at all. He stopped at a McDonald's to get me an ice cream. I felt sick, why an ice cream? So he could watch me lick it? I felt so afraid. I didn't know what was going on or why this guy was taking me out. He'd taken Gio and Trent to do stuff before, but never me...I didn't know what this was. He offered to smoke me out while we were driving across the bridge to East Wenatchee, I can't remember if I accepted or declined.

We went to the mall. While we were walking around he grabbed my hand. It was just like that night in the bunk bed, and the morning on the couch, I froze and hated myself for it. How could I freeze? And why was he freaking holding my hand? I wondered what would happen if I broke away, but then where would I go? I wondered what would happen if I told the first security guard I saw he touched me in the night. I wondered what everyone else was thinking seeing a middle aged man holding hands with a petite young girl. I felt violated, and it was only holding hands. I saw a knick-knack and found my excuse to twist away. I 'needed' my hand to hold it. After I was finished "looking" I put my hands in my pockets to keep out of his reach. He said we were killing time, but I still I didn't know for what and still he didn't say anything. For the man who ranted and raved, he was acting weird.

Then the time was right, we left the mall and drove to a church. I still didn't get it, Lester was taking me to church on a week day in East Wenatchee? If he wanted me to go to church he could have dropped me off at Gramps church, why here? He finally spoke. He said he found the empty whiskey fifth in my room and the other bottles too. I told him Megan and I had enjoyed vodka and peach schnapps drinks together, I didn't drink it all myself, like he was implying. I was careful to imply the whiskey was shared too. Suddenly it made sense. The creeper was all of a sudden getting parental in the only way he knew how. It had to be totally foreign territory for him to try and actually do something slightly good. He was taking me to an AA meeting? That's why he was so quiet...he was nervous? What a joke!

I lost it! I went off on him using all the expletives I had in my vocabulary. Did he really think that I had a problem with drinking? Didn't he realize it was his wife that bought it for me? They were the ones that told me to ask for it. A stupid meeting wasn't going to make me stop drinking and for that matter who cared how much I drank? My grades were all A's. Wouldn't someone with a drinking problem have problems in their ability to produce such good grades? On and on I went on my own rant in the cab of his beat-up blue pick-up while it clouded with smoke from both our cigarettes. It didn't matter, he had me here and we were going in. What a joke!

All of the guys looked like old or greasy creepers to me and the women were tattooed and had harsh, raspy voices. It was NOT cool! If getting sober meant hanging with the likes of these people I was never going to stop drinking! I think I might have even said it out loud, but at least in my head I did. They did this little round robin thing and took turns telling the group about past exploits and how bad it was to be drunk all the time. I passed when they said it could be my turn. Lester didn't say anything on the way home. I went straight to my room and got high after I yelled at my mom because she was the one who bought me the booze in the first place. We never talked about it and nothing really changed after that except that I made sure to throw empty liquor bottles away immediately.

CHAPTER 19

CHRISTMAS MY JUNIOR year was different in every way than the year before. Mom blew-out one of her lungs, go figure, and was in the hospital for almost a week. I think she ended up getting pneumonia too. I went to visit her after school, as the hospital was right next to the high school. She asked me to help her with stuff around the house for the kids and what not. I did. I'm sure Lester had to re-work his schedule too, but I avoided him at all costs so I don't know how Mom's sickness affected him.

Mom freaked me out in the hospital because she had hallucinations while on the morphine drip. They were bizarre; apparently she had some sort of crazy allergic reaction from the morphine that really messed her up, almost as bad as the lung thing itself. I didn't like seeing her that way, so I visited as little as possible, while still being sure to check in.

When she came home she was still pretty weak and needed my help getting ready for Christmas. She gave me money and asked me to take Trent and Hannah shopping for gifts for each other. I took them separately and despite their rambunctious natures they were great one-on-one. I had fun shopping with them and seeing what they'd get each other. They helped me put up the decorations and make sugar cookies. They sang Christmas carols while I played at the piano and that Christmas was extra special. No matter how her moods hit her, our mom was still our mom and we seriously thought we almost lost her and yet she'd recovered.

The night before Christmas, after returning from the obligatory visit to the Gianelli's, Gio and I found our special presents us under the tree. The parents let us open them that night away from the little kids' eyes. By the smell and size of the package I knew it was weed. We each got an eighth of a pound for ourselves. It was a lot of weed, even for us. We all smoked out together, there in the light of the Christmas tree and mom, for the first time since coming home, found her way to the piano and played "O Holy Night." For a family full of drug users, it was a precious moment. Just for that moment things were perfect; Mom was alive, I was thankful Lester had given us each such a big stash of herb, my twin and I were getting along, we were a happy family unit.

The next morning was one of the best Christmases I remember even though I knew what almost every present was. Mom had managed to stuff stockings the way she always did, it was her thing at Christmas. So while the parental units woke up and had their morning cup of coffee, we kids opened our stockings and goofed off with the goodies inside. Mom put nicer than expected gifts in the stockings but for the life of me I can't remember what they were. The little kids passed out their gifts for everyone and were excited to see if the others liked what they had chosen for them. It was the first time I'd seen joy in giving. The kids had given with no strings attached, they thought about what everyone else liked and got gifts for them to match. Sure the jade coaster little Hannah picked out for Gio, I think, was laughable but everyone else got nice gifts full of thought from each other. Mom got me the most beautiful emerald necklace I'd ever seen as a special thank you for all my help. It was a petite little thing with a perfect little emerald in the center and three little diamonds on each side. I loved that necklace and that morning so much. I could never have imagined how drastically things would change.

After Paul and I had our day, my need and desire to chase and tease boys had significantly decreased but I was a teenage girl and I still very much liked boys. My new goal had become to get a boyfriend. I felt innocent again and really had no desire to go "all the way" until I was married, or at least until I was in real love. Boys still asked me out, but the thrill was gone so I only accepted if I was attracted to them and they could hold my eyes. Most boys looked away after a second or less, or checked me out, but precious few could match my gaze; fewer still would lock eyes with me. It became a game to me to see how quickly I could make boys look away.

It had become a normal part of my existence to lock eyes with people; I was usually never surprised by what I saw reflected back, but in the winter of my junior year, Caleb McDonald surprised me. I was entering my advanced Chemistry class the same time he was exiting a lower level science class. He was in my seat, or I was taking over his. It was a perfect excuse to stare him down. I recognized him by his Gilligan's hat. He was a football player. He sat with the team during pep rallies and his distinctive hat set him apart. He stood and walked toward me; he was exactly what I liked, thick, broad and muscular. Then our eyes met. He knew my game and stared back, a subtle, playful grin upturned his lips. For those few seconds my mind was frozen, no boy had ever played my game. I was lost to the world, but determined to win with him. We held eyes as we passed and turned our heads to stay connected. We both almost laughed and he winked a victorious good-bye to which I nodded my head. I had an intense desire to know him, who he was and why he didn't look away or check me out. Then I was slightly offended that a boy with his seeming self-confidence didn't check me out, was I not pretty enough? I had to know who he was, so Caleb became my mission.

Gio knew of him and approved of my interest and gave me more details. He said he was a cool guy. He wasn't a great athlete, but played football and was a wrestler too. I liked him more after learning that. I told Gio I wanted him over a plotting and planning session filled with roasting bowls that day after school and Jazz band practice. We analyzed the effects of me dating a jock like Caleb and decided, in our supreme plan to rule the world, that it would be fine if I ended up getting together with him. We planned for Gio to give Caleb my number. I pretended like I didn't care if he called me or not.

I hadn't pursued a boy since Jackson, because I knew it never worked when girls chased boys, but I wanted that blue eyed boy so badly! He had Gio give me his number, but I refused to call him first. I would not give chase, I would be chased, but I held onto that piece of paper like it was a million bucks. He seemed to leave his science class late, and I imagined it was because he wanted to see me.

"You got my number," he whispered once as we brushed shoulders and passed each other.

"You got mine," I winked back. I wanted to call so bad. I wanted to hear what his voice sounded like and hoped it wasn't annoying, that would ruin the whole thing. He didn't call the first week after Gio gave it to him but I knew he was interested or he wouldn't wait around after his science class to stare me down. I waited and passed time with drinks and tokes every dark night after school.

I was flustered and infatuated and preoccupied with Caleb. I tried not to obsess, I told myself to chill or I'd be too much for him to be interested in. I tried to find other things to occupy my time and not call him or pine away for him to call me, even though that's exactly what I was doing. Everyone in the house knew I had a crush and was razzing me, but I didn't care. One day, I found my way to the laundry room to fold clothes. There was always a perpetual mountain of laundry strewn the floor or in baskets; it was a perfect distraction. I'd folded two or three loads not at all day-dreaming about having another wrestling lover, when I had a hankering to smoke a bowl. I turned to go to my room but had the strangest sensation overtake me. I still can't effectively explain it; it wasn't a voice, it wasn't audible at all but something spoke to me. All it said was, "If you do this now, you'll never have a chance with Caleb." That was it, no reason, no vision, no light from heaven or appearance of an angel or ghost. It didn't cause me reason for me to question the existence of God, or paranormal experiences but it, whatever it was, shook me enough to stop me mid-stride.

I was completely infatuated with Caleb, a boy I hadn't even talked to. The thought of not having a chance with him halted my desire to get high. The "knowing" of that inaudible voice wouldn't leave me. It was something outside myself and couldn't be ignored even if I couldn't explain it. I knew that if I got high, I wouldn't be, couldn't be with Caleb. I was re-wired, re-made in that moment. My addiction was completely gone, and stayed gone, for the entirety of the eighteen months Caleb and I were together.

Caleb called that instant; we flirted on the phone and hung up after a half-hour or so of getting a feel for one another. I was more infatuated than ever. He didn't get great grades, but not everyone could be an honor student. He was funny though, and nice and he was taking my heart from me. I wanted him more than I wanted to drink or get high. I wanted to know him, to watch him wrestle, to meet his family he'd told me about, to ride in his cherry red and black 1973 Mustang. I couldn't risk losing the chance. I gave Gio the rest of my weed with a shrug.

"What's this for?" He questioned me curiously

"I don't think Caleb smokes. I really want a shot with him. I can't."

"Whatever, more for me."

I got a call to the office on Valentine's Day. There was a beautiful red rose for me, from Caleb of course. The note said, "Will You Be Mine? –Caleb," I figured it was a canned sentiment, I was not overcome by emotion, but it was nice to have someone give me a flower. I thanked him sweetly at school, but it was just a rose, no commitment there. I was a little bummed because I'd been hoping he'd ask me out or take me to dinner or something more significant. I thought we were so into each other it didn't make sense why he would invest that much time into me at school and on the phone and then make Valentine's Day so bland. Maybe he wasn't as into me as I was thinking, maybe I was being played the way I had played all those boys, maybe this was going to be like Jackson all over again.

That night on the phone he asked what I thought about the flower, I told him it was pretty and thanked him again. Then he asked what I thought about the card.

"The card?" I asked a little confused.

"Yeah, the one that said, 'Will you be mine.'…

"Oh, that card, um, it was nice?" I still didn't know what he was getting at.

"Yeah… Will you?"

"Will I what?"

"Be mine, Gia. I want you to be my girl."

I was in Gio's room, sitting in his video game chair. Gio and Trent were right there. I was trying to play it cool and sound normal on the phone, but I started rocking like crazy in the chair and getting all excited. Of course I said yes and then told him how I'd gotten all worried it was just like a nice little Valentine's saying he didn't mean. He assured me that he meant it. Caleb and I were officially boyfriend and girlfriend and his purple and gold letterman's jacket was my new winter coat!

Like usual, my family partied that Friday night, unlike usual, I stayed in my room and talked to Caleb on the phone while Hannah listened to every word. I hoped their music and ruckus wasn't hideously loud to him. Now that he knew I was his girl I guess he felt safe to tell me all about his life. He too had a flaky mom, evidently I must have unconsciously been drawn to people like that, or them to me. He said he loved her but had come to live with his dad about the same time I'd moved in with my mom because she got her third husband and Caleb was not a fan. He had a same-aged step-sister who was the brains and favored child in their home. Though they weren't twins it was another point of commonality between us. It was a love-hate relationship that couldn't be escaped.

He had all these ambitions that were so thoughtful for a kid our age. I felt sort of sorry for him that his grades weren't great, but they were good enough that he could get on the sports teams. He did sports because he wanted to look back when he was older and show his kids his high school letter and sports picture in the yearbook. He involved himself in other clubs, drama and student leadership among other things to have the full high-school experience. He wanted to build memories to treasure when he was older, he wanted to meet the expectations he put on himself and set impressive goals to achieve them. It was novel and inspiring in someone so young, it was a shame he wasn't a little more intelligent.

We planned our first real date for the next evening, Saturday night. He was going to pick me up in his shiny red car! I was simply giddy when we hung up sometime past midnight. I had a date with a boy, a boy who was my boyfriend, and he had a car and my life would never be the same. I didn't want to smoke or drink, but had fun being the center of attention when I came down the hall that night. The euphoria of having a crush was very much like a high in itself. I was on top of the world and though I had nothing in my system, I went to bed later that night with my head spinning and heart racing.

The next morning there was some kind of funky tension between Mom and Lester. Since it was a winter weekend and Lester wouldn't be going to work, a fight was sure to break out. Everyone knew it, we just didn't know when. As luck would have it, Megan called to hang out, and Gio and I got a ride with her into town. It sucked being there when they fought, so the escape was appreciated. I didn't particularly like leaving the little kids, but didn't know how to protect them from the fights either. I'd been forced to listen to far too many fights myself, so I justified leaving; they had to learn how to deal with it like Gio and I had. I coped by running away. I'd spend the day with Megan and have a date that night with my boyfriend. If I was lucky, I would miss most of the drama. I was not lucky.

CHAPTER 20

MEGAN DROPPED US off around five so I could get ready. Hannah met us at the door, she was flushed and worried and said, "Mommy and Daddy got in a fight and Mommy fell down. Daddy was going like this..." She put her hands around her neck. I was shocked and stunned; it had been a long time since there had been any physical violence between the two of them. I thought they'd grown out of it. I almost didn't believe what she was saying but I remembered all their fights in my youth. I remembered how Mom would chase after him and how Lester would go after her. I was horrified that my younger siblings had seen it too.

Mom was at the piano, Lester had apparently locked himself in their room. We ushered the kids into the boys' room and got more of the story. Hannah watched the whole thing, she said it had happened in the laundry room. Mom had been folding clothes and started yelling at Lester about something. She said they argued all over the house. Trent was afraid, and tried to get Hannah to go into his and Gio's room, but Hannah wouldn't leave. She yelled for them to stop fighting. Trent gave up and sat on the couch. He reenacted the whole fighting scenario with his ninja turtles. They said the parents went back into the laundry room and they didn't follow but said Mom screamed and there was a lot of crashing and noise and then it got really quiet. Their dad came out of the room and locked himself in their bedroom. The kids found Mom on the ground, but she wasn't dead. Trent's chin quivered when he recounted how he leaned over her to make sure she was breathing. They had to wake her up, but she eventually came to and told them she was OK.

By the time Gio and I had gotten home she was in a mood and making music. She had bruises all the way around her neck. It was so scary and I didn't know how to react to it all. I was horrified that my little siblings watched that. I was mortified that my brand new boyfriend was going to pick me up on a night when all hell had broken loose. I should have been worried about my mom but I blamed her as much as Lester.

Mom got up from the piano and started to clean. The more she moved around the house the more distraught she became. From what I gathered from her shouts at the locked door, Lester must have cheated on her, or she thought he did. She was egging him on again, banging on the door, cursing him from the closed side. Her mood was over, she wasn't dead, and she wanted to fight again. I told her to shut up, we all told her to shut up, but she was bound and determined to call Lester a wife beater and cheater every way she could come up with to say it. She kept on going on and on. I wanted to strangle her myself. I couldn't figure out why she just didn't keep her stupid mouth shut or call the cops and let him get arrested. Actually, I knew why no one called the cops, we had too much weed in the house and it would have been way more than a possession and paraphernalia charge if the officers decided to look around at all.

Lester came out of their room with a stuffed duffle bag and garbage sack. He announced his decision to go to his parents, the faraway grandparents' house indefinitely. He didn't know if he'd be back but he needed to chill and Mom, he said, needed to figure herself out. Mom kept yelling it was done, they were done, it was over, he was ruining their marriage. That made the little kids cry, they were sad their parents might divorce. Divorce was no big deal to Gio and I, and I knew Mom was just saying stuff to make Lester mad, maybe she didn't mean it, maybe she did, but at that moment all she was doing was trying to keep the fight going.

Chaos, drama, fighting, crying and it was almost time for my date! I never forgot that it was coming even in the middle of all the fighting; it was always in the back of my mind. I decided I'd have to call and cancel and tried to fabricate a believable enough story that wouldn't involve making my family sound like a bunch of fruit loops. I can't remember what story I came up with, but I told Gio I was going to call and cancel the date with Caleb. He didn't want me to; he wanted me to get out of the house. Lester had guns and might come back. Gio wanted me out of there. I didn't want to leave my mom or siblings but I didn't want to stay and deal with any of it either. I felt horrible for listening to him and keeping my date, but I didn't want to stay. I got ready quickly and Mom switched into this overly happy mood when I came out of my room. She ooohhhed and aaahhhed over me. I felt so guilty. My home was falling apart and I was leaving for a happy little night out.

When Caleb came to the door to get me, Hannah was right there jumping at his heals with all her nervous energy. We were close enough by then that I kind of crumbled into him when he hugged me. He could tell something wasn't right, I remember he shared that his mom had a sort of rough life and hoped it was enough for this whole thing not to totally freak him out or make him insist we call the cops. Gio filled him in on the situation all man-to-man like. The more details Gio gave Caleb, the tighter his arms wrapped around me. It was surreal having my brother hand me off to Caleb with instructions to take care of me and be there for me and try and understand it'd be a rough night for me. I was mortified and relieved all at the same time. I didn't have to lie about it, with Gio validating what had been going on Caleb wouldn't question whether I was being a drama queen or not. I can't even remember leaving the house or where we went, I only remember him coming to pick me up in the middle of all of that mess.

It bonded him to me. I think he was attracted to the fact that I sincerely needed help. He wasn't going anywhere. We became inseparable at school outside of class, and talked every day on the phone. I kept waiting for him to say I was too much to handle, the psychoness of my life was too much, but he never did, he just stuck with me.

Mom stayed away from the house for a while so we pretty much fended for ourselves while she and Lester figured things out. They took turns calling us to let us know what was happening. Lester sent money for groceries and Caleb took me to the store to buy them. Mom came to visit me at school. She was a mess. She said she was staying at her mom's house because she was afraid Lester would come back. She said it was so hard to be away from her kids. I can't remember how long she was gone but I remember thinking that if I were a mom instead of coming to my oldest kids' school after a long time of not seeing and telling them how much I missed them all, I'd have figured out a way to be with them. She did eventually move back in and Lester was officially out. He moved to Arlington to live in a trailer on his parent's property and started farming and he came over to get Trent and Hannah every weekend because Mom worked all of them.

Everything was different after that. I didn't block my door or worry about a creeper coming in in the night. I was still reeling from the infatuation Caleb and I had going on. My body was normalizing to not having any foreign substances in it so that probably factored into the overall feeling of goodness that pervaded my soul as well. It was as if I'd finally taken off a heavy backpack I totally forgot I was even carrying. I was free, I was light, I could breathe and move and dress however I wanted and not worry about Lester. There was no porn when Mom wasn't there to keep secret. I was able to walk around my house unafraid or on alert. I didn't realize that I had been so conditioned to watch out for Lester until he was gone and I didn't have to. Life felt great. The only things I barely missed were weekend parties and visiting Trent and Hannah's grandparents, but those were sacrifices I willingly made.

It would have been perfect if Mom hadn't started to party away from home and completely flake out. She'd work, sleep while we were all in school, and then go out, largely leaving Gio and I alone to care for the littler kids during the week. At first it was fine because we were free of Lester's wrath, but it got old fast. After a few weeks, Gio started to go to wrestling practice at Caleb's recommendation, so Mom had to at least be up when the little kids got off the bus; up until then he had been watching them while I was at jazz band practice. It helped a little, but there were plenty of evenings she was already gone or still asleep when we both got home. We fed them, helped them dress in the morning and get ready for bed at night. We tried to keep the house clean too. It was exhausting for Gio and I to be mock parents.

I couldn't do anything with Caleb during the week because the kids needed to be watched and I didn't want him to come over. It didn't matter how bad my home life was with kids like me, but

Caleb wasn't like me, he was a well-kept boy who was used to a higher class of living. When he offered to bring Gio and I home, we both declined, opting for a ride from one of my jazz band friends or the city bus that got us within a mile of our house. I didn't let him come over too often because I never knew if Mom would be up and high, or getting high and the house would smell like weed, or in a mood, or worse than all of that, coming on to him.

When he did come over and Mom was there, she sometimes flirted mercilessly. It was humiliating and disgusting all at the same time. My mom was more than twice our ages and she'd put her arms around him and bat her eyes like a high school rival. I'd seen her do it with plenty of Gio's buddies but, first of all, they were not my boyfriends and second, she had Lester to answer to so she had to keep herself in check. I hated watching her flirt with him, it was gross and it made me mad. It fed my anger and resentment. I confronted her about it and all I got was the whole, "You're overreacting. You're such drama queen," speech. She insisted she was just being friendly. I'd seen her friendly with Mark and Lester's friends and that friendly didn't have her up in their personal space. She was flirting with my boyfriend and I didn't want him around because of it.

The more days passed, the more Mom went off into her own little world away from her kids. After one of Trent and Hannah's visits, we found out that Lester was with a new lady who was some sort of teacher. It gave me the willies to think that Lester might be around lots of little girls, but at least he wasn't near me. Gio and I griped and moaned about the whole situation to each other constantly and would berate Mom's lousy parenting.

During one of our mom-bashing conversations we brought up the fact that she didn't even make Trent shower. He was starting to smell pretty rank and his hair, naturally light brown, was literally so dirty it looked almost black. We asked him when the last time he had a bath was and he couldn't remember. Gio and I were convinced it'd been way too long, and he needed one. He refused to shower, so we filled the tub and prepared to give him a bath whether he liked it or not. We stripped him to his skivvies, I grabbed his arms and Gio had his feet. We carried his kicking and screaming form into the bathroom and dunked him in the warm, sudsy pre-filled tub water. We had to work fast but scrubbed him and his hair clean. He was so dirty that the water turned brown. And he was so mad that we washed him. He yelled and cussed and hit, but we triumphed and he was washed.

At that moment, Mom decided to make an appearance. She heard Trent going off on us and us going off on him. She got pissed at Gio and I.

"What do you think you're doing?" She bellowed, holding a soggy Trent in her arms.

"He's filthy," I answered, "We gave him a bath."

"You traumatized him..." She yelled.

"We traumatized him?!" Gio screamed back, "We traumatized him? How about you and Dad?" I hated it when he called him Dad, but he always had. "We're trying to give him a bath. That's something his mom should make him do. But you're never here, and he stinks! Look at the tub! It's black! What kind of a mother lets her kid get that dirty?"

"I don't like the way you're talking to me," was all she could come up with for an answer. Her nose flared and the vein in her forehead throbbed.

Adrenaline raced through me too. I tapped in, "I don't like the way you're acting. You have kids, grow up and take care of them!"

"Don't you speak to me that way or I'll..."

"What Mom? What are you going to do?" Gio asked.

"I'll kick you out, that's what."

"You wouldn't kick us out because then you wouldn't have anyone to take care of your kids."

"Really?!" She challenged, "Then I suggest the two of you find another place right now, because you can't stay here anymore."

Shocked silence filled the room. Had she really just said what we thought she said? The little kids were crying. She stared us down defiantly. I took the cordless phone off the wall and called Gramps and Nonna and told them Mom kicked us out. They said they'd be there soon and to be ready, so I started to pack. Like the day of the strangling, I felt horrible leaving the kids. They didn't deserve this kind of a life, but I had no options. I wasn't going to let my little brother not bathe and I got kicked out for trying to take care of it. I figured if she thought she could do better without us, it was her opportunity to prove it.

CHAPTER 21

AN HOUR LATER, we were loading up to leave. Mom had been doing her typical chase-the-person-you're-pissed-at deal for about twenty minutes. She alternated between telling us to start walking and meet Gramps and Nonna on the road, and saying she never actually kicked us out. She said we made that choice to leave then begged us to stay. Gio and I both tried to ignore her, but sometimes engaged. We knew what she told us. She kicked us out because she was mad and now that reality was sinking in and she knew she'd have to take care of her kids herself, she regretted her decision. She'd never before told us to get out. We knew her crazy too well. She gave us the escape. We had no choice but to take it.

Gramps and Nonna listened to her arguments patiently but they didn't encourage us to stay when she said we didn't have to leave. Gramps even helped pack our stuff into the bed of his new-to-him Ford F150. The kids ran after us on the road; Trent bawling and begging for forgiveness. I cried watching them until they were out of sight then let the tears stream down my face, my neck and soak into the collar of my tee-shirt. Gio, ever the stoic, stared straight ahead with a clinched jaw.

My grandparents never asked about what had led up to us moving out, they just offered us a way out. It didn't even bother me, I didn't even want to talk. I welcomed the surreal Gianelli denial of all that is bad. I wanted to take what was mine, my clothes, music and keyboard and get as far away from my crazy mother as I could get. I figured she'd get back together with Lester and since I had a way out, a place to go, and was no longer hungry for their drugs I knew I didn't want to be there. I was gone.

Those last months of my junior year are kind of a blur and it's weird to me why they are; it seems like I should remember more about when I was clean and sober than when I was getting drunk and high. All I can make of it is that a mundane life doesn't leave too many traumatic memories to hang onto and life had become safe, predictable and almost boring. Lovely Leavenworth was my town again, and nowhere was as wonderful as my Bavarian town! Returning to Dad and Vickie-Jean was a non-option; as far as I know they never offered, and we wouldn't have accepted even if they had. Gio and I preferred living with my persnickety, pastoral grandparents to them. We remained enrolled at Wenatchee High School. I asked to stay there because of jazz band, my friends were like family by then, and of course, I couldn't leave Mr. Kearny. Gio didn't like school anywhere but had proved to be remarkably good as a wrestler and didn't want to leave mid-season. We rose extra early every morning to catch the city bus that took us to school nearly an hour away. Almost everything was safe and good.

We started hanging out with our cousins and Leavenworth siblings again; Billy, Andy, Martin and Alex were almost always still at Nonna and Gramps when we got there in the evenings. It was just like old times except we were all older. Billy was the first to drive and got what everyone called a "starter" car for Christmas; an old, rusty, gas-guzzling Suburban. We didn't care, he had wheels and it was cool! He drove our little Italian family gang around town when there was nothing better to do. We drove back roads blasting music and awaited the turning of the seasons, when we could go up into the mountains. We were the gang again, at least when I wasn't busy at some jazz band competition or function.

There was a lot of pressure from Dad, my grandparents and even Aunt Maria and Uncle Joe to get Gio and I licensed and driving. They didn't like us taking the bus; if we had our licenses and a car it would be better for the Gianelli image somehow. We had no problem with public transit and were quite used to hitching rides from Billy or Caleb or other friends to get anywhere we wanted to go, but didn't argue when they put us through driver's ed.

Church at the good old AG of LV was a non-option. Since we lived with Gramps and Nonna, we had to go. It was different going back after the long hiatus. The people seemed frumpy, fat, old and weak and weary of society. I don't remember attractive church members there or people who looked like they had it all figured out. I remember the smelly, disheveled, migrants struggling to learn English and old folks from the local nursing home. It was as if my grandparents' church was an oasis for the "less thans" of Leavenworth society. The church was the Island of Misfit Toys in Rudolph the Red Nosed Reindeer, only in real life. But they were good and kind and always had smiles and what seemed like genuine love for the LORD, a LORD I still didn't know.

I began to read the Bible again. Gio had actually started before we got kicked out of Mom's. It had something to do with us ruling the world; we needed to know the Bible. He'd get all excited about what he was reading and sort of preach it to me in his room at Mom's. I questioned if God was even real. Gio's new found excitement added to my confusion, but I guess I sort of forgot about it when the ritual and routine of church-going and religion resumed. I prayed to a God I wasn't sure of, I read a Bible that was truth to so many but so often left me with more questions than answers. I'd go to Gramps and Nonna's church and do all the churchy things. But it was once again a lifestyle I was embracing, not a God I was meeting.

I liked the church kids, though no one I knew from before remained, I liked my family, I liked my boyfriend; I felt mostly normal, but I knew the filth I was. I knew the secret raging I still did, when running just wasn't enough and no amount of music could play the pain away. I knew the bad things I'd done and never told to a Christian soul the way a good Gianelli did. I knew how much and how often Caleb and I were making out and how not OK it was compared to the "good Christian" standards Nonna was always preaching to me again. I was a garbage kid, who did stupid things and was never going to be good enough. That horrible dreadful feeling of being a failure started to eat away at me every time Nonna corrected me for something I did wrong or could have done better, and she corrected me all the time.

I don't think the move or hell-fire sermons affected Gio the same way at all. I doubt he felt anything less than master of his universe, or if he did he never let on. I'm not convinced he ever quit using, but we didn't talk about weed in our new world. I wanted to stay far away from it because of the "knowing" I had about Caleb so I never asked or offered to smoke up with him. He was the same old macho, tough, Italian loud mouth he'd always been but instead of being a thug, he totally morphed into a stereotypical jerk of a jock through and through. He put his heart and soul into sports and got so good Dad even came to one of his wrestling matches.

Caleb accepted the new, churchy me as unconditionally as he had always accepted me. It was totally foreign to me that someone would like me just the way I was at any particular moment. That boy confused me worse than the Bible. He was outspoken in his questioning of God's existence but would still respectfully attend church with me and accept my religious practices. He even participated in some of the other church activities but kept his steadfast agnostic stance.

One of the first times he joined in on a youth group event, we got caught making out. The youth leader, a fun, old wrinkly grandpa-man named Pastor Jack who was probably twenty years older than Gramps, scheduled activities for us about once a month. One night we did a scavenger hunt all through town and ended up at the church for pizza and pop. It was fun hanging out with the kids and getting to know them and watching my twin have a good time doing legal, honorable things. All the kids I knew from living in Leavenworth before had moved on, but the new group embraced Gio and I and Caleb too.

After pizza and clean-up, Caleb drove Gio and I the short distance home to Nonna and Gramps. It was late, they were already in bed and Gio went straight to his room. We were alone in a safe, warm house with full, happy bellies and hot, teenage passions. It was dim and quiet, the tic-toc of the clock in the kitchen invited us to enjoy some sweet moments together before he left in time to get home for his curfew. Good-bye kisses on the couch got intense until everything disappeared except for his lips on mine, his hands touching me, his hips grinding with mine. All of a sudden I heard the signature sound of Gramps's presence. He had a habit of sucking air through his teeth. And he was there, sucking air, while we were sucking face. We heard it too late though, by then he'd seen enough for Caleb and I to both be mortified. Caleb pulled his hands out of my shirt. I jumped off his lap.

"Whew, I should have got a picture of that." That was it, that was all he said. He took his white underwear and tee-shirt wearing self into the kitchen for a drink of water and then back to bed. I wanted Caleb to leave so I could go and rage on myself for being so stupid and careless. I needed to feel the pain of my stupidity. Caleb insisted on apologizing to Gramps. That would mean Nonna got involved too. I would have rather died than for Nonna to know I was making out. I tried to make him understand the Gianelli code, no bad shall ever be confessed or discussed. We just move on. I tried to tell him it was as good as over. I tried to keep him from going down the hall. If he confessed our sins and apologized it would only bring Nonna into it and only make me need to purge more evil from my body.

He wouldn't listen. We disrespected Gramps home and he needed to apologize. I stood outside their bedroom door after Caleb's quiet knock was granted entry. Baseball cap in hand, he made a humble apology. Nonna, bedsheets to her chin, start crying and asking God why, "Why God, why?" and she cried her pathetic cat cry of sorrow. I was really going to make myself pay for this screw up! Caleb came out feeling much better; his conscious was cleared, his handsome face free of stress lines. He'd made his apology, we wouldn't be making out at the grandparents anymore, all was good for him.

He hugged me under his chin and told me not to be so upset. He didn't get it. If he'd have kept his mouth shut, Nonna never would have known and the shame wouldn't have been so bad. I knew Gramps and Nonna would never speak of it again. Gramps would treat it like his counseling work, it was something to keep confidential. Nonna would find something else to endlessly shame me for, but really she'd be shaming me for that night. It sucked so bad being me, I hated me everything about me.

Gramps was a great guy; he made living with Nonna tolerable… almost. I loved waking up with him early in the morning for school. Nonna slept in later, Gio did whatever he did to get ready for school. Gramps was my morning pal! He was as steady as that ticking clock

I loved so much. Brew the coffee, suck air through his teeth, sing a hymn down the hall to wash his face, suck air through his teeth, whistle a tune as he dressed in the bedroom to start the day, share a joke or two and push some toast and peanut butter onto me.

"Manja Gia. It's-a good for you!" he'd say in a zesty mix of Italian and English. Sometimes I said yes, sometimes no, if I ever said no, he'd go into a good natured lecture about a body needing nutrition and peanut butter being a great source of nutrients and on toast, well, that was just delicious. I never really got it back then, but his jokes were often like Jesus' parables. I thought they were just funny stories, but he was trying to impart wisdom, share a truth or draw me into a relationship with Something greater than myself and the little world I lived in. Seeing I couldn't see and hearing I couldn't hear…to me, they were just jokes, just stories, but he was using our light-hearted morning conversations the way Mr. Kearny used music. He spoke in riddles, fed me toast and nourished my soul and sent me and Gio off to catch the city bus with a smile.

Getting Gio and I back and forth from our extra-curricular events was a pain for everyone. We were the extra burden the family had to take on for my dad. We were family, that's what good Italian families do, but we were burdensome. Most days after jazz band and wrestling practice we caught the last bus west to Leavenworth. Some days Caleb would bring us home. Every day I would rather have stayed anywhere than have to go home to Nonna.

Her non-stop picking at us didn't bother Gio but it wrecked me. All the comfort and safety of their house, all the patience and predictability of Gramps couldn't buffer my feelings around Nonna. The woman drove me crazy. Any time I questioned her reasoning, which was often because she was a little wacko with her idolization of her dad and her obsession with over cleanliness, she'd cast the devil out of me. I knew I had something in me, but not the devil, it was aggravation at her, and a hate for myself because I could never, ever, even once please her. I tried to clean just so, I couldn't do it good enough as a little girl and I still couldn't get it right as a teenager. Nothing I did was ever good enough. So after a few months I started to avoid her like I had avoided Lester and Vickie-Jean. I had so much anger inside me, though that we got into a couple yelling matches. She refused to acknowledge that she went overboard on the cleaning and rules and casting out the devil and I wanting so badly for her to understand how she made me feel. She never got it.

I usually took off on an angry run and ended up banging the church's baby grand's keys fiercely because I couldn't cut or scratch anymore. By then Caleb knew my body as well as I did, maybe better. He cared about me, if he'd seen something like cut marks, he would have tried to get me help. He was always trying to help me, always trying to make things better. He understood that I was broken, but he saw the good underneath the brokenness and wanted to help me get fixed. I kept on telling myself it was only until I was finished with school then I could move out with Caleb and leave Nonna forever. I couldn't graduate and turn eighteen soon enough.

CHAPTER 22

SOON ENOUGH GIO and I finished driver's education and Billy and Andy's dad, my Uncle Joe, had a friend who gave us the least cool car ever. It was a tan Pinto with a broken driver's side window, but it was our ticket to freedom. I named the little turd Tanner and loved him like he was a Corvette, Gio treated him like a hunk of junk. Neither of us cared that he was a goober of a car. He took us where we wanted to go, all I wanted was to be away from Nonna! I'd convince Gio to stay out as late as we possibly could with Caleb or the cousins or anywhere, just hoping Nonna was in bed by the time we got there. I loathed the drive home and went as slowly as I could when it was my turn to drive Tanner the turd.

I didn't hate her but I hated never being good enough and she perpetually reminded me how not good I was. Nothing I did was ever right. Conversations, or more accurately shaming sessions, where she told me what I messed up and I was supposed to silently acknowledge obediently, ended one of two ways: either I yelled and or she casted the devil out of me. Sometimes I reverted to my childhood technique of staring into her eyes until I disappeared into my own world while she went on and on. I knew she loved me but at the same time she didn't like anything I did.

I got in the habit of staying over at Auntie Maria's whenever I could; she became a sort of surrogate mother to me. She welcomed all the kids from the church and school into their house so I never felt "special" but I felt far more tolerated at their place. She knew what it was like to be a female under Nonna's thumb and let me stay to be free for a while. She discussed it with Uncle Joe and the cousins, and of course Nonna, Gramps and my dad and offered to let me move into their six bedroom home because everyone knew the tension between Nonna and I was getting ugly. I didn't hesitate, but said yes!

Gio wasn't happy about my decision; he hadn't been asked or didn't want to move again and accused me of deserting him. I threw it back in his face and reminded him how he left me when he first moved to Mom's. That shut him up; but if I'm honest, things were never the same between us after that move. I tried to justify things to him and to myself. He had his own life with the guys on the sports teams, he didn't even want me around him at school corrupting his tough image, we both knew I mattered very little to him. Besides all that, if I stayed with Nonna I'd end up saying or doing something that would really hurt her or me. I didn't want that. Nonna guilted and shamed me but she was the only woman in my life who'd always been there. I didn't want to hurt her and it was far easier to listen to Gio bellow than to deal with Nonna's guilt. I knew I'd still see them both all the time, it wasn't like I was leaving the family, just leaving her house, because it wasn't a safe place for me. Nonna's shame was toxic to my soul.

For a while Gio kept Tanner the turd and dropped me off and picked me up on his way to and from school. My new house sat on top of five rolling acres next to a vineyard. It wasn't the biggest house in sight, but it was by far the largest I'd ever called home. Aunt Maria, Uncle Joe, Billy and Andy were about five minutes out of Leavenworth toward Wenatchee. More often than not Gio would stay for a while when he dropped me off, then leave only to pick me up the next morning. About a month into the new routine, Dad found Gio a little pick-up and gave him the keys over an otherwise mundane family dinner one Sunday at Gramps and Nonna's and that effectively ended our twinning, not that we ever "twinned" much.

School days became a regular barrage of classes, grades and activities. Caleb was involved in a little bit of everything and I was his girl so I went along. For me it was a chance to see how the other half had experienced high school; what they did when they didn't hurry home to get high. It was fun for me but I noticed that Caleb wasn't passionate about anything. He was avoiding home too. He didn't love sports, leadership, drama, going to church with me or anything really; they were just things he did out of some sense of needing to do things. It was good natured fun, he was a good natured boy, but he had no passion, no drive for life. He was steady, he was sure, he was everything I'd ever hoped for physically but he was a little too safe, a little too predictable, a little too into me.

In the beginning I was so into him, and figuring out what was going on in my life, that it was cool that he was so attentive. We went everywhere together, did everything together and we really bonded over the messed-upness of both of our families. He wanted to be with my family to avoid his and I wanted to be with his family to avoid mine. Auntie Maria's became an oasis for us both. They were liberal, affluent, open-minded and their house was always full of good kids hanging out doing good things. We spent most of the rest of my junior year hanging out with my cousins and brothers and the drama crew he practiced with.

Uncle Joe and Auntie Maria were better off financially than my dad or mom had ever been. Aunt Maria had her vet practice and Uncle Joe was a techie titan who spent most of his time out of town. There were actually only a few times, the whole time I lived with them that I remember both Auntie Maria and Uncle Joe home at the same time, it was rare because they both worked a lot, but I was used to that from living with Dad and Vickie-Jean. On those occasions, after all the other kids and Caleb went home and it was just their family and me, I pretended we were a normal family. I dreamed and wished these boys who weren't always trying to pick a fight or insisting they were right were my brothers instead of Gio and his cocky, arrogant attitude. I pretended Uncle Joe with all his dumb dad jokes and teasing was my dad, Auntie Maria with her cup of tea and chat at my bedside each night was my mom and that we were all one and we were all happy.

Sure, they had issues but their problems were normal. Billy and Andy got grounded for talking back to their parents or forgetting chores, they didn't get beat. Auntie Maria sometimes had a bad day, but she didn't shut down for days on end and leave us to fend for ourselves. They were entrenched in Gianelli culture though, so the debt they were buried in wasn't spoken of but sometimes eeked out. I figured Aunt Maria was my best hope of getting someone to break the rules and validate my memories of being sexually abused. I worked to get her to tell me the truth. During one of her bedside check-ins I asked about me being in the hospital. She defied Nonna, and the Gianelli code of silence, weeks earlier over a girls' dinner we all had together and affirmed Gio and I had both been examined. She didn't give many details because Nonna clearly disapproved of the conversation. Alone that night, just the two of us, with no one there to stop her, she told me what she knew.

Gio and I had both been horribly sick after returning from my Mom's house one weekend. A woman named Meredith was my babysitter. She had taken us to the hospital without my parents' permission. She was dating my dad and Aunt Maria commented that she may have not been the most stable of women. With my dad's choice in women, it didn't come as a shock, but I'd heard all of that before, I didn't want to go there again. I wanted the truth about what Brad did to me, so I redirected Aunt Maria back to the real inquisition.

"Did they say he had sex with me?" I held her doe brown eyes in mine. I defied her to look away or ignore the question.

She stumbled over words, neither answering nor dismissing my question, "Oh sweetie," she sighed painfully and touched my foot. It was a comforting gesture and I was sure I was ready to finally hear what I desperately needed to know, "They said something happened but...what, we don't know. You were too little for anyone to understand what you meant. Your mom, she was in a bad place. And no one knew how to take Meredith. Sweetie, I just don't know." She couldn't look me in the eyes any longer. That was a lot of purging, she changed the subject to my upcoming prom. That was as close as I'd ever come to a Gianelli admitting such an evil had occurred. I took it to heart and moved onto talking about the prom too.

I was going to prom! Caleb hadn't officially asked me yet, he was always so tight and careful with how much of his allowance he spent, but I was sure he'd eventually ask me. It was the single most importantest day in a high school girl's life; he just had to ask me. Turns out, he wasn't going to ask me. He wanted to save for the summer, he already had big plans for our summer and every dollar he earned went toward it. But this was prom, I countered, and I made it clear to him in no uncertain terms, I was going, so, of course, he went too.

Auntie Maria took me dress shopping and we settled on a gorgeous emerald, off the shoulder mermaid dress that made my auburn highlights pop! Maybe it was a little too Princess Ariel, but the dress gave my stick straight frame curves and I felt grown-up, majestic and absolutely beautiful! The only annoying thing were my healing scars, still very prominent, on both forearms. Auntie Maria assured me they were my past and I didn't have to be ashamed or hide behind long sleeves on a hot spring night. Caleb did spring for the tickets, but pictures were my deal. I got the biggest, best package I could afford, with money Auntie Maria had given me. He questioned if I really needed to get that big of a package, he was so very predictable.

He did the dance for me, because I wanted it, but he wasn't a showy kind of guy so he didn't get on the dance floor more than twice. I danced with everyone, my jazz band friends, his drama and wrestling pals, even goofy classmates. He'd been to prom since he was a freshman, the event was checked off his goal list, so one more prom with one more girl was just one more thing he did without passion. We found a place to make out in his car after the prom, the way we always made out after a date or being together for the night. Hot, horny, heavy petting and genital explorations brought both of us to climax. I appreciated that he didn't get off and then leave me hanging, but all our fooling around up to that point had been technically "pure." Caleb was a good guy, a virgin guy, a safe guy and I didn't want to corrupt him, if he didn't want to be corrupted. He drew the line he was comfortable with and I toed it with him but we didn't cross it...even that prom night. It was so sugary sweet, so good, so pure, so not the dirty girl I was. I felt like I would contaminate him if I asked for sex, or told him I was ready, so I didn't say the words and simply followed his lead. That night led me back to Uncle Joe and Auntie Maria's house by curfew.

Caleb was a balanced, mellow guy, not one to give into his emotions but far more emotional than the Italian guys I'd grown up with. I always figured it was because he grew up with his mom for so long. Caleb had goals and he attained them but he didn't get charged up about anything. After a few months of dating, I felt like I was just another goal on his list; goal #5,501—*make that chick that stared at me be my girlfriend.* I was right before goal #5,502—*learn how to change the oil in my car* and after #5,500—*letter in one high-school sport.*

If Caleb had a passion, I'd guess it was theater. His eyes would light up when he talked about the sets or costumes. He was a behind the scenes guy and was obsessed with getting the right props and scene set-up. It was nice to see something stir him up. I tried to get him to think about making a career out of theater work, chasing a dream, moving to a glitzy, bustling place, living for his ambitions, but he wouldn't bite. Plans like that were too lofty, too dreamy and not realistic enough to set as a goal. We spent hours in the set room or behind the curtain stage left, getting things just right as the other kids would act out their parts on stage. It gave us plenty of time to talk and know each other better.

Caleb was a talker, he shared his feelings, and I suppose for such a steady, strong guy he had lots of feelings. We dreamed of someday living together in *our* house, with *our* family doing white picket fency things. We talked about *our* goals for the summer, which were really all his goals, but I had none, so I played along with his. It was like playing Barbies when I was a child, making up dream worlds that may or may not come to fruition. But it was all too sugary sweet, too good for someone like me, too predictable and too boring. I thought, if I could get at least get him into a career in theater production we could live somewhere other than a little valley in the middle of nowhere, and always be into a new and exciting play. We might even be able to travel, to see different theaters and performing houses around the world or at least in America, but, no, that would be frivolous, silly and a waste of money.

He always circled my fantasies back to reality. He liked theater but didn't want to pursue it as a career. He didn't know what he wanted. He was great at setting goals, but was afraid to take risks associated with dreams. He said his biggest goal was to love me and be loved by me and his life would be happy. Another sugary sweet answer from my sugary sweet boyfriend who was way too sugary sweet and good for me. I thought I loved him and I believed he loved me, and I thought our love would send us on a whirlwind romance of fun and excitement and adventure like Johnny and June or Bonnie and Clyde without the whole law breaking parts.

My junior year ended so differently than it had begun, I was part of a we, we were more inseparable than my twin and I had ever been. We went everywhere together, did everything together, were practically one. The only time we really had a problem was when we were with "his" people. Caleb had been with the drama kids for two years. He knew them and they had a history I wasn't a part of. Unless we were talking about music, I was still pretty awkward in group settings. I had a hard time coming up with the right thing to say or the right time to say it. I had a fear of sounding like an idiot and since I was part of a package deal, I was worried that if I said something dumb it would reflect poorly on Caleb. They had after-parties when a performance came to an end and they were always so uncomfortable for me. The girls, in their made up faces after the finale, intimidated me and reminded me of all the girls who had ever belittled me. They weren't like mountain parties where I could grab a drink of liquid courage or offer to smoke them out and then they'd all be my friends. I was lacking in the social skills and graces necessary to comfortably interact with them.

CHAPTER 23

I HATED GOING to the parties with him and would actually pout before we left because of the energy I knew I'd have to expend to get through a night of social pleasantries. There weren't even games or music to occupy myself with, it was just a whole lot of standing around talking about how great or lackluster their performances were. I had nothing in common with those upper-middle class goody-two-shoes who'd never had to suck anyone's anything or risk having their little brother be killed. I'd really get in a huff about going. Once at a party, with punch and cake and even a few teachers congratulating the cast and crew, I'd faked all the smiles I could for Caleb's sake and barely talked to him on the way back to my place. I did try to talk to people, but I didn't know how to start or how to finish. I either said too much when asked a simple question, or made a stupid comment nobody understood, or timed entrance into a conversation incorrectly, or kept drifting off in my head when someone was talking about something that bored me. It was so much work to be part of a group for the sake of someone else. I copped my attitude with Caleb and yelled at him after every party and called them dumb. It was easier to say I had nothing in common with those people than to consider that I might benefit from the effort it would take to get to know them.

Caleb was so patient, it was part of his sugary sweetness. He would love me so sweetly through my bad attitudes and moods. Seriously, that poor boy put up with a lot. He said I reminded him of his mom. He went through it all with her, female emotions and menstrual cycles, temper tantrums and irrational bad attitudes. He was definitely there for me. He wanted to help me; fix me. I sure kept him on his toes, there was never a time when I wasn't high strung about something. My anxiety oozed from me, I lived at the edge of a crisis at all times and vomited what I was feeling onto him. I think I let so much out to overcompensate for my family's denial of anything bad. If I was mad or sad, I had a right to voice it, if I had been devastated by a traumatizing event, I had a right to vent about it, hurt about it, purge it from my soul. But I was raised a Gianelli, I was not supposed speak about the bad. And I was the child of drug dealers, I was supposed keep my mouth shut. I hated it, I hated them, all of them for being like that. I wanted vindication, and if he couldn't give me that at least Caleb gave me a safe place to let it all out.

Unfortunately, the very fact that Caleb was my new "safe" place made him an innocent bystander in hurricane of my emotions. After I got my license, I regularly visited Trent and Hannah and took them to do something special just to let them know I remembered them and loved them. I would get so upset to see Mom doing the same crap and they were effectively left on their own. I'd go from seeing that to visiting Martin and Alex and seeing all their privilege. It wasn't fair that two of my siblings lived on the edge of crisis and two of my siblings had anything they wanted and Gio and I were the throw-away kids neither parent wanted. It wasn't fair and I couldn't talk about it. If I tried to mention I thought my mom was using drugs Nonna would start pleading the blood over her and the kids and sing hymns, Aunt Maria would change the subject to something fun and lighthearted.

I couldn't communicate with my family, so Caleb was my outlet. I'd make out with him and go as far as he'd let us go just to bury my feelings in a fury of sexual lust. I'd yell at him and beat his chest or cry on his shoulder until it was soaked with tears and snot. He'd take it or hold me the whole time. He let me get it out, reminded me I couldn't fix my mom or make my dad love me. I could only be a stable figure for my little brothers and sister. He never left during one of my fits, never yelled back, never said I was too much. Sometimes I'd shut down completely on him, like Mom did. That was usually after a fight with Nonna or Gio or Mom herself. I'd pull a Cinderella and go into my own little corner in my own little head and, like Mom, would refuse to talk. We would drive around for hours listening to music he knew I liked until I was back to me again.

More often than not, I'd snap out of my mood long before I let on, just to see how much he could handle. Mom and them made fun of me at the slightest show of emotion. The Gianellis ignored emotion all together because to show feelings was weakness. My feelings never mattered to any of them. Caleb responded to me, to my emotions, to all I was. Caleb knew me, he knew I was hurting and he loved me anyway. I wasn't too much for him, all he had to offer what his steady strength. He could handle all of me, or maybe he was a door mat I could step all over? So I'd keep my mouth shut and see what he'd do.

The quietness frustrated him more than the anger or crying, he'd do anything to make me talk. He wanted so badly to fix my brokenness. I wanted him to get that I was too broken for him to fix. He'd beg and plead for me to start talking. When I was bored with the game I'd start talking again but not before. It was a rush to be able to control him like that, but it was also unnerving that he was so into me that he couldn't leave me be until I was over it on my own. I loved that I mattered to him but I didn't like how much power he gave me. I was a big wrecking ball of confusion, I needed a rock I could crash into, that was strong enough to take it. I was lost and afraid and I wanted a hero. I wanted him to be steady then like he was all the rest of the time, but silence made him desperate. Desperation seemed weak to me. I don't know what he could have done that wouldn't have made me perceive him as weak. That poor, poor boy. He tried so hard to fix me.

Summer before senior year, Caleb and I were inseparable. There was no him without me, or me without him, we were we. If Caleb was one thing other than cute, it was that he was goal oriented. He was always making goals and attaining them. I admired his initiative, but in time I realized that his goals were always easily attainable, predictable, rational, and safe… there was never any risk. But that's what he did; he set goals and achieved them. He set a goal to get his own personal computer, and he got one. He set a goal to letter in sports, and he did in football and wrestling. He set a goal to make me happy, that was the riskiest goal he made. I was his enigma, and I was the only thing he risked his stable little life for.

Not surprisingly he wanted us to set some summer goals, we, and by we I mean he, came up with three, easily attainable, somewhat memorable goals. We were going to: go Seattle and visit the Woodland Park Zoo, hike to the beautiful blue alpine Colchuck Lake, and both of us were going to have jobs before school started. He set them and we attained them. The zoo was a childhood memory of his that he wanted to relive. I remember the graceful giraffes and goofy orangutans; and I remember looking at the families. There were mommies and daddies with sticky little cotton-candy covered kids. It was sweet and disgusting to me all at the same time. I liked watching the kids who were excited over the animals. Truth be told it was even kind of cute to see the kids who were afraid of an animal. But I wondered how many dads were like Lester and touched their little girls at night and how many moms were like Vickie-Jean and freaked out and hit their kids when they didn't obey. The families looked so happy and, maybe they were, maybe mine was the only really screwed up one. If there were truly happy families, I decided I would have liked to have grown up in one. Caleb wanted us to be a family and to bring our kids there someday. Another goal, in the future with kids and zoo days. I didn't want that future. I wanted to see the world, to live in New York, to drive across America. I didn't want kids or a family. I wanted to live. It was a lovely day and I thanked him for it but I was terrified to have a happy family of my own.

The hike to Colchuck Lake was a little more fun, and a whole lot more adventurous. It was a popular hike, and we couldn't go more than a quarter of a mile without passing other summer nature enthusiasts. I was a cute girl and caught eyes in my hot pink halter and sports shorts. Passing guys, their girls in front of them, checked me out. I said a nice little "hello" but my eyes lingered too long, my coy smile grabbed their attention, my backpack strapped chest highlighted healthy, tan cleavage they couldn't avoid. It was quick, innocent flirtation but it didn't go unnoticed. Caleb's arms wrapped around me tightly on quick breaks. He pulled me close and kissed me more passionately than usual. The mountain air, the rush of running water and sexual energy, the comfort of a safe companion combined and made me feel like I was the queen of the world.

I didn't care at all about the other boys, they were only a means to get Caleb to pay more attention to me. He was a polite and respectful young man and propriety was in his nature, but he was hot for me that mild summer day. He'd pull me off trail to catch a glorious mountain view and take me into his arms. We made out as much as we could until other travelers came upon us. He sat me on his lap once by a cluster of rocks alongside a roaring waterfall. We sipped our water and drank in the day. It was just us, no worries, we were expending energy and turning each other on over and over again. Everything about it was wonderful. I loved the way I could turn him on with a kiss and suggestive look. I was powerful and I liked it. It was risky and adventurous, always there was a chance we would get caught kissing and still we kept taking make out breaks. It was bold, beautiful and so much fun; it was one of the best adventures we had, that's probably why I remember it so well.

We got our jobs before summer ended too, as luck would have it for us, right in the same shopping plaza. The easiest job would have been at Dad and Vickie-Jean's shop, it made sense to ask Dad if they were hiring, at least for the summer. He said he had to check with Vickie-Jean and they offered to hire me, off the books, for two dollars an hour less than minimum wage. I politely declined, but noticed my nearly adolescent brother, Martin, in the photo gallery dusting the precious art the day I checked in. Of course they didn't need to hire real help, they had a new wave of child labor. I wondered if Martin and Alex felt the same way about it that I had, but I was too much of a Gianelli to ever ask.

All the other places I applied were in Wenatchee. It made better sense to work where I went to school and practiced. Caleb got a job at a small-town hardware store, and I was hired on at the mocha stand at the edge of the plaza's parking lot. We were part-timers, but it was liberating to have so much money to spend on myself. I bought lots of nice clothes, kept my turd-mobile clean and took all my younger siblings out to the movies or on little adventures and shopping trips. I don't remember ever having to pay for dates but do remember Caleb was ever frugal so saving was always a top priority.

I snuck over to Caleb's house on summer mornings any chance I could get, no longer intimidated by its poshness, my new digs with my aunt and uncle were bigger and better. It wasn't like I was lying to Auntie Maria when I said I worked morning shifts at the mocha stand but I left just as early on mid-morning shifts so I could spend an hour or two with Caleb before starting. His dad and step-mom left by seven and his step-sister, Lisa, honored sibling code so we were golden. The first time I snuck into his room totally surprised him. He was still sleeping and Lisa let me in. We visited for a while, whispering in the kitchen, then I snuck up the steps as quietly as I could, stripped off everything but my tank and panties and slid under his covers. We did everything in that big king bed of his that summer, except have official intercourse. It was all legal in his rule-bound mind as long as vaginal-penile penetration never occurred, it was all fun in mine.

I don't know why we didn't have sex. I suppose it was because I said no, like once, way back in the beginning and he always respected me, and he was a good boy and we were taught abstinence in church and school. I'd experienced Paul and enjoyed Caleb and my foreplay immensely. It was really, usually all about me. He liked to get me off, with his hands and mouth; he explored my body with sensual kisses and touching. I liked being pleasured and orgasms were not difficult to come by as long as he hadn't yet ejaculated. I figured if I pushed for full on sex all the petting and kissing might go away and I'd be nothing more than his personal porn star to take him in and get over myself when he was done. I really liked sexual pleasure, I didn't want it quick or just about him in me until he could cum.

Even with as amazing as my official first time with Paul had been, it was still more about the foreplay and adventure than the actual intercourse. I didn't want to lose the heat and...I didn't want to let go of my memory with Paul. It was like that first kiss with Tyler, no one since him compared. As the years passed and I added new boys to the list I forgot how good it was, but knew no one was that good again. I was concerned it would be that way for sex too. It was great with Paul, I found the right boy and he didn't disappoint me. I didn't start dating Caleb with sex in mind, he was hot and I wanted to get to know him, that was all. He was so cautious and concerned about me and my feelings I knew it'd be a softer, sweeter, gentler kind of sex and I didn't think I'd be disappointed but I wasn't ready, so I didn't ask for it and he didn't pressure me for it, so we didn't do it. It didn't stop us from sexually gratifying ourselves in all kinds of other ways. I had an insatiable sexual appetite, I'd been primed since childhood to be stimulated and, well, I was a whore, I liked it. So week in and week out, I'd go over in the summer and we'd get it on.

I felt no shame about the whole thing, I still felt sort of cheated and was making use of a willing participant. Caleb was clean, not a man-whore, we were exclusive, it was safe, it was between us and it was fun. I hated going to church and hearing, blah, blah, blah, save yourself for marriage, don't give away your heart, like the two, my body and my heart, were connected; they weren't. Making out was about physical, sexual pleasure; it was easy to disconnect the actions and the pleasure from 'my heart.' When Pastor Jack preached on sexual sin and the importance of purity I wanted to ask him how he would classify a girl that was molested when she was pretty much a baby, and then again before she was 10. Was that girl guilty according to their God, and if so, why not have fun with it? I knew I hadn't given any part of my heart away to either of those nasty men when they took my innocence, I didn't have to give it to Caleb to feel good. What about with Paul? He gave me back what Brad and Lester took from me, was that wrong? The church had its nice little rules from the thick onion page book, but I was out of compliance already. I was dirty according to them and their rules so what was the point of "saving" what I never had to save?

That summer Aunt Maria made it her mission to make me feel at home in her house. The room I'd moved into had been her craft room and even months after my official move, it was still stuffed with her paints and ceramics and boxes of someday projects and ideas. Auntie took me to Pier One and let me pick out fuchsia and turquoise decorations that matched the new bedspread I purchased for myself out of my second paycheck. She pulled an old mission style bedroom set out of storage and was pleased it had been put to good use again. She filled in the empty storage gaps with crafts and projects she was still going to get to someday. It was dreamy to have a place of my own and not have to share with a sister or someone else's things. It was all mine. I felt like the room fit me to a tee. There was a part of me that was nice and presentable, the Pier One showroom floor bedroom, but behind the dark wood shoji screen, a nook of musical chaos. A keyboard, a stack of well-worn music books, a wall tacked with ripped out magazine quotes and pictures; a mess of confusion and solitude. It was a wonderful little room and I was so grateful that Auntie Maria let me move in. She and Uncle Joe must have really loved me, but I couldn't see it. I figured they were the kind of people who would do that kind of thing for any loser kid off the street, I was just the lucky recipient.

CHAPTER 24

BY THE TIME school started there was no me without considering Caleb. It was fine, it was comfortable, it was my life. I liked having him to hold me and take me out, to talk to and cry to. I loved the security of waking up every morning and knowing Caleb was there for me. I loved the idea of us and all we were and did. We were good, he was good, I gave up silly dreams like ruling the world with Gio, like living in New York and backpacking Europe. I settled for a predictable life with a nice young man and figured it was a good as a bad, worthless girl like me could hope for. Caleb was better than what I deserved and I knew it, everyone knew it, compared to him I was unsteady, unpredictable and a mess, so I tried to make it work, but I felt like life was more than what I was living. I wanted adventure and a little bit of unpredictability in the day-to-day.

There was this one boy, Jeff, who joined jazz band that year that I couldn't get out of my mind. He played the guitar, it reminded me of Paul, but nothing else about him did. He was slight but ruggedly handsome in a down-home country kind of way. He wore Wranglers and cowboy boots and when he looked at me, it made me want to throw it all away with Caleb. I wanted to know how he kissed and if he was a safe and sweet lover like Caleb or if he was bold and would dare to cross the line. He didn't look at the other girls that way. Kate, Amy and Steph got friendly, cordial treatment but only I got that 'I want you' look he threw me from under his hat. He challenged me, dared me to break rules, or was it all in my head? It was only a look but brazen, playful, risky and bold…not at all like Caleb was.

It felt like Jeff was bad enough for me to be myself with, like I could stand up on the table and start dancing and he wouldn't be mortified, might even cheer me on before pulling me into his arms for a big wet kiss in front of everyone; not that I would ever do that, but if I would, he'd be all for it. I was willing to bet I could chug a beer or hit a bowl and he wouldn't have been horrified. He knew I wasn't available but it didn't keep him from looking too long and smiling too playfully. I knew Caleb wasn't going to be the one to keep me, but I never stared back at Jeff long enough to let him think he was the one either.

I had respect for Caleb. I would not cheat on him. Quite honestly, I'd never had anyone put up with me so willingly and patiently before and I didn't want to lose that. I could count on him, he was there for me. I really did like Caleb, he was a nice boy, but I was too much for him, or he wasn't enough for me, I wasn't sure then which. I was coming to terms with the fact that our relationship couldn't last, but he was such a nice boy, and it felt good to be loved and safe. I was tried to make it work despite what my heart said, what Jeff's eyes asked, and what I knew to be true.

I tried to switch as many of my classes to be with Caleb as I could, but I was more advanced in most subjects so it didn't work out. Out of the blue one day, Mr. Kearny asked me if I was settling.

"What?" I asked as I hefted my backpack off my shoulders and rummaged in it for the music book our jazz band was practicing out of.

"Look, I like Caleb, he's a cool kid. I'm not about to tell you how to live your life or who to date or anything like that... but don't give up who you are for someone else, kid." He looked at me a long time waiting for me to answer.

"I won't."

"But you switched out of Physics for a Biology class he was in. Why? You love science."

"I do... but..." checkmate. Mr. Kearny read my mail and called me on it. I shrugged, "I don't want him to feel bad."

"Why would he feel bad that his girlfriend is one of the smartest kids in the high school?"

I had no words that time, just looked down at the keyboard and dusted imaginary dust off them.

"Gia, there's greatness in you. You've fought your whole life to be who you are. Don't let her go because of the first nice guy that comes along. There are lots of nice guys out there you won't have to dumb yourself down for."

"I'm not dumbing myself down," I spat back. It might have been the first time I was ever angry at Mr. Kearny, but it was because he was right and we both knew it. Caleb never said anything derogatory about me having advanced classes and good grades, but it wasn't like he cheered me on either. Mr. Kearny's words made their point and he didn't need to say anymore.

Mr. Kearny was right, I felt bad for Caleb because his grades were only OK and he wasn't even in the toughest classes. I imagined he felt the way I did in seventh grade when the school placed me in all the hardest classes and I really had to work for my grades. It's not that he didn't try, or wasn't smart, it's that "getting by" is where he did life. Caleb skated through everything, Cs and easily attainable goals were enough for him. Sometimes I felt like his vanilla life was a front because deep down he really wasn't as smart as advanced students, as fit as star athletes, or as cut out to lead as the other kids in leadership. Whether he was mediocre by choice or by design I could never tell. Either way, I assumed he felt like I had in middle school when I couldn't cut it compared to the smart, popular kids, and asked for easier classes. I tried to help him with school work, but I couldn't make the concepts stick in his brain. I felt bad but at the same time I was kind of embarrassed that he was not as smart as me. I didn't want a boyfriend I could outsmart, so, Mr. Kearny nailed it, I was dumbing myself down to stay at his level. I visited the guidance counselor the next morning to set things straight. I didn't switch back to the college-prep English class I'd dropped but did re-enroll in Physics. Mr. Kearny was proud of my decision and Caleb and I had one class together. The two men that mattered most to me were satisfied with my decision and I started to finalize my decision to break up with Caleb.

He was such a good boy, such a nice guy. I told myself he loved me and I'd be safe with him, but I started to question the "safe" part. Would he keep me safe from a bad guy? I had never seen him push past his comfort zone, for anything, fear, love, goals. Athletically, once he'd lettered, he quit trying in sports at all. He gave up track and football and probably only stayed on the wrestling team because of me and Gio. He wasn't the fastest, strongest or most spry out there, in fact he usually always lost, and that without breaking a sweat. If he cared about keeping me safe, was he even strong enough to do the job? It was OK to lose, but he didn't give his heart and soul to the match, or to the effort to get to the mat. It was embarrassing to be the girlfriend of the guy who didn't even get a little upset when he lost. He just kept his same even keel, nothing shook him and nothing invigorated him. He had the most beautiful body, he looked strong, but he didn't perform the way he should have, it was the same as if I only ever played Chopsticks on the piano. A waste of unknown talent. A question mark as to whether he could keep me safe, or would he be like my family and let it run off his back like it didn't matter at all.

We got into several fights about his apathetic approach to wrestling matches, even Gio got in on a few. We'd both tell Caleb that he needed to have more of a hunger to win, he needed to hit the mat hard and wrestle with all that was in him. He listened respectfully, he nodded, but he remained mediocre. The next match would be the same as all the last, minimal effort, barely any sweat, three seconds on his back, a handshake to the victor and his coach and a shrug as he walked to me for his consolation hug. He didn't even smell like other wrestlers, and I'd been around plenty, he smelled like apathy. I didn't want a boyfriend that couldn't protect or wouldn't protect me. I tried to ignore that too. I was determined to make it work. He was such a good boy, such a nice guy.

We started to argue over church too, me and all of my religiosity didn't appreciate his lackadaisical acceptance, which was really lame because I questioned so much about it but did the things church-y people did out of respect for the ritual. I wanted him to fully participate, even though my heart wasn't even in it. He was steady, the way he approached religion was the way he approached life, half-heartedly. He went because I went but wasn't going to put any more time or effort into it that what he had to. As best as I can remember he attended occasional Sunday morning services with me, when he didn't work, and had the gas to get to Aunt Maria's so we could carpool the rest of the way. He never really got too into church services and never really seemed to care. I had become a compulsive

Bible reader, mostly to pick it apart and question the seeming absurdity and inconsistency of it all, but I couldn't talk it through with him because he didn't read it. He just wasn't that into it. It vexed me.

Years later, just like with Mikey, Nonna told me she'd run into Caleb; he actually helped her and Gramps move from their house in town to the house they built for their golden years on property in the woods near Lake Wenatchee. At that time I was hardcore into my drug addiction and she was trying to give me some kind of hope things could change. She told me Caleb had become a Christian and was serving the LORD. I smiled and nodded, through a slight drug haze, and ruminated on the irony of it. Two different boys, two different times in my life had poo-pooed the religion I introduced them to only to succumb to it later. They credited me, a lost, sinner of a druggie, with introducing them to God. It was so incredibly ridiculous it belonged in the Bible too. I didn't even believe in God at the time she told me, or if I did it was only as a mean God who wrecked people and I'd brought two people to His alter. Those were living sacrifices. The irony was psycho!

But back in twelfth grade, I felt like I was wasting away. The end of the calendar year was approaching, my graduation was sneaking up on me and I had nothing to look forward to. I knew I wanted a career where I could make a living with my music. I had several college offers come in, not surprising with my honor roll grades, but I knew they meant nothing. I wasn't going to college. I was a throw-away kid that neither of my parents wanted and even if they did, they weren't the kind of people who could pay for the Berklee College of Music, or Julliard, which I was really interested in because they were the best for music majors. I was a pathetic little girl who lived with my Auntie and Uncle because I couldn't stand my semi-legal guardian, Nonna, and neither of my parents wanted me. Auntie Maria and Uncle Joe loved me, but no more than any of the other girls the cousins brought over. They weren't going to fork over the dough to send me to a prestigious four year school. Gramps and Nonna were pastors of a humble little church, they didn't have the kind of money it took to send one of several grandkids to college or the favoritism toward me to make it happen.

I knew the best colleges were out of the question, or I'd been with Caleb too long to dare to dream of them. I settled on the attainable. I thought maybe I could get into a nice state college, with scholarships and my hard-luck story. That's the route I took. I applied for hundreds of scholarships, entered at least a dozen music competitions with money for college for winners. I did it all by myself. My parents and Gio could care less, my grandparents, aunt and uncle were too busy with their own lives to pay attention. Caleb was being a melancholy jerk about the whole thing. He said he didn't want to hold me back but lamented over which school I'd choose because we'd be apart. It didn't occur to him to leave his mediocre life and follow me wherever my music would take me. I applied myself to so many different scholarship programs it was like a job, or at least an extra class at school.

Mr. Kearny; Ms. Schram, the guidance counselor; and Lacy, a cool, youngish para-educator lady with big blue eyes and pink cheeks in the career center at school helped me most. Unfortunately all my efforts had come a little too late. The real hopefuls had started applying for scholarships years earlier, sometimes as early as their freshman year. It was hopeless, I saw it in all of their eyes, though they tried to keep it out of their encouraging words. It wasn't just the timing either, it was the whole process. The question was always, "What will you major in?" How the heck did I know? Music! Wasn't that good enough? I was barely surviving, let alone looking out into my future. My best hope was to stay together with a sweet, steady guy and be half of a sweet, steady couple that never did anything great or exciting for the rest of my life. I was good at school, and great at playing the piano. I wanted to major in being a musician, it's what I did well…it was all I did well. But it was a lame answer for applications. Millions of people wanted to be musicians, I didn't have anything to offer that made me stand out. I was as mediocre as I ever blamed Caleb of being. With help from my educational team, I eventually came up with something I thought would score me points, and get me scholarships because of my scholastic achievement more than musical abilities. I was going to be a music teacher! I loved music, I liked kids, after all I regularly visited my siblings and did special things with them by choice. It seemed like a good major.

It wasn't good enough, I wasn't good enough, the autumn before graduation wasn't early enough. I wasn't going to a four-year college, not a big name one, not a state one, not any four-year college. I was too late and was not enough and it wasn't going to happen. It was the story of my life. I was an insignificant little nothing in a little nothing town. I wasn't going anywhere. Maybe if I hadn't screwed up my sophomore year and I had a higher GPA I would have stood out, but in a class of over four hundred students I was barely in the top ten percent. It was not good enough for any academic awards. Jazz band usually placed well, but in solo competitions, except two, I didn't win. I sucked, my family sucked, my boyfriend, sweet as he was, had aspirations that sucked and the rejections were making me really mad.

I was depressed about none of the scholarships panning out; I was resigning myself to a life of less than what I dreamed of, even though my only dream was simply to escape the valley and go to a four year college. Caleb was perking up with each passing day and rejection letter. He was so disgustingly there for me, to wrap his arm around me when another letter came back saying, 'Thank you for applying, but you didn't get the prize.' I wanted to leave my family, my childhood, my very existence behind and start fresh somewhere else. I wanted to go somewhere and to be someone who did something with their life instead of languishing in a vacation valley with family secrets bubbling under my skin. I wanted to run away from my life like I had when I moved from Dad's to Mom's. Caleb didn't want that. He wanted to patiently climb the career ladder where he worked… a hardware store, and aspired to someday be the manager. Whoopee! He thought a respectable degree from our local community college would suit me and my teaching goal just fine. He wanted us to make a boring, steady life there in Sleepy Valley USA. I don't think he ever admitted it but I don't think he wanted me to go because he was afraid I'd push him into college too, or would leave if I advanced my education and he didn't. In his mind it was way too risky to leave our steady jobs and our vanilla future. Caleb McDonald did not take risks; and I remembered my mother fuming out the door insisting she was meant for so much more than being a lounge pianist, and her life flashed before my eyes. I had to make him understand why I needed to escape.

CHAPTER 25

THERE WAS ONE frivolous thing, one, risky adventure Caleb had ever mentioned; skydiving. For a boy who was grounded and cautious and safe it was interesting to me he would even consider it. It sounded fun to me, to jump out of a plane and into the sky. I told him I'd do it with him, we could jump together. He politely declined after finding out all the information from a salesman at a mall kiosk during our Christmas shopping planning trip. We didn't actually buy anything that trip, we simply planned what we'd like to buy for our friends and family; it was very sensible, just like Caleb was. Skydiving cost one hundred twenty dollars a person, far too much for us to be spending on something so frivolous and risky, but he said he sure would have liked to do it as we walked off.

I couldn't get it out of my mind, the thought of him actually doing it, would he really jump? Did he have it in him? I projected some of my passion for life onto him and imagined that he would, if only he were given the opportunity. I was the person to give Caleb the opportunity! I wanted to push him out of his safety zone. I wanted him to feel the rush life could give if he did something with a hundred percent of his being and he couldn't get more one hundred percent than jumping from a plane. I snuck back to the mall by myself before Christmas and bought Caleb a tandem jump out of a plane. The expense about busted my Christmas budget, but he was what and who mattered most to me, so he was worth it. I really did like him, I thought I loved him, I just needed him to live with a little more passion. That was all I was trying to do, give him a moment where he could live life full throttle. I needed adventure, excitement, activity and passion in my life. He wasn't giving it to me and I could feel myself pulling away from him. He loved me and wanted the best for me and what girl wouldn't want that? I hated myself for being bored with him, I just needed more from him. I thought if he jumped he would understand what he was missing in his safe, riskless life.

Christmas came and the family went to Gramps and Nonna's, like always for Christmas Eve. It was Caleb's second with the family, and he was like family by then. Everyone loved Caleb, polite, sociable, wrestling boy that he was. Everyone was so happy I settled down with such a good boy. Settled. I was settling for a life of boring, but I smiled and nodded because they were right, he was a sweet boy, a sugary sweet catch. I felt like they thought he was he was better than a damaged girl like me could possibly hope for. We went to his folks'. We went to my mom's. I gave gifts to Trent and Hannah and she gave me, and Caleb, stockings.

Mom was less flirty with Caleb since she and Lester had reconciled sometime the previous season. But she'd grown a big old root of bitterness toward d Lester and his mom for her part in the hook-up between Lester and the other lady. I guess they dated for several months before Mom and him got back together. The wound was still fresh for Mom so visits, even on special days like Christmas, were sure to be watered with reasons why she couldn't bring herself to sleep with him. She told me, her young daughter, she worried about how she compared and it froze her up. I really didn't need to hear it in the first place, but in the second place, I wondered if she ever wondered if he compared me to her. I accused him of molesting me way back when and it was always there hovering in the air. She had to know what he had done to me. Did that bother her just as much as another woman did? I wondered if that was part of the reason why she'd sometimes totally flip-out and make fun of me or cut me down for no reason, especially in front of him. I didn't know, but I was never eager to stay in that nasty house after moving from it. As soon as gifts had been exchanged, Caleb and I took off. I always felt dirty leaving there, the place was littered with bad memories. Mom and Lester kept it clean, but soap suds didn't cleanse away cvil. Lester was there again, the place felt yucky in my bones.

After all the family stuff was done, it was Caleb and I alone together at Auntie Maria's. We'd waited until last, the two of us; to exchange our gifts. I was so excited! I fantasized that the moment was going to open his eyes to all he had been missing. I can't remember who opened first or if we opened together. I must admit I was slightly expecting a ring. He had talked about it, we had perused jewelry stores, he mentioned our future together enough, it seemed like a reasonable assumption. I didn't get a ring. I got a cute little giraffe piggy bank, cute and safe. It was a lovely little bank, we'd seen it on our Christmas planning trip, it cost thirty-five dollars, for Caleb, that was a lot of money and reminded him of our very special day at the zoo. It seemed so fitting. No risk in a piggy bank, it was safe, secure and dependable. I was a little disappointed in the price because I'd spent over a hundred dollars on him, but it wasn't really the price that erked me. I knew what our agreed budget was and I'd totally gone over of my own free will. I couldn't put words to it then, so it probably came off like I was upset over the difference in price, but it wasn't the dollar amount.

Our gifts were a tangible representation of what I was feeling. I wanted adventure, excitement and to sometimes take risks and do things that were crazy, safe but crazy. Skydiving was risky, but not like the drugs or life I used to live. I got him a tandem jump with a professional diver, sure there was risk, but it was controlled. I thought the expense was worth the once in a lifetime adrenaline rush. The piggy bank was from a display I was most intrigued by because they were so uniquely made. I admired an artist's creation coming to life. He remembered a warm summer day, accomplishing a well planned goal, when we were both happy. He loved me, he cared about what I liked, he watched to see what thing I liked most, he paid attention to me, but he didn't get what I loved about it. He was a wonderful young man so full of devotion and care. He was so much better and more stable than I was. He deserved someone more stable than I was.

The bank part was all about him. He was offering me a life of security, of planning our future and saving for a rainy day so we would make it through just fine. I felt like he was saying, "Stay with me and I'll keep you prominently displayed, up on a shelf, where you never go anywhere, for the rest of your life." I had way more problems and nervous energy than he could handle. I hadn't even told him about the closet, only Lester. I hated myself. I had a great guy, handsome, nice, personable, stable, all the things a girl like me should be happy with, and I didn't want what he had to offer me. I felt like being with him was like burying all of the hopes and silly dreams I had for myself. I was trading ambition for a steady life and predictable boy I could count on FOREVER. FOR—EVE—ER! Forever bored, forever living a pretend life of OK-ness, something I wanted so badly, but also monotonous and mind-numbing. On second thought, I was not disappointed that he gave me a piggy bank, it was so much better than a ring.

I was sure Caleb loved me, I was sure he'd probably give his life for me if there were no other alternatives available. That poor, poor boy. I remembered how it felt to have Jackson not return my affections; I simply could not do that to Caleb. He cared about me so much and I really did care about him enough that I couldn't leave him. I wasn't a good person like he was. I wanted too much out of life and had been screwed up too much by life to fit into his safe little world. I cared about him though and didn't want to break his heart, but by Christmas I knew I would. I was going to leave after graduation but I decided to love him good in the meantime. I emotionally checked out though, I just couldn't do it.

I changed my mind once at spring break. I decided he wouldn't be too bad to stay with forever. He told me it was our senior year and he wanted to go crazy for spring break! That's what I was talking about! We were going on an adventure!

Just kidding, Caleb would never do anything crazy, but he did want to take me to the Coast and across the peninsula to visit his fabled mother. I knew lots about her from the stories he told. He'd visited her before, but he was inviting me to tag along. For me, it was an adventure, a good, exciting, fun adventure, even though it was part of his normal life. It was enough, a little something out of the ordinary, not too risky, but new, not dangerous but wondrous. I'd never been on a ferry, never been over to that part of the state, never been anywhere with him overnight let alone for a week! It had all the makings of the kind of fun and excitement I needed in life. I ignored the part of my brain that told me this was not an adventure for Caleb. He regularly visited his mom, he grew up in the house, he knew the roads and route, it was normal to him.

Of course, any venture needed to be planned for, and even with my hunger for more out of life, I liked to plan and prepare and know what to expect. I researched the Coast a little, asked around to see who'd been there, it was bliss to dream of getting away. It wasn't without challenge. We had to get time off work and get my family to sign off. Had I still lived with Mom, it would have been no problem at all, but with Auntie Maria and Uncle Joe and my religious family it was a more controversial deal. They passed the buck to my dad, where the decision should have landed anyway. Caleb, responsible young man that he was, went with me to the shop to ask Dad if I could go. I didn't know my dad anymore. Except for occasional Sunday dinners when he and I both weren't working and able to attend at the same time, I never saw the man. I didn't know the look that played across his face. I didn't know what he thought of me or Caleb. All I knew is I needed his permission.

"If I say no," he eventually said, looking at me, "you'll get mad and hold this against me too." Then he looked at Caleb, "If I say yes, I expect you to treat her right and respect my request that you not sleep in the same room." Caleb told him his mom had the same rule. She had a spare room on the lower level of her house and I'd stay there while he slept upstairs in his old room that was now his younger brother's. Then Dad looked between the both of us and said, "You know what's right, make the right decisions. You may go." I wanted to jump and scream and shout, instead I went around the corner and hugged my dad's neck. I was going away for spring break!

As anticipated it was no problem getting the time off from work for either of us. I'd been taught by the Gianellis how to clean and keep busy and work hard. Those traits got me my choice of shifts after a few months, and immediate approval for vacation time off. Some of the other girls were jealous, but I was a good worker, they were slackers and gossips that wasted company time, what did they expect? It hurt my feelings, though, to be grumbled against, but my boss, family and Caleb assured me they were only jealous and being spiteful. Caleb was so great whenever I was upset, always there for me trying to make me better. He was a jewel at his job; dependable, honest and overly responsible for a boy his age. He was the weekend assistant manager as a senior in high school, that meant he was managing people twice his age. His plan to climb the company ladder, however unglamorous it was in my eyes, was working well and quickly. He had to be home for both the weekend before and after spring break but that still left us with five glorious days of vacation time.

Anticipation about the trip fueled me. I felt refreshed and renewed inside to have something out of the ordinary to look forward to. New roads, new landscape, new smells and surroundings. It would be so fun. Caleb asked if I'd be open to having sex with him on our get away. I blushed and my heart rushed and affirmed that yes I most definitely would be! Action, adventure and sex. There was that whole church and God thing I was doing and I suppose I should have been more prudish in my answer, but I was excited about it. Caleb and I had been together over a year and the church's rules didn't apply to me anyway because I was already a dirty, nasty, sexual sinner. I liked sex and feeling aroused too much to care about it being wrong. If I was evil and a sinner for wanting to share physical affection with my boyfriend, so be it, how dare the church or a book or a God who let the nasty stuff happen to me begrudge me having fun and feeling good?

Excited as I was, I was nervous about having sex too. It had been a long time since Paul. Caleb and I gratified each other often but it was always mostly PG stuff, over the clothes or hands inside them, grinding, dry humping, hand jobs... We'd never even seen each other naked. I wanted it to be as good, or better as with Paul, I wanted it to make me fall totally in love with Caleb all over again, but Caleb wasn't that kind of guy. To even ask me to make love was a big risk for him. Nakedness and penetration was way past his comfort zone. I doubted there would be any dressing room or shower sex with him. I guessed it would be safe and probably quick...hopefully not as quick as Greg, but he'd be so excited I didn't think it would take too long. A part of me feared he would chicken out since he promised his mom and my dad we'd be good.

CHAPTER 26

SPRING BREAK CAME and we packed up and left the valley for the ocean coast! We drove over the rivers and through the woods, into metropolitan cities and onto the ferry terminal. After his car was parked in position, we went up to the observation deck and watched the water and seaweed and jellyfish pass by. His mom's modern beach house sat on the edge of the ocean at the tip of the peninsula. It had huge ocean facing windows upstairs and down, from which we could watch the surf slam the rocks below. I was at home there right away.

His mom and her husband were nice, his little brother a little cutie. We visited, had dinner together and downright enjoyed each other's company over dominoes and old stories of Caleb's childhood antics. At ten o'clock, his mom showed me to my downstairs bedroom. I was alone in the basement which was almost a separate apartment. I could taste being on my own. I imagined the place was mine, clean sheets, no Gio to be compared to or protect, no Nonna or Vickie-Jean to make me feel like I sucked at life and taking care of stuff, no Mom to keep me down and shove booze and drugs down my throat. I imagined it was all me, all alone, Caleb didn't even fit in the fantasy, only me.

The place was dreamy, I loved it! In the mornings I woke up to the smell of coffee, just like at Gramps and Nonna's, and to sweet Caleb coming in to gently wake me up. It was surreal and wonderful and peaceful. His mom and husband left early for work and took his brother to daycare, so we were alone most of the day. We made and ate breakfast like it was our place and watched the ocean's dance from the well-weathered porch. We scampered over the rocks and walked along other nearby beaches. We drove to quaint little tourist places and hiked to beautiful waterfalls and we made love.

It must have been Wednesday morning when we did it. It was like the other mornings, I woke to the robust Colombian coffee brewing and hustle and bustle of the family leaving for the day. Then it was quiet again save for the ocean surf. I'd drifted to sleep again, then he was there, the sweet boyfriend I said I loved. He didn't just wake me up, he crawled into the bed with me. I brought my best panties for the week, knowing it was going to happen and wished he could see me in them. He started kissing and fondling me. I started to respond but then it hit me that his breath was minty fresh and mine was morning nasty! I couldn't get away from the thought of my breath. I didn't want to kiss him or even open my mouth, I didn't want to say anything and ruin the mood. I let him proceed but tried to keep my mouth shut. It didn't take too long for my excitement and his moves to get the better of me. I was aroused, as he was.

Then it got all kinds of awkward. He reached for the condom package on the nightstand but struggled to open it. The weirdness of Caleb putting on the condom coupled with my morning breath, took all the romance out of the moment. This was his first time and he wanted it so badly. I let him have it, I wasn't into it anymore but was warm and wet from the sexual foreplay and it wasn't horrible. He was not quick, he was into me as much as himself, but it was weird. I don't know if he picked-up on my feelings about it or not. I tried to pretend like it was great and fun and super fulfilling (without talking or moaning in the direction of his nose) but I liked his foreplay a lot more than his sex. He got me off touching me, the whole sexual episode didn't. It was juvenile and awkward. I suppose if that morning had been my first time by choice the thrill and excitement of the moment would have carried me beyond the awkwardness, but it wasn't. I was no innocent, it wasn't my first time in any context. I wasn't disappointed in him, I was disappointed in me. This should have been my first time by choice, but it wasn't my first time, and he wasn't my first lover and I wasn't going to stay with him, so maybe I was nothing more than a good for nothing whore.

I tried to keep my anticlimactic emotions to myself as he hobbled, juicy condom in hand, to the bathroom across the hall. He flushed, but the condom wouldn't go down the toilet.

"Ahhhh, it won't flush!"

"What?" I asked only half aware of what he was doing as I stared out the window, lamenting my life.

"It won't flush," he popped his naked, still half-hard self back into the room, "I don't know what to do."

I got up, and stood naked in front of him for the first time in my life. Our eyes lingered on each other, knowing smiles budded between the two of us. "Just pull it out." I shrugged.

"That's what she said," he joked. I laughed. It lightened my mood. He fished it out, wrapped it in a wad of toilet paper and tossed it in the trash while I brushed my teeth. The humor, more than the sex, bonded me to him. We played with each other's slippery, soapy bodies in his mom and step-dad's fancy walk in shower and familiarized ourselves with, until then, secret parts. A friendly, mutual exploration; a light-hearted finale, another fun day wandering around the peninsula. I made sure to brush my teeth as soon as the coffee woke me all the remaining days of our vacation and we made the most of a few more days of playful morning sex. Other than that I don't remember ever having intercourse with him again.

The rest of spring break was a blur and before I knew it we were back to the same old school, same old faces and same old melancholy future. I was tired of my life, it was bland and boring and unfulfilling. I wanted 'more' but I didn't know what 'more' was. Caleb was content, he had no aspirations for college, the hardware store was his big plan. Since I didn't have a shot at college I gave up. I didn't follow through with the SAT, though I'd taken the PSAT to prep for it and scored well. There was no point in an SAT. I had no scholarships and no financial way to pay for school. I didn't let my grades drop though, I kept plugging away, knowing the end would come.

I tried, I really did, to get into Caleb, the way I once had been. When he picked me up the day of Mom and Lester's fight and promised Gio he'd keep me safe, he briefly became everything to me. He was strong, and safe and cute. He held me close and I felt like I fit somewhere, even if it was in the arms of a young man with a completely different plan for his life than I had for mine. His safety, his hold didn't feel good anymore, it felt restrictive. He was going to keep me from my dreams. Yes, he would keep me safe and love me good but it would cost me every aspiration I'd ever had to be more than another American living the American upper-middle class dream of houses, cars and kids.

It's not that I didn't want what he had to offer me, but I wanted more too. I got so mad at myself and fought over if I should or shouldn't break up with him. I was done with boring, I started not to care about not using, I imagined getting high again, so what if I lost my chance with Caleb, I didn't want it anymore and was the only reason I quit. I was boxed into a life I could not live forever, I felt how my mom must have felt when she left me and Gio and Dad. I couldn't walk out on kids the way she had, so I decided to jump ship before we had any kids. I'd leave him with a chance to have a solid, stable life with a girl who wanted what he had to offer and save my children from the pain of step-parents.

It wasn't all Caleb's fault; I raged against his future ideals so fiercely because I felt trapped in my life. I thought escaping the valley was the only way to escape my life. I had no purpose, no vision for my future, no hope. I was sinking fast into depression and I couldn't hide it from Mr. Kearny. He heard my music and asked why the foreboding mood. I told him I hadn't heard back from any scholarship boards and I was afraid I wasn't going to college. He refused to hear it. He told me not to give up hope, he was sure something would work out for me.

Something did work out for me. I came home from jazz band one hot, dry summer-ish day in May to a letter addressed to me on the solid oak dining table. Aunt Maria and Uncle Joe used the table as a catch all. The return address wasn't from one of the many foundations or programs I'd asked for scholarships, it was from my own high school. Inside, my dream come true. Mr. Kearny and a few of my other teachers had given me a scholarship!

The "Teacher's Scholarship for most Improved Student" was awarded by ten of the teachers from my high school, ten teachers I knew personally. It said it was good for one full year of full-time education at Wenatchee Valley Community College, books not included. It didn't even occur to me to be sad it was for college in the valley. It was for college! I was going to stay in school. I was so excited that I never bothered to find out if it was an award unique to me, or if they hand-picked some down on her luck loser every year to send to school. All I know is I did not apply for it. My teachers appointed me the recipient on their own. I was humbled and overjoyed.

Another letter found its way to the table a little while after that. I was one of one hundred students to win some musicians' scholarship that was enough to pay for my books that first year. It was a huge honor and yet it highlighted in my mind how insignificant I was. My mostly affluent jazz band friends were going to Berklee and the University of Michigan and Gonzaga and UW for the next four years. The best I had was one year of community college. I didn't appreciate what an amazing gift my teachers had given me because I couldn't brag or boast about what I got to my friends. It was like showing off hand-me-down, off-brand sneakers when they were all sporting shiny new Reebok's.

The scholarship, like Caleb, promised a good safe start to a good safe life in the heart of Washington far, far away from Nashville, Los Angeles, New York or any musical dreams of fame or adventure. I should have been happy with my awards like I should have been happy with Caleb. I should have taken what I was given gratefully, let go of silly dreams that probably wouldn't happen anyway and live the good life I was being offered. I confided in Pastor Jack, told him I was struggling but I wasn't really sure why. He proposed that maybe I was running from God's call on my life and that's why there was so much pain and confusion inside me. Maybe instead of raging against what I had, I could try being grateful for the good things I had been given. It was good counsel. I tried it.

I tried to be grateful. I was grateful for my sweet, mellow boyfriend, for my college scholarships. I was grateful for my aunt and uncle who took me in when neither of my parents wanted me. I tried to be grateful I was only fingered and not raped by my step-father. I tried to be grateful Jose never hit me with batteries, only boys I unwittingly lured to him. I tried but the rage was heating up inside me. The pain I tried to bury being grateful was rolling to a boil. Confusion over my existence and why the horrible things happened was rolling to the surface again. Then one Sunday at church, I simply boiled over.

Pastor Pete, a portly man with puny hands, came up to me and asked a simple question. The unsuspecting assistant pastor couldn't have known what his words would do.

"Gia," he said with a big, friendly smile and appropriate side-hug, "How are you doing for the LORD today?"

"The best I can," was my honest reply. I was doing my best.

"You know, your best will never be good enough." Did I know that? Yes I knew that, every day of my pathetic existence I knew that, how nice of him to remind me.

If he said more after that, I do not recall it. That's all I heard and wasn't it what I'd known all along, since I was the baby trying to wash out my diaper? My best wasn't good enough; my best attempt to love Caleb didn't feel right. My best work as a student still didn't make me stand out. My best attempt as daughter and granddaughter didn't make me someone people were proud of. My best sucked, I sucked. I was a nothing, a no one and I wouldn't ever be more than that. I was destined to a life of less-than, nothingness; the sooner I gave up hoping for more, the better I'd be. There was nothing for me than to be battered, berated and abused, it started to make perfect sense. My life was a Rod Stewart song, "Some guys get all the luck, some guys get all the pain." I got all the Pain, he was coming back because my lot in life was to be a nothing. The sooner I accepted it, the sooner I could live my meaningless, pathetic life. But I didn't want to accept that was my life.

I wanted to get high, I wanted to dull the pain bubbling up in me. Auntie Maria and Uncle Joe weren't drinkers. They'd had the same few wine coolers in their fridge since I moved into the house. They lingered in the bottom and never got taken out. I took one out and hid it in my room. I took another one later when no one noticed the first was missing and hid it too. I tried so hard to be everything everyone wanted, and I couldn't be her, so I would go back to being numb.

Caleb couldn't keep my pain in check, he loved me but he let me walk all over him. If I pushed, he caved, I needed a rock to smash my pain into and break it to pieces. Caleb was steady but not immovable, I wanted him to stand firm when I crashed into him, but he gave in to my ramblings. I got mad when he went out with his buddy one night and threw a big fit. He apologized and said he wouldn't go out alone again. I got mad that he took me out to the drama parties with him, I hated having to interact with people I didn't know that well, he apologized and said we didn't have to go out to group things. He had no backbone when it came to me. The "knowing" that I'd never have a chance with him if I used disappeared. I "knew" he'd find a way to look over it. I wanted him to be strong enough for the two of us, to control my craziness. It wasn't his job, but I held it against him. My best wasn't enough for the world and Caleb wasn't enough for me. I hated myself for being so petty. I wanted to beat my head against a wall and bloody my fists, I wanted to stop being so dramatic, I wanted to get high and block it all out.

CHAPTER 27

GRADUATION WAS AROUND the corner and Caleb talked of us moving in together; even marriage was too big of a risk for him. We did fight about that, my religious background dictated that I marry, not move in. I was absolutely opposed to moving in with him, especially since I had lost all interest in him except as a sexual partner I did everything but have intercourse with. I refused to move in with him. That was his next goal. He wouldn't budge and do the marriage thing and I wouldn't budge and move in without being married; I would have panicked if he asked to marry me, but he never would. It was a stalemate we kept coming back to. He wanted out of his house so badly and couldn't afford it alone, we had to go in on it together, but I was OK at Auntie's. The closer to the end of the school year it got the more desperate he became, but I couldn't do it, and he wouldn't cave. I was proud of him for sticking to it. I wish I could have rewarded his resolve. Instead I broke up with Caleb the week of graduation.

The poor boy was absolutely heart-broken. I felt so bad for hurting his feelings; I really didn't want to or mean to hurt him but I knew I wouldn't change my mind, I was done. It wasn't personal, it really wasn't. He was a great guy and had treated me well, with respect and love. I wanted to comfort him through the break-up. I wanted to find him a steady, stable, normal girl to fit with. I wished him all the happiness in the world. I tried to console him while he sat in the passenger seat of my car, begging for another chance and I kept saying, no, but I was sorry. He wanted to know what it was so he could change it, and I knew if I told him what it was he would change it because he always caved. But back then, I didn't even know what it was about him I wanted away from. I just told him it was over, we were done, I was done.

I got out of the car to go to class or graduation practice or whatever we had to do; he followed me, begging, almost crying there at school where someone might have seen. I felt so bad for him, but I felt embarrassed by the groveling too. I wanted him to man up. Then he sealed it for himself, one question. If it had been any other question in the whole world, I may have rethought the break-up, but it was the one question that would assure me we were done.

"Will you marry me?"

Would I marry him? I was running from normal, stable, predictability; I craved frivolous, uninhibited, adventure and all he could offer me was more of the same old Caleb. If he would have asked me to take off after graduation with him to Spain, I'd have said yes. If he had asked me to streak across the graduation podium, I probably would have done it with him. He could have asked me to do a road trip across the country, or backpack the Grand Canyon, or even move to Seattle with him and try to make our way and I'd have said yes. Of course if he'd asked to get high with me to see what it was like, I'd have said yes. I probably would even have said yes to just going back on the ferry to visit his mom, whom he said gave him the advice to ask me to marry him. He didn't ask any of those things. He asked me the one question I couldn't say yes to. If I married Caleb, I'd do exactly what my mom did and ditch him with a kid or two to go live a senseless life out of nothing more than rebellion to monotony. I didn't want to leave him like that. I didn't want to bring kids into my dysfunction. I didn't want the same old routine. I wanted to go crazy, I wanted to live for the moment. I wanted more than Caleb could possibly give me.

We were civil the rest of the week, we had a routine together and it was easier to keep it than make up a new one. We agreed to be friends but he kept asking me if I'd changed my mind, or if we could have one last kiss. He knew me too well, he could talk me into a little more time with those lips of his. I kept it platonic because I knew if I let him kiss me I'd let him do more, my body responded even if my mind didn't agree at first. I liked physical, sexual contact. I craved it. He had taken the place of masturbating and we regularly gratified each other. Barely more than virgin or not, he knew what got me off; we'd spent over a year playing our lover's game. I liked him a whole lot better than my own fingers inside me. I think it was because I could watch him, or stare at him while he pleasured me. I thought about doing the one last kiss thing but he would have seen it as a chance to get back together. It wasn't just him, my resolve wavered if I let him touch me, it might have changed my mind. I just needed to get through graduation and our routine togetherness at school and get on without him.

Graduation day came, and I had a troupe to watch me walk the aisle. Of course Gramps and Nonna made it, but so did my mom, Aunt Maria, Uncle Joe, Gio, Martin, Alex, Trent, Hannah and, much to my surprise, my dad. It was hard for me to believe he was actually here. I'd gotten to the place I didn't believe he would ever come to see Gio or I do any school events. He always promised to watch me perform or Gio wrestle but never followed through, work, always work was in his way. It was a nice surprise to have him there. He would finally see me, and my jazz band cohorts, perform. The irony of his first being my last with the jazz band wasn't lost on me. He gifted me with a beautiful cedar hope chest, and a nice wad of cash. In fact several people helped to pad my pockets and I had over three hundred and fifty dollars of graduation gift money. I was the queen of my world and with no steady, predictable boyfriend to encourage me to use it responsibly, it was going to be adventure money!

It was awkward being there with my "friend" Caleb whom I'd just broken up with. We had done the last eighteen months of life together. We got jobs together, took our senior pictures together, had gone to church together. Everyone was confused by the situation and it was hard for me to answer anyone about it. All I could say was I was done with him; I made up stupid excuses because there was no good excuse for breaking up with him. They seemed to appease all those who questioned me.

Our outside stadium ceremony was as elegant as the purple and gold we walked down the aisle in. I didn't have to walk with Caleb because our band was playing songs through out the evening and we were positioned in the back corner of the portable metal stage. When they called us up for our diplomas, they announced any scholarships or honors we carried, where we were going for college, or what our plans were. My name came with a respectable tag:

"Gia Gianelli, Teachers Scholarship for Most Improved Student, Walter H. Miller scholarship for musical accomplishment, academic honors, lead piano in jazz band. Gia plans to attend Wenatchee Valley Community College." The only part I was really proud of, as I shook the principal's hand and smiled, was being lead piano for the last two years. The smile belied the fact that I was slipping off a cliff, no one saw it. Caleb was stuck in his grief, my family was confused by the break up and my insensibility, Gio and I had lost what we had—we barely talked anymore, the school teachers only heard what I said and Mr. Kearny what I played; I said all the things a functional kid should say and played only happy, fortuitous tunes. I guess I played the part convincingly because no one picked up on the fact that I was losing my hold on reality.

The ceremony concluded, the jazz band packed up and left the stage, the production was over. It was done, like my relationship with Caleb. Twelve years of school, eighteen months of togetherness the only two things I ever did right, be a student and his girlfriend, and the wandering ship that was my soul set sail. If I'd had an anchors in my life, they were that school and that boy and I just pulled them up. I was a ship lost at sea and no one knew it.

My ship left port, but there was no captain to guide me. I spiraled into darkness; a deep, thick darkness that consumed me. I sailed, like a ship without a rudder in a torrent, into the depths of hell on earth. For weeks after the break-up Caleb tried with all of his might to get me back. He begged and pleaded and promised a happiness I knew he couldn't give me. His ever presence and persistence freaked me out a little, but in some sick way I liked it too. I can't explain it, but it was nice to have someone want me that badly, but it was too much. I finally had Uncle Joe tell him he needed to stop coming by, following me and calling. I repeatedly told him we were over and he needed to move on. It was better after that, but he still waited at my car after he was done with work. I let him take me out to dinner once, trying to be friends, but he circled the talk to us getting back together. After that, I broke all communication with him, there was no point, I didn't want him and he couldn't be just my friend, I wasn't cruel enough to keep leading him on.

I had always been a flirt in school and at work, which was my own little world away from Caleb, even though the main mocha shack was in the parking lot of his store. There were a few boys that had made advances at me, and, now free, I took them up on their offers when I ran into them. Unfortunately for me, the one boy I really wanted to run into, Jeff from jazz band, never crossed my path again. Merrick, an Italian exchange student, did though. I went out with him only because he was from Italy, my motherland. He talked about me visiting him there and told me about his home that was a mythical, wonderful place in my mind. He had none of the physical attributes I liked except that he was very tall. He wasn't well-built, he was thick, almost overweight and only slightly attractive. We made out plenty but he flew away and I remained in the valley. I went on a date with a presidential hopeful. Seriously, the young man, home for the summer from Seattle where he was getting his law degree at the UW, wanted to be the president and loved to debate politics. He was really formal and proper. There was no making out with him. We shook hands and went our separate ways, but I promised I'd vote for him when his name showed up on the ballot.

I got a job at the Valley Music Store working the counter and floor between private piano lessons in their beautiful sound booth. It was a sweet job and there were tons of my kind of guys who walked through the doors looking for picks and strings and musical things. I dated several boys, and one older man I met there. My favorite was a boy named Jason from Entiat. He was petite and feminine, but had a fabulous sense of style and smelled so good. We went out several times, never more than an arm around my shoulder though. Had he made a move I'm not sure I'd have accepted his advances, maybe that's why he never did. He was too soft to handle me; but my, that boy was a good time! We'd run around the mall together like giant airplanes, with no drugs to influence it. We played lava monster in parking lots. He was a kick in the pants but started to monopolize my Friday and Saturday nights. When I told him I was coming off a long relationship and wanted to be free and have fun for a while, he lost interest.

Another boy, Jack, who I thought was a goody-two shoes homeschooled kid, asked me out. We went to his house where he lived with his family to have dinner and watch a G-rated movie upstairs in their sitting room. They seemed so perfect, like Dad and Vickie-Jean perfect, the package was pristine but, sure enough, it was fake. We dated off and on and later that summer he called me and asked a huge favor. He wanted me to come pick him up because he and his mom got in a fight and she bit his chest. I didn't ask what he did, but I got to him right before the cops got there. Like me, the ugly hiding behind the perfect, plastic smiles turned him down a long, hard road to nowhere. We met up again later, funny how the roads to nowhere in a small valley all have the same dead end.

The older guy liked to jam to hippy music from the sixties. He was thirty-two. I was not yet eighteen but had finished school, so I said yes. Going out with him creeped me out, we were clearly not the same age, but it was a free breakfast date and it was so nice to hang out with someone who spoke music. It was a nice enough date, but he was so not my type and I must not have been his either so I never went out again although he still frequented the store as often as ever.

This spoiled, rich college kid, Devin, came in to buy instructional guitar videos, to learn to play so he could impress a girl of course. I showed him the most popular, the easiest to learn from and up sold him a Fender from the base model starter guitar he originally had his eye on. He came back, once or twice with stupid questions before finding enough the courage to ask me out. He was fit, hot and rich. Yes, was the easy answer. We went out several times over the summer, usually ending up at his folk's house on top of the west facing ridge of fancy Fancher Heights. We made out and he kept it pretty PG the first few dates. I wanted more but I was learning that good guys didn't push, they let the lady lead. I wasn't completely depraved but he was an opportunity I didn't want to miss. The whore in me asked for more, my kisses more insistent, my touch more intimate, my desire spurred him on and our clothes came off. It was hot and heavy and I was so wet and horny, but I had enough of my wits about me to ask about a condom. He didn't have one. Diseases didn't seem like a real fear to me, but I remembered the fear of pregnancy with Paul. He didn't have a condom, I didn't have it in me to go bareback. We ended with a nice "safe" or at least pregnancy safe hand job and called it good.

Later that summer Devin invited me to go to a kegger at his fraternity house near the University of Washington. Despite my desire for adventure, I said no. It was his rush week and I was not going to be put through some sort of humiliating ritual, or caught on video with him because he was a pledge. I knew there'd be alcohol. I knew I would drink and not want to stop and would end up driving away drunk or crashing there and finding myself having unsafe sex or even in the middle of an orgie. I'd seen enough of Lester's videos to know one girl with lots of guys never really worked out too good for the chick. They always looked pained, half drugged and oh the penises in all the parts! It was too much of a risk, I wasn't going to take the chance. I was not emotionally attached to Devin and I felt a little profiled. He wasn't asking a girl he knew well but some unknown face, and there was a fair bit of pressure included in the invitation. It was his rush week, I'd seen enough movies, I didn't want to be the butt of a joke, or worse. I was a risk taker, but it seemed foolhardy to travel three hours away with a guy I had only dated a few times as my only connection. He never called me again.

CHAPTER 28

AUNTIE MARIA FINALLY sat me down and asked me what had happened. She said she understood I was having fun dating, but couldn't understand why I'd broken up with Caleb, he was such a nice boy and the whole family had grown to love him and she missed him. She wanted an answer and I didn't have one. I couldn't explain what I did. I didn't know why I broke up with him. I felt bad for breaking up with him and wanted to get away from the feelings. People kept asking me questions I didn't know the answers to. Everywhere I went someone was asking what happened, why I broke up with Caleb. I tell anyone it was because he was too boring and I wanted adventure, what kind of a lousy reason is that for breaking up with someone?

Thinking about why I did it frustrated me, I wanted to rage, or to run. I needed a hook-up or a ticket out of the valley. I know, I took my graduation money and flew by myself, for a solo senior trip, to New York. I honestly don't remember anything about it. I took some pictures in Central Park and Little Italy. I wandered around Times Square and watched *Wicked* on Broadway, but I don't remember anything significant about it. Not how long the trip was, not the hotel, not the flight to or from, it's all a big, fat blank...like an extended black-out...it's weird. The trip stilled the need to move in me, but not the desire to escape. I needed a break from the questions and the stress of life after graduation.

I decided I wanted to get high again, just weed, I told myself no pills or whiskey, just weed. I wanted to feel the old high, I wanted to fade out into thinking about everything and nothing. I wanted to disappear from life. My first thought was Mom, she'd smoke me out, maybe. Our relationship had been strained since she kicked Gio and I out but I visited regularly. I'd come by and take the kids out, so they wouldn't forget me, but didn't like to stay long. It wasn't home anymore and Lester was there again. Mom was out.

Megan and I were still friends, it was easy to reacquaint and blame the separation on me having a boyfriend and her earlier foray into adulthood the year before. I asked her once if she had a hook-up, she did, and we scored a bag. We drove up to one of those mountain lookouts I partied at all those months before and roasted two bowls while we caught up. It was like the first time all over again. I'd never driven high and didn't really think that part through too well. I couldn't drive like that. Who knows how long we sat there watching the wind kick up dust and talking in Tanner, my turd car, before I felt good enough to take her home. I smoked the rest of the bag alone out the basement window at Aunt Maria's. I drank the wine coolers too and wondered if they had any good pills. It was scary and wonderful. I wanted more of a high than what I had. I was hooked. It felt so good to be numb, to not think about Caleb and why I broke up with him, to not think about life and what I would do now that school was done, to float above it all in nothingness. I never wanted the high to end.

The rest of the summer was filled with sneaking tokes, dating lots of boys, going as far as they wanted to go and trying to plan for a college year I had no clue about. No one came with me to find out how to register for college. I didn't ask because I didn't want to bother anyone and no one offered. People in the financial and career offices at the college were busy and unconcerned about whether I understood what I was supposed to be doing or not. I was passed off from one person to another, met with a busy advisor who could have really cared less about my career path and I gave my class schedule my best guess.

I picked classes that sounded fun because I didn't know what else to do, I was doing my best but, like Pastor Pete said, it probably wasn't good enough. Maybe if I hadn't been so high it would have been easier to figure out a plan as I sat alone in my room at night with the sample schedule for an Arts and Sciences teaching degree so I could play the piano for a living. I picked my classes: Spanish,

Psych and Introduction to Music Theory, that was it, three classes, three hours. I'd never not been in school all day and I could only take three. It made me feel like half the person I was in school.

Then, alone, confused and bored in my bed, high and isolated from the family I lived with, I called a number I used to dial every day and still had memorized. It was not Caleb, it was a number from before Caleb, a boy who had only ever been a friend and who had encouraged me to date Caleb. It was Adam. It was like old times all over again only we were grown-ups. He had a job, still lived at home, and hadn't really changed since I saw him last. Not surprisingly he dropped out of school. We were both wandering through life aimlessly. He had gotten himself into quite a bit of trouble with the law. He only told me enough to know he couldn't drive yet. And he got high, I knew I'd have a chance with him even if I was a stoner and that somehow felt comforting to me. I knew with Adam I didn't have to pretend to be someone I wasn't, I could be the loser I was and he'd still accept me. I wasn't afraid of being rejected by him.

By the time school started in September I was talking to Adam regularly. He had a chip on his shoulder toward all authority, and Uncle Joe didn't like his attitude. I didn't get why he had a problem with Adam, it made me feel closer to him because no one liked him. It's all a big blur in my head because it happened so fast, but my life changed when I called Adam. Nothing was off limits, we fed off of each other's adventurous energy levels and tended toward illegal or illicit activities. By the time he asked me out for our first real date I already knew I was in love, apparently so did he.

Our first official date was on or around my birthday in mid-November. It wasn't memorable. We went to Denny's because we wanted to stay out and warm all night. I could be "real" with Adam, there was no pretension. He knew me as a person already so we didn't have to get to know each other and he was cool with me getting high, so I didn't have to sneak or hide it. At some point during that first date the first red light went off, but I ignored it. He didn't like it when I talked about Caleb, I could tell by the way his jaw clenched and eyes darkened so I knew telling him about all the other guys would not be a good thing. He was coming off of a break-up with a girl he'd been with for several months. I didn't think it would be good to tell him he was one of many boys I was fooling around with. I said something endearing about how Tanner took me to all the places I wanted to go and he flipped out.

"Who's Tanner?" He asked, his face turned bright red. No one could have missed his anger. He was horribly mad for a few seconds. It weirded me out. I looked at him funny and told him Tanner was my car. He didn't believe me and I had to physically show him the opalescent "Tanner" magnet I specially ordered to attach to the side of my little tan turd. After he saw it he laughed it off like it was no big deal. It should have been a big deal to me. I thought going to a frat house on rush week a bad idea, why I didn't identify Adam's jealousy and avoid it, I don't know. I thought I knew Adam because of our friendship before. Back then I talked about other boys and it didn't phase him, he even encouraged me to go out with them, he gave me tips on how to get them to like me. The rules changed in his head once I accepted a date. I was his. A possession, a belonging. I just didn't know it yet.

Less than a week later we had sex for the first time and I was his and knew it. Adam was persistent. He never took no for an answer. He wasn't like other guys that would tuck their tail and stop asking me out or stop where I drew the line. Adam drew his own lines and he was the only one who moved them. If anyone said no to him, he took what he wanted by force, persuasion or by breaking in when no one was home, or when everyone was sleeping, and stealing it. He took me by persistent persuasion.

I said, 'no,' I don't know how many times, but no didn't mean no to him, it only meant ask and try again until he got what he wanted. It was not romantic like Caleb had tried in his sweet innocent way to make it, it wasn't redemptive and powerful like with Paul. It was for him to score, like Greg, only longer and more possessive. I think part of Adam's goal was to rule me, to be the winner, therefore making me the loser. He didn't hear my no, he was only slightly concerned with whether I got off. He refused to respect my boundaries and kept pushing until he got what he wanted. Eventually I gave in, exhausted by his persistence. We were on the floor of his parents' house, under a blanket, watching a movie, or more accurately fooling around while it played in the background.

There was lots of foreplay, probably one of the reasons I gave in; I'd been well pleased, he made me feel like I owed it to him. He didn't have a condom and wouldn't slow his roll, wedging himself between my legs. I didn't put up a huge fuss but said we shouldn't without a condom. He didn't respect my wishes and I just let it happen. I was all of a sudden intensely aware of my need for birth control with a boy like Adam. I made an appointment and was seen within two weeks. In that time we had unprotected sex multiple times. The Planned Parenthood doctor who did my exam asked when I'd had sex last, how many times, if there was protection involved, blah, blah, blah then politely refused to give me the shot because I was more than likely already pregnant. I tried to tell her I wasn't and I could just get the shot, but she wouldn't give it to me. She may have mentioned a follow-up appointment, options available to me, but I was not hearing her. I refused to believe I was pregnant. I told Adam, and he didn't believe it either. It just wasn't a possibility for either of us. So we pretended like I wasn't, and continued to have lots of unprotected sex. Our biggest commonality turned out to be that we both liked sex. I was a tool for his needs to be met, he was decent at getting me off along his way to climax in all the different ways and places he wanted it. I didn't pursue birth control.

Adam's hostility toward authority was not a good influence for me, especially at a time when I was floundering so badly. I had a lot of pent up anger inside toward my family, and between Adam's reinforcement and my drug use, it came to a head in an ugly fight over Adam being able to stay at their house past midnight. Adam and I thought it was a stupid rule, but they insisted. Uncle Joe would knock on my door about five to midnight and tell us it was time to say our good-byes. I argued that I was a grown woman and didn't need to be told who could stay with me and for how long. They wouldn't have it, under no circumstances was he welcome after midnight. I thought it was a stupid rule. I hated it so I ran to my mom to complain. The further into the pit I fell, the closer I seemed to get to my mom again. She lived in the pit; it wasn't hard to find her there. She had a grudge against the Gianellis too so she let me complain over drinks and a just-like-before jam session one night. She agreed that I had every right to have someone over at my house whenever I wanted, and then she too stuck up for Aunt Maria and Uncle Joe's rule.

"Do they make you pay rent?" she asked.

"No, they never have."

"Well, then you got no dog in the fight, it's their house, their rules."

"It's stupid," I countered.

"I'm going to say no, it's fair. Now... If you paid rent it would be a different story. You think they'd let you pay rent and let him stay." I highly doubted it. The rule put a huge wall up between me and my aunt and uncle. They weren't upset with me, they blamed it all on Adam and had no problem making sure I knew that. It made me even more upset. It was my life. I complained to my mom again and again, instead of having me take personal responsibility or for a problem or deal with it, she found a way for me to avoid the problem all together. She recommended I move out on my own.

CHAPTER 29

MEGAN JUST SO happened to be looking for a roommate. She and her boyfriend, whom everyone called Buddah, had broken up and she couldn't pay rent on her own. I packed up my stuff and moved out on my own without so much as a conversation with my aunt or uncle about it. I wanted to get it done when no one was home. Adam helped me move during the day but, for some reason Uncle Joe ended up home early and caught me. I knew Adam wasn't above arguing with him and hoped he wouldn't get in a fight with my uncle. He was going off about how they shouldn't have tried to keep us apart and maybe if they'd have let him stay, I wouldn't be leaving. Uncle Joe watched me move my stuff and at the end, when my car was packed full, he let me know in very clear terms that if I did this it was going to be a huge mistake. I did do it, and he was right, it was a huge mistake.

When I left Uncle Joe and Auntie Maria's home that freezing cold December day, I punched out as a Gianelli. Except for one or two phone calls to my dad, I don't think I had any contact with any of the Gianellis for over a year after that. I was done with the family and their secrets, I was done with the fakey Jesus thing. I was done with trying to fit where I didn't belong. I was a loser, I had my loser mom and my new loser boyfriend who drank too much with me and smoked too much with me and didn't get mad if I did it too. We were high on our infatuation with each other as much as, if not more than, we were from the stuff we were putting in our system. With the exception of one addition, I stuck with what I knew from my past; whiskey, weed and pills when they were available, and I was a daily user all over again.

The addition was ephedrine. Mom introduced me to it earlier that summer, maybe even right after my break-up with Caleb. Ephedrine was this wonderful sharply pungent little weight-loss and energy pill the bottled called Quick Thins. Popping quickies killed my appetite but filled me with an overwhelming sense of well-being, joy, attentiveness and energy. Mom liked them because they helped her clean. I liked them because they made life all kinds of better. I started with three or four once a day and within weeks was up to a bottle of thirty every other day or so. I loved the buzz, I loved the rush of my heart palpitating inside me and the feel-good shivers that swam inside my body. I loved the way it felt when I mixed them with whiskey, weed or other pills because it changed the nature of any high. It wasn't like weed where I sat around and did nothing or whiskey where I couldn't do anything but sit without falling. I was free to do as much as I wanted and more. I could play and write music like one of the greats. I could stay awake and look like I was paying attention at school, on the days I still went. Often, though, Adam and I stayed up until the day dawned in my little rented room talking about our lives and dreams, then slept the day away, skipping class and ditching work. We justified it all because we were in love.

In love or not, the red flags were waving all over the place about the kind of guy Adam really was by then and I couldn't ignore them. He was ridiculously persistent and used his persuasive tactics to convince me he knew what was best for me and I ought to always do what he recommended. His extensive criminal history rivaled Jose's, the kid I had been desperate to escape from. At only eighteen Adam had a felony for robbery and countless misdemeanors for possession and minor theft crimes and he only planned on making it bigger. He was Clyde and told me I was his Bonnie, so I better learn to drive fast, he'd laugh. He said he wanted a rap sheet that stretched to the floor. He said he liked breaking into people's houses and taking their things, especially while they slept. He liked the rush and power of it all. He told me a story about guns he'd stolen from his dad's friend's house. He sold the stolen items and later one was used in a robbery in another town. The police shared the news with the friend and Adam reveled in it. He thought it was super cool that a gun he'd lifted and sold had been used by someone else in an unsavory endeavor. Adam told me he liked doing bad things. I was already too far down the rabbit hole to escape from him. There was no fading out of his life the way I had with Jose. I was Adam's girl, I couldn't drift away unnoticed, and if a good guy like Caleb went a little mad when I broke up with him, I dared not see what Adam would do.

His sexual appetite was insatiable, like nothing I'd ever experienced. Once he nailed me it was an everyday, multiple times a day, occurrence. At first it worked for me well, I enjoyed the stimulation and gratification and it was easier to climax with a new, exciting partner than it was on my own the way. As the days wore on it got exhausting. I was over stimulated and he was always hungry for more; not for me, but for a sexual rush. Regular old normal sex was boring for him. We always had to amp it up; try more things, use more toys, watch more videos. It rapidly went from fun lusty playfulness to raunchy nastiness that would soon lose its shine and have to be replaced by the next sexual deviance. In short order what had seemed nasty the first time, made the next thing he wanted to try or do look sweet and innocent. I followed him down the rabbit trail at first because it was fun and exciting. I did like the rush exploration and experimentation and the thrill of pushing past socially acceptable norms. But the further into depravity we got the more I went along just because I was trapped and afraid to say no.

Sex, if it ever was sacred, became nothing more than a primal act of gratuity. It had nothing to do with sharing affection for one another, certainly not love, what we did was a gross mutation of what I'd asked Paul to redeem for me. It was sensational, dirty and nasty, never satisfied; a beast, like any addiction demanding more and more and more. Love making lost its appeal and I was so over stimulated and inundated with sexualized talk and videos I could only get off anymore by increasing the nastiness of it. Sometimes what we did humiliated me, and I took it. Adam made me feel the way Brad did, but I wasn't even trying to save Gio's life, I was just pestered into the next thing to try. It was clear from that first time, though, that he wasn't willing to stop and wait for me even to use protection. He wouldn't take my repeated 'no' as 'no.' I was his and it was expected that I would give myself over to sexual depravity.

And sex, so briefly bought back from the bad guys, was a bad thing all over again.

Adam was intensely jealous too. If he came to see me at work, which embarrassed me because he usually always came noticeably high or drunk, and I was talking to a male customer or co-worker I'd get grilled up and down about who he was and if I wanted to sleep with him and if I liked him more than Adam and on and on. I'd have to tell him over and over again that they were just co-workers or customers and I didn't want them. Adam had me pegged as his little whore because of the things I'd do to satisfy his sexual appetites. He didn't think I was faithful, he was convinced I'd do those things to anyone. I felt a little guilty; like I was lying to him, because he kept on questioning me.

"Don't you want that guy just a little?"

"No, I don't."

"You've never thought about him pounding you? Giving it to you?"

"No... I promise."

"Are you lying to me?"

"I'm not lying to you!" It was frustrating because it didn't matter what I said, even if it was the truth. If Adam believed the truth to be something else. If he was sure I was flirting with some guy that's how it was. We could go on for hours over his certainty that I wanted to have sex with some other guy especially if I insisted it wasn't true. Sometimes I'd agree with what he said, just to make the interrogation stop but then I'd have to apologize and promise never to talk to that guy or customer ever again. The further into the relationship I got, the easier it was to not argue. I learned to never talk about guys for fear he'd terrorize them the way he did Caleb for a while.

He didn't beat Caleb up, but it was just as bad. He picked me up one night from work to go partying and he and his buddy, Will, were in a rage over nothing. They wanted to do bad things; it was a usual occurrence when they were together, unless they were so high on weed they were lazy. They drove over to Caleb's car in the dark hardware store lot and slashed all of his tires. I begged them not to, I told Adam to leave Caleb's car alone. That pissed him off. He said I was his girl, not Caleb's anymore so I shouldn't care if his tires got slashed. It served him right, Adam said, for sleeping with his woman. It was so low and mean, he was just like Jose and he marked me his. Adam had all of the control in the relationship. There would be no escaping him, even if I wanted to, not that I wanted to yet. He was still pretty exciting to be around even though it was getting scarier by the day.

I maintained my job at Valley Music Store, it was to sell picks to people, listen to them try the different instruments and teach people to play the piano. My drugging and drinking didn't affect my job too much at first. I'd never called into work for anything before and since using had only done it a handful of times so I figured I was OK with them. I enjoyed my work. I didn't want to let go of my job not only because of the money but because I liked working there. I was able to see lots of kids, now young adults, from school and catch up on their lives. Emily was one of them, she'd stop in with her new boyfriend, Carlos. She'd had a long-term high-school boyfriend too and, like I did with Caleb, she ditched him around graduation. I was struck by Carlos, he was so not what I expected her to go for. He was quiet and kind of geeky looking, a real contrast to her sporty, energetic personality. But I wished her well in her life. I saw Mr. Kearny too and I tried to make it sound like I was doing fine, just fine, in school full well knowing I was having a tough time keeping up with it all. I didn't want to disappoint him so I told him things were good with my classes, but I couldn't see a point to them anymore. I started skipping classes all the time, sleeping in or hanging with Adam.

My whole dive off the deep end happened so quickly. One day I was a normal kid with graduation blues the next a druggie spiraling downward with an abusive boyfriend and promiscuous roommate. Megan told me she didn't care if I had guys...or girls over. She filtered lots of guys in and out. I suspected she might be a prostitute, she turned "dates" over like one and had regulars like one, and she wasn't particularly quiet. I never felt bad when Adam crashed there for the night or for a few days. I wouldn't have been surprised to find out they had sex with each other. Both of them were insatiable, but if it happened they never said anything. Adam, though, said plenty about my choice in roommate. Her behaviors did not help his jealousy or accusations in the least.

Then I missed my period.

CHAPTER 30

I KNEW, WHEN I left the doctor's office after my failed birth-control consult, I was either pregnant or would be if I kept things up the way I had been with Adam. I was getting sick every time Adam and I would eat out at night. No matter where we went, I kept getting what I thought was food poisoning. The manager of the music store laughed when I came down from a bathroom run.

"You're pregnant," is all she said.

I was in denial, like at the Planned Parenthood office. My head was swimming. I couldn't be pregnant, I mean, technically I could, but I couldn't. It didn't fit into the life I was living, it didn't fit into the things I was doing. It didn't fit into how old I was or anything. I couldn't be pregnant.

"I'm not," I shrugged, willing the nausea away.

"You're not a sickly kid Gia and you've been running to the bathroom for the last two weeks."

"It's food poisoning from dinner."

"For two weeks? That doesn't even make sense. Take a test," she encouraged.

When we closed up for the night, I drove my car west toward the mountains but stopped shy of Leavenworth. I bought a test while grocery shopping at Martin's Market in Cashmere, a tight-knit orchard town, sandwiched between the mountains and Wenatchee. I didn't dare get caught dead with one of those tests in my hand by someone I knew from Wenatchee or Leavenworth. I took it home and Megan found it while we were putting away groceries. She was on the cordless phone with her mom and laughed about it. Her mom knew my mom and I freaked. I made both of them swear they wouldn't tell. It was probably just a scare but I needed to be sure before I could get prescribed my birth-control.

Megan left to go pick up some guy and I was left holding the phone because her mom felt a need to mother me. I barely knew the woman but she was telling me how pregnancy would ruin my life. I had school and this and that in front of me and a baby would mess it all up. I thanked her for her concern, told her there was nothing to worry about even as I was watching a second line appear on the test stick. I told her I had to go. My life had changed with one purple line. The doctor said it was possible, my boss said it was probable, neither of them changed my life, but the purple line made it absolute. I was pregnant.

I angsted over how many people would be mad. I had no idea how Adam was going to react; he had to be in some sort of denial like me. My mom was going to be pissed but I knew I had to tell her before word got to her that I'd taken a test. I worried about what Lester would think and I don't know why. I hated him but I didn't want him to think I was a whore. The Gianellis would be collectively disappointed but what more did they expect from me? I was a series of poor choices as far as they were all concerned. It wouldn't surprise any of them that I got knocked up.

I was numb. I was done doing anything that could mess up the baby. I didn't have a supernatural "knowing," like I had with Caleb, but quit it all that day and didn't do anything but smoke cigarettes from that moment until after I delivered. I went right back to it, but I was at least able to quit for a baby that didn't need that pushed on it. I wasn't going to be my baby's drug dealer like my mom was for me. I hoped and prayed it wouldn't be a girl. Bad things happened to girls, especially around people like Lester and in a lot of ways Adam reminded me of him. He was controlling and would go off and yell and scream forever if he didn't like something. We watched way worse hard-core porn together than Lester ever had on the TV with the kids in the room.

I didn't want a girl because I didn't want her to have a life like mine and I didn't know if Adam, or anyone else, would misuse her. There were a lot of bad men and I couldn't get it out of my mind. The one thing, one thing, I absolutely refused to do for Adam was shave my pussy for that reason. I tried it once, at his request, to look like the porn stars, he said. He enjoyed it too much for me. I endured for a while until I was almost physically ill when we had sex. It took me back to being a little girl in the closet, or a bigger little girl trapped in the bunk bed, with fingers exploring my hairless privates. I didn't know why men liked hairless so much. I feared Adam liked little girls and that's why he wanted me bare. It was sick and wrong and I couldn't stomach it. It didn't matter that he never once did anything to make me believe he was a pedophile. I never saw anything that would lead me to believe that. What we watched and did was all with adults. But there were other evil men out there. I was afraid if I had a girl she'd suffer my fate. I wanted a boy.

I think the first person I told was my mom's best friend, Rachel. She was like a parent but more level headed than my own ever were. I thought if I told her first she'd buffer me with Mom. She'd had a son of her own a year back and had mellowed out quite a bit. She didn't go to Friday nights at Mom's anymore. She offered to pass down some of her boy's clothes if I had a boy and any of the things he had should I need them. She also offered her house as a neutral territory for me to tell my mom that I was pregnant. I took her up on that and had Mom meet me there. I didn't get a chance to tell her. She looked at me, smiled and said, "You're pregnant aren't you?" In her own mom way she was mad. I think she went a while without talking to me and then it was back to normal.

The next person to tell was Adam. I used to meet him at his work for his half hour lunch. He worked a graveyard shift at a packing plant and would meet me at my car to get high. He got in and I looked at him, told him what was up and waited for whatever would come next. His response, to my relief wasn't an accusation about cheating on him, it was worse.

"I guess we're getting married then," he said, then hit the pipe. I rolled my window down for fresh air. Neither one of us was exactly excited about the prospect of a kid. I stayed at his place that night and we told his mom, Michelle, in the morning.

Michelle Cross was a short, loud, jovial, white woman. From the first time I met her I fell in love with her. She was the typical Italian mom, without being Italian. Food was her language of love. It was essential to life and happiness. She cooked Mexican food and oh boy could she cook it! I could never figure out how a lady as loving as she was could have a boy as mean as Adam. She had a heart that held all the people she loved close. She wasn't perfect, but she was everything I'd dreamed of in a mom and might have been one of the reasons I didn't take off on Adam those first few months when escape might have been possible. She had an alcohol addiction that kept her and her husband, Mason, out to all hours of the night when her kids were younger. They'd mellowed out by the time I really got to know them, but the effects of the lifestyle had caught up with them. Their relationships with their children were strained, Adam's trouble with the law may have been a result of too many unsupervised nights, and financially they were always stressed.

I wasn't used to hearing about money hardship. The Gianellis kept bad things a secret so if there were financial woes they were only whispers I never tuned in to. My mom made a point of paying her bills first, and paying them in front of us so we all knew where the money went. She always had a twenty dollar bill to hand us whenever we bugged her for money. Lester kept the cabinets stocked with plenty of food, even if it was off brand and bland food. I'd never known financial stress until meeting the Cross family.

What they had, despite the poverty and alcoholism, were kind, open arms. Adam's dad, Mason, was a decent man with well-behaved eyes. Michelle made me feel right at home in her house, she hugged me, talked to me, listened to me. I loved Adam's parents and they loved me. I was afraid to tell his mom over an egg and chorizo breakfast that I was pregnant. I think she cried and then laughed and said something like she always figured she'd get her first grandbaby from Adam.

By winter I was dealing with recurring urinary infections that went all the way to the kidneys. I was in constant pain and yet every day Adam needed sex. A lot of the times I could talk him into other things to satiate his appetite because I was hurting so badly, but I think part of the reason why I kept getting one infection after another was because of all of the sex. I'd never been much of one for the hospital, so for me to go see a doctor, it was pretty bad. I made an appointment at some office I found in the phone book. I developed an allergy to the first antibiotic but the second one he offered worked better. They didn't have anything else they could safely offer while I was pregnant. I couldn't stop the pain or blood in my urine. It got so bad it looked like I might lose the baby. I was sort of sad about that because I'd spent a month thinking about being a mom and realized I might like the opportunity, if it was a boy.

With Adam's demand for all of my sexual attention when he wasn't working, or at least my physical presence, and the pregnancy, and the infections, and work, college fell to the way side. I barely attended, I hadn't done my assignments, I was failing. I dropped out a week before finals. Sick and trapped in an inescapable relationship, I felt like a sorry loser, so dropping school didn't phase me; it was just another notch in my belt of failure. I was so out of it I didn't try to finish the quarter, the permanent withdraws scarred my transcript, ever a reminder of being a failure. Adam encouraged me to quit. He was perpetually concerned with me liking classmates and professors at school. Every day I'd go to class he asked me who I wanted to have sex with and what I wanted to do with them. If I said nothing and no one he pushed and pushed and pushed, insisting I did and was lying to him about it. I really hadn't. Because of his accusations I stopped looking people in the eye. I got in the habit of floor scanning so that Adam couldn't accuse me of looking at some guy.

I was no longer Gia, I was Adam's woman, and his woman didn't need to be in college, so he was glad when I withdrew.

I kept my job though, I refused to give it up, I needed the money for bills and rent and extra things. I couldn't let it go and he couldn't make me, although his behavior made it hard to keep. Adam was always sure I was cheating on him, or thinking about cheating on him with customers. There was nothing I could do to assure him I was faithful. My words meant nothing. He didn't accept them. He was convinced I was a cheater so in our reality that's what I was. I stopped chatting with fellow male employees. Because of Adam's constant berating and the fact that I had done a lot of dating I felt guilty of cheating on him even though I never did. I couldn't win with him, he was convinced I was a cheating whore and there was nothing I could do about it.

I felt worthless, but for some reason I still got a rush being with Adam. He was funny, hilarious in fact, and I loved to laugh. He was

a handsome young man with bright blue eyes and a well defined
movie star jaw line. He could be so charming and endearing. His
arms were always around me, holding me close or our hands were
interlocked. He wasn't afraid to tell people what he thought,
something I hardly ever did. He wasn't necessarily nice about
sharing his feelings, but I liked hearing someone else say my family
was messed up. He could be mean, but he was also charismatic, his
energy was infectious, he was like a drug. I especially liked that he
was adventurous. He was always going places, doing stuff and
trying new things on his days off. Granted most of the adventure
was laced with illegal or illicit activity but it made the days go by
fast and blinded me. I couldn't see that the constant accusations were
a warning sign and I should run far and fast away from him. I was
caught up in him. There was nothing ordinary or mundane about life
with Adam and I loved it. If he wanted to do something he did it and
nothing and no one held him back.

Often times, he and Will would pick me up after work and we'd
cruise all around in the city and outlying areas. They sold drugs and
did a lot of delivery runs, some took us out to long, frozen dirt roads
where almost no one else lived. When they knew they were going
out that far, they brought their guns and drove Adam's four wheel
drive pick-up out into the woods as far as the snow would let them
go and shoot off dozens of rounds. It was hard-core redneck fun and
my first exposure to those loud banging things. They showed me
how to hold them, load them, shoot them and take care of them.
Guns scared me but fascinated me at the same time. I took my turn
shooting the rifles, but was leery about the hand guns. Luckily, we
never got stopped by cops. That would have been bad, getting
caught with all the drugs and guns in Adam's truck.

Just because I was pregnant and didn't drink anymore, didn't
stop Adam or any of his buddies. He was a big drinker, and a
prankster when he drank too. Once, after I was pregnant and the
only one not under the influence, he and Will picked me up and had
a scruffy bearded buddy, Dylan, in the back who was totally and
obliviously wasted. In their circle, if someone couldn't hold their
liquor and drugs, they paid the price. Dylan's turn was up, they all
had been where he was. It was the "too-high" game. We messed

with him something fierce. We would accelerate into a turn, drift sideways and watch him hit his head on the window, then slam on the brakes fast and watch he'd whip forward then back before he could even react with a single word or hand up to save his face. The other boys thumped him on the head and we all laughed hysterically at his condition. We finally dumped him out of the car. It took Adam pulling, and me and Will pushing, to get his body out of the car. He couldn't move at all. He did try to say "stop" but we were having so much fun we ignored him. When he was out, we tossed him onto the grass and took off. I remember looking back and seeing him lying there, a fetal pile of drunkenness. I'm not sure to this day if we dropped him onto his front yard or a stranger's. I don't know what ever happened to Dylan after that…he stopped hanging with us.

There were other times Adam would get a wild idea to take off and go for a drive to some place in nature far, far away and we'd go, no planning, no prep, just random adventure for no good reason. Those spontaneous adventures were my favorite! He or I would think about a place; Spirit Lake, Mt. Rainier, the ocean coast and we'd go. I came up with a trip to the ocean "randomly" and never told Adam I was there once before with a boy I knew in another life so long ago and really just months in my past. Always we tried new, off the map restaurants. We hiked to the most beautiful lakes and he fished if they were in season (fishing and hunting rules were the only things he almost always obeyed). He was an intoxicatingly charismatic guy, when he was happy.

When Adam was mad he was neither amusing or endearing or anyone I wanted to be around; I started to question the fitness of our relationship but I got in a wreck and literally couldn't get away from him even if I had decided I wanted to.

CHAPTER 31

I LEFT HIS house once, on my way to who knows where, on a cold winter morning and spun out on the ice. I was fine, the baby was fine, but my car was totaled. I didn't have enough money to fix it. I certainly didn't have enough money to buy a new car. I still only worked part-time hours at Valley Music. I had rent and my part of the utilities that consumed most of my income. I all of a sudden had no way to get to and from work to make money. I couldn't call any of the Gianellis after two long months of not talking to any of them to ask for help. Adam and his folks were always broke and couldn't help, not to mention the fact that Adam didn't like me out on my own anyway. He wouldn't have helped me get another car of my own if he did have money. I sat on the edge of their worn recliner and cried. I was stuck.

Adam had never been so happy, he promised he would take care of me and the baby. He wanted me to move out of Megan's to save money. He said we would save up, get a place of our own and I could quit my job and stay home and grow our kid while he worked. He didn't want me working pregnant and sick as I'd been anyway. I had no reliable way to get to work from his parents' place so, with his encouragement, I put in my notice, with his arm around my shoulder, one day after my shift in the middle of winter. Adam hugged me and nurtured me all that day, he liked it that I would be home all the time, there were no men for him to fret about there. He moved me right into his bedroom at his parents.

Most days I was completely alone with their cat until they all came home from work and Tommy came home from school. I watched TV, played on my old trusty keyboard that had moved with me everywhere I went since I bought it years earlier with saved up money working odd jobs when I lived with my dad in Leavenworth, and I ate. I ate a lot. Michelle always had good Mexican food cooking up or left-over and I sampled it throughout the long, lonely days. I embraced being a loser. I knew that I had let down anyone who had any hopes for me. I was a waste of Mr. Kearny and the teachers' scholarship. I proved to the Gianellis I was nothing but a failure. Between the isolation, my own self-doubt and physical abuse, I was back to hitting my head and pulling my hair, and Adam's jealousy and put-downs when he was mad, I felt like nothing and that no one cared for me. I was disgusted that I'd gone from where I was when I was with Caleb to where I was with Adam.

The only things in that house that made me feel good were my keyboard and Michelle. I had to be careful about playing too much on the keyboard when Adam was home because he got jealous even of the time I sat at it, but he never discouraged time with his mother. She was nurturing and kind. She loved me. She'd take me into her arms and hug me when she saw I'd had a rough day or after a fight between Adam and me. She never got into the fights but was there to hug me and love me once they were over.

There were lots of fights. The most common theme of the fights was me looking at guys. It had gotten so bad so quickly I tried to not make eye contact with any men at all. I walked beside Adam, hand in his or his arm around my shoulders, and looked at the floor unless I needed to see where I was going. I didn't want to deal with the accusations and it was the easiest way to avoid them. One time Mason got into the middle of one of our worst fights. To this day I do not remember looking at the guy, but Adam told me I checked a guy out. He fumed all the way home. He accused me of looking the guy up and down as we turned a corner in the grocery store. I denied it because it wasn't true. Adam was convinced that it was, so it didn't matter what I said. I didn't let up, I hadn't looked at the guy much less looked him up and down. I wasn't going to give in that time and admit I did something I didn't do.

We fought about it all the way home and at his parents' house too. He yelled and screamed and slammed stuff around. I yelled back that he was wrong and a jerk for accusing me. He'd get right up in my face and call me a whore, his spittle landed on my face. I vehemently denied it because I hadn't looked at the guy. Then he started taking my things and throwing them out his bedroom window. He threw out my clothes, my shoes; pretty much everything I'd moved in with, he was shoveling out the window. When he went into the living room to get my keyboard, Mason stepped in. Mason rose from the sofa and told him to lay off of me. Adam told his old man to shut up and mind his own business. It wasn't like Mason couldn't have done more to put Adam in his place, he may have been able to, it was more like I wasn't worth him getting into a fight with Adam over. After that, though, Adam told me to get out. I obeyed and left.

Most fights ended with a break up like that. Adam accused me and kicked me out or I called him a jerk and threatened to leave. I would usually take off, on foot, with or without a bag full of my things. That time I almost got away. I should have never gone back. I walked about two city miles to a friend of my old friend, Willow's. I felt pathetic walking in the cold, winter, Washington snow, pregnant, in my boots, with a stupid cartoon sweat shirt on that made me look even younger than I was. When I got to her house, about ten o'clock at night, she and her parents were gracious enough to let me in. I was humiliated and embarrassed and still so mad. They let me stay the night. She shared stories she remembered about Adam from school, how he'd crack up the whole class with his comedic antics, and entertain them all with his animated stories of hunting and fishing and partying. Even though I hated him at the moment I did love his energy. I loved how goofy and exciting he had seemed when we were "just friends" so long ago. I missed that about him. I don't remember how or why I went back but I did.

I knew the situation was bad, I also knew I was bad so I figured my life was as good as it would get for a pregnant loser like me. Most fights ended with him finding me, wherever I was, and begging me to forgive him and promising that'd he'd never yell at me like that again. Then he'd buy me something nice, let me pick out whatever I wanted, and we'd start the whole thing all over again in less than a week. It was a clear pattern and cycle of abuse, and I knew it wasn't right, but I was stuck in it at the time and couldn't see a way to get out. It would have been easier to leave him if he was always mean. But when he was nice, he was so very nice, and I wanted to believe that was who he really was and eventually he would see I wasn't a cheater. I'd forgive the bad parts over and over again, hoping things would change.

Adam defended me too. It was weird and misguided, but he gained my allegiance by being my bull dog. He got into it once with my dad on the phone. My dad had called and asked me to come home, to his place or to anyone's but Adam's. Adam was livid. He took the phone from me and challenged my dad.

"You got a lot of nerve, old man. You're trying to defend her now? She finally has someone who loves her and protects her. Where were you when she was a little girl? She needed you then, man. She don't need you now. Do you, Gia?" He handed the phone back to me, "Tell him you don't need him."

"Dad, I'm fine."

"Just come home Gia, please," my dad pleaded.

Adam took the phone again, "She is home."

I don't know why, but I had never felt so loved. I didn't want Adam to say mean things to my dad, but it felt good to hear someone finally call him out for allowing the abuse to happen and not helping me. How could anyone ignore the fact that their daughter was abused like that? How could he still deny it ever happened? I relished every minute of it. For once in my life someone was doing something about the abuse! It cemented me to Adam, he was a hero to me for standing up for me. Despite the abuse he himself inflicted on me sexually, emotionally and physically, I was grateful to him for being the first person to say to my dad what I could never say for myself.

I didn't realize how bad my situation was getting. I had alienated myself from virtually any connection that didn't involve Adam. If I wasn't stuck at his parents, waiting for someone to come home, I was wasting the day at my mom's. We had become close again. When I divulged her drug history to Adam, he was suddenly interested in me mending that relationship. He was enterprising and entrepreneurial and his side hustle was drug dealing, my mom and Lester, new potential suppliers. Because of the pregnancy, I didn't do drugs with them anymore, but she let me hang out there with her and that's what I did a lot of my pained and jobless last two trimesters of pregnancy.

I was in the dumps and Mom was so happy. I felt like when I was rising above my problems and achieving goals, she was constantly saying and doing things to pick away at my self-esteem and make me question if I was good enough to dream the dreams I had. But after I got knocked up, was getting fat, was together with an abuser, and no home of my own, she had nothing but nice things to say. She still made snide remarks and laughed them off as jokes, but her general attitude toward me changed. She was less competitive, more commiserating and seemed to approve of me so much more.

Now that she was my biggest supporter, she wanted to know what she could do to help me shake my depression. I told her I felt like a loser since I had to move out of my place with Megan. I wanted a place of my own again and preferably before the baby was born. She said if I could find a place we could afford, she would help with the deposit.

Adam was great at getting good paying side jobs but had a horrible time keeping them. For legal work, he took a lot of temporary construction work that didn't last long. Usually things were fine at the temp jobs until the project was finished or until Adam got pissed at a boss or co-worker and up and quit over it with no notice. It was a somewhat steady flow of money, but it was meager. There simply wasn't enough coming in consistently to afford a place of our own. I knew if I went to work again, I could count on myself and we could get a place, but I didn't know what would happen after the baby came. I was desperate for a place of our own, and in all of the subtle ways I could without setting him off, I let Adam know that's what I wanted.

He took another steady but lower paying job at a productive, local fruit packing plant and managed to keep it for a few months. I figured up what he made working full-time, assuming he could keep the job, and what he made off the few regular drug deals he worked for my mom, and was convinced we could get a little place of our own. I begged my mom to help with the deposit, I wanted my baby to have a place of its own to live in. She did and that spring I got my house. It was a little, tiny one bedroom apartment made out of a converted garage four miles out of town, heading west toward Leavenworth.

I was alone almost every day, Adam left early for work with the sandwich lunch I got up and made him, and didn't get home until very late at night. He usually claimed he was working "overtime" which I never believed because of the whiskey on his breath. Sometimes, though, he wouldn't even hide the fact that he was out partying, what did it matter he'd say, I had my place didn't I? And besides, he was selling stuff for my mom at a hefty profit to us. He'd throw me money which I couldn't spend because I had no vehicle to go anywhere and expect it to shut me up.

I mostly liked being alone. I had no real friends anymore and had completely alienated myself from my Gianelli family, which I seldom regretted. To mend fences with them would likely mean apologizing for moving out for no good reason and accepting their God. I had too much pride to apologize and no use for their God. I wasn't convinced there even was a God anymore. It didn't make sense to me why God would let my life happen. I should never have existed let alone suffered the way I had. Nothing good had ever happened to mc, my life from my second memory forward sucked. How a god could let a kid go through what I went through was wrong. For that matter my life compared to other kids and people who had it way worse looked blissful. It was easier for me to not believe in God at all than to believe a supreme being would assign me my sorry, pathetic life. I didn't want to have anything to do with Nonna and her Jesus. I was too ashamed to talk to Gramps. Dad, surprisingly, tried to stay in contact with me, but I was so closed off to all of them and their "take it to Jesus" answer for everything and denial of anything bad happening that I don't remember much communication.

The only person I really missed was my twin, Gio. For so long it was us against the world, or planning to rule it, and I hadn't talked to him since he found out I was pregnant. He was so disappointed in me. I heard he was a star wrestler on the team that past season, his senior year. He was a letter man and a real big man on the campus. I was so proud, I wanted to watch him wrestle, but Adam never would have allowed that.

Alone in my apartment I got lost in food and soap operas, cleaning and eating and forget about the family I had abandoned, or had they abandoned me? I couldn't tell. Alone in my apartment I could pretend that my boyfriend didn't yell at me all of the time and want me to participate in sexual games that were getting more and more deviant. Alone I could pretend we were married and our child would have a great life. I could pretend Adam wasn't writing bad checks the little money we had couldn't cover. I could pretend a large amount of his earned income wasn't going to drugs and alcohol. Best of all I could pretend I was happy and not gaining ridiculous amounts of weight. But I was lonely out there.

For the first time I wanted my baby to come.

CHAPTER 32

ADAM STILL SOMETIMES took me out with him, if the outing was acceptable in his mind for his growing woman with a baby in her belly to go on. It wasn't like when we were first dating and we went everywhere together and I got to be a part of the antics and joy rides. I was his woman now and his kid was in me. My job was to marinate. He didn't think I should be going out with him at all when he partied, if I asked too hard to go with him so I wasn't alone all night after being alone the whole day he'd ask which of his friends I wanted or why I wanted to put the baby around that kind of atmosphere. It wasn't worth the fight, so I usually just made him dinner and bade him good-bye for the night. When he went out, especially on the weekends, it was common for him to not come home until late the next day or not show up at all until Sunday night to get good sleep before work on Monday. Sometimes if it was a dull night he'd be home a little before dawn, alcohol seeping through his pores, the sick, sweet stench penetrating every corner of the house as he lay passed-out for the whole of the next day.

When he would take me out, it was either fishing, eating or hanging with his married buddies at their places. He was nicest fishing because we went where people weren't. I couldn't get accused of looking at other guys because there was no one but him to look at. I caught a huge fish once and he was so proud of me. He took me over to his mom's, they took pictures of me dressing the fish and for a moment, it was like we had a perfect family. I wanted it to always be like that. I imagined in my head that it was and, like a true blooded Gianelli, tried to throw out everything that was bad.

Eating had become my refuge. I didn't have much excitement or adventure in my life anymore, unless I counted wondering if Adam would come home drunk or not at all, so I loved to make different things to eat. I tried to cook or bake anything I was interested in and always cleaned my plate even if I was unimpressed with how the dish turned out. I was well on my way to obesity. Fighting with and being put down by Adam had become my reality, but food never yelled at me, never made me feel bad, never left me alone. The side benefit to my newly found appetite for anything edible was that the bigger I got, the less jealous Adam seemed to be and the less he demanded from me sexually. I suspected he was cheating but I didn't do anything about it except cook more, bake more, eat more to ignore the feelings.

Towards the end of my pregnancy Adam started to make some friends that had 'women' too; discarded girlfriends, lonely beaten-down wives. Birds of a feather flocked together. Our relationship and the pregnancy had affected him on some level. He identified as a man with a family and started to hang out with dudes who had fat, barefoot, pregnant and lonely women at home too. I made them my friends and I became theirs. Life started to have a little meaning in it again. Adam would take me to those buddies' houses; we were too far out, so no one ever came to us, but we started to hang with them a lot. All of us were in similar predicaments, the men wanted their women kept at home and liked to drink and drug their income away. We were all young, impoverished and struggling financially. The other couples had cheap little one or two bedroom apartments too.

Cameron and Mindy were my favorite couple. Mindy was nice and sweet and easy to get along with, and like me, she wanted to think only about the good times. She had long, thick, wavy brown hair, but her blissfully ignorant, perpetually bubbly temperament would have better suited a blonde. Her guy, Cameron, was more of a drinker and cheater than wife beater, and they'd landed in Wenatchee to get away from some of his legal problems in another state. She was pregnant too and due just a little after me, so we got to enjoy being pregnant together. Like me, she kept her little cinder block apartment clean, but latch-hook picture making, not food was her coping mechanism. There were at least ten different carpet pictures hung on their walls and she'd even given us one, of a mountain scene, for our home.

Chris and Jen were a little more complicated and Jen was plain old difficult. I'd gone to school with Chris. He was Emily, my dear high school friend's, cousin. We hung out here and there a few times back in the day. He slept with anything with a vagina and got one extra-large sized vagina pregnant. And that's where Jen came into the story. Her family had enough wealth and muscle to talk him into marrying her since she was pregnant, but he didn't love her and I don't blame him. He really should have had a conversation with her before sleeping with her. He would have realized right away there wasn't a lot going on upstairs. She was younger than the rest of us, maybe seventeen but their little boy, Blake, was already three months old when we were first introduced.

She had no clue how to take care of her baby. She let him cry and cry and sit in wet diapers. Chris would yell at her to do something about the baby, but never did anything with Blake himself. When I hung out at their messy, unkempt two-bedroom townhouse, I would hold him and feed him and say out loud when and why I was burping him. I talked to the baby but hoped it would help Jen be a better momma; that poor baby. Jen's immaturity was actually disgusting. She fought with Chris like a toddler and to rebel against his late nights, she didn't clean their house at all. It was a mess! Adam and I played a game called "see how long it stays" when we visited them. We each identified a random piece of trash strewn around their messy apartment, and who ever's stayed the longest, was the winner. The hands down winner was a fruit pie wrapper that stayed on the trash piled kitchen table for over a month. But she was my friend so I never told her how gross I thought her house was.

Those ladies made life almost bearable again. I wasn't happy, but I had friends to talk to, and every day over was a day closer to the baby coming. The summer was hot and dry and if I wasn't fishing with Adam on a day that was too good for him to waste at work, I was at home alone, at Michelle's, Mom's or with my new friends. I could almost pretend like things were OK. As long as I looked down, didn't confront Adam about where all of the money went and why we needed financial help from his doting grandparents when he should have been working enough to cover our bills, and didn't ask him to mellow out on the drinking and partying, things were OK. I had my life, and my baby was coming soon. I was excited for the baby to come, and I was extremely uncomfortable with it in me and I wanted to know if it was the boy I desperately hoped it was, or if I was bringing another poor girl into this sad, sick world. Unfortunately ultrasound technology was still developing and each attempt to positively identify the sex was inconclusive.

The bigger I got, the more uncomfortable everything was. I just wanted the baby out. Mom, true to always be there when life sucked, was my champion delivery tech. She helped me come up with all of the ideas I could possibly do to induce early labor. When I reached thirty-six weeks, enough for a baby to be fine if born, we started trying to get it out. I walked, I ran, I did sit-ups, I had all the sex Adam wanted, I tried castor oil. I'd started having little contractions at home, went into the hospital or doctor's office and they told me I wasn't ready yet. I didn't want to stay alone all day, so Adam brought me in to Mom's while he worked. I took castor oil again and spent the day on the toilet, clearing my bowels but had no luck getting the baby out.

Evening came, Adam came to pick me up, but the baby stayed inside. We went home and tried to go to bed. Adam was out in no time, but I kept on having pain that made getting into a comfortable position difficult. Adam got frustrated because I kept on moving around so I got up, shut the bedroom door, and nested. In the middle of the night, I cleaned the tub, the sink, the toilet, the grout on our tile counter top and anything else I could do quietly. The pains were getting worse and were coming and going regularly. Then it dawned on me that those pains were the real thing. I was going to have the baby! Because we were so far away from the hospital, I woke Adam and asked him to take me to his parents'. Contractions got too painful though and I told him to take me straight to the hospital instead.

The contractions came regularly but I wasn't dilated. I didn't want any drugs because I wanted the baby to be OK, but it hurt so bad, and the nurses kept telling me I needed to relax and let my body work. Finally, with Mom and Michelle's encouragement to take something, and Adam holding my hand and whispering in my ear that it was OK, I allowed them to put the drugs in my IV. The first shot knocked me out. They said I was only out for seconds, but I was a girl that never felt anything the first time. I was amazed at its potency. I dreamed of cereal cartoon Toucan Sam flying over a real tropical rain forest. The next cervix check a few minutes later showed that I was at an 8. I had just needed to relax. Mom and the nurse coached me on what would happen next. Adam kept saying the same stupid things over and over again and hitting my forehead with the bill of his hat when he leaned in to hug me. I was so frustrated with him, and this was my chance to get it out and not get in trouble, so I yelled at him a good bit while waiting for the baby. I pushed then took a break, he leaned in and whispered soothing words and his hat hit me one last time. I had enough, I took his stupid hat and threw it across the room and remembered hearing the ladies in the room chuckle.

They told me it was time to bear down and push again. My doctor came in to the room, gloved up and told us all baby would be here soon. He said he knew it was painful and I was hurting but he wanted me to bear down and push hard. I was worried about pooping on the table. Chris made so much fun of Jen because she'd pooped. I didn't want Adam to do that to me. I didn't want the baby to have to deal with it either so I focused all my effort on a front push not a back push.

"Wait, wait," I heard the doctor say. The baby was half way out, I couldn't wait, my body wanted it out so I pushed again and it was out! The doctor held her up for me to see.

"Here she is!"

"No!" I bawled. I was devastated. They had to take the baby right away to the oxygen station. They'd wanted me to quit pushing and wait because the cord was wrapped around its neck; I hadn't and it'd put the baby in a little bit of stress. All the attention shifted to the baby, the girl baby.

I was alone with the news...

Here she is.

A girl.

How was I going to take care of a girl in the sick and twisted world I lived in?

ALSO BY LUCY H. DELANEY

Gia's Secrets (Just Gia – Book 1) *Gia's Secrets* is the first in a trilogy chronicling the life of Gia Gianelli, a young girl, who struggles to deal with the effects of a traumatic sexual assault at a young age. In Gia's Secrets, Gia tells how it all began and how she learned to cope with the secrets, shame and abuse. It is a raw look at the effects of childhood sexual abuse as told through the eyes of a survivor.

Catching Tatum (Road to Love – Book 1) After a high-school romance left her heartbroken, Tatum turned love into a game; the boys either followed her rules… or they were out! Everything was fine until Cole and Justin decided to play. Will Tatum's rules help her navigate two very different men, or will she strike out at her own game?

Waiting on Justin (Road to Love – Book 2) Amidst tragedy and despair, Justin and Haylee seek an answer to the age-old question: can love endure the harshest of climates and passage of time? A touching and poignant story about a love worth waiting for.

Finding Jordan (Road to Love – Book 3) Jordan's life was great. She had an amazing job traveling the world, and a super hot romance with a blue-eyed guy who was almost too good to be true. But, just one night and just one decision was all it took to put both in jeopardy and leave her with a secret that could ruin everything.

Scandalous Affair - Nate appears to have it all, but he is torn between two sexy, powerful women. Chelsea, one of Hollywood's hottest leading ladies, has warmed his bed for years. Sofia, has beguiled him for far too long but she wants him to leave Chelsea for good. Is it a choice between two women or a tale of something more dramatic than a Hollywood love triangle could ever be?

Made in the USA
Las Vegas, NV
17 April 2022